TURN FOR HOME

Lara Zielinsky

Supposed Crimes LLC • Matthews, North Carolina

Published in the United States.

ISBN: 978-1-952150-99-9

www.supposedcrimes.com

This book is typeset in Goudy Old Style.

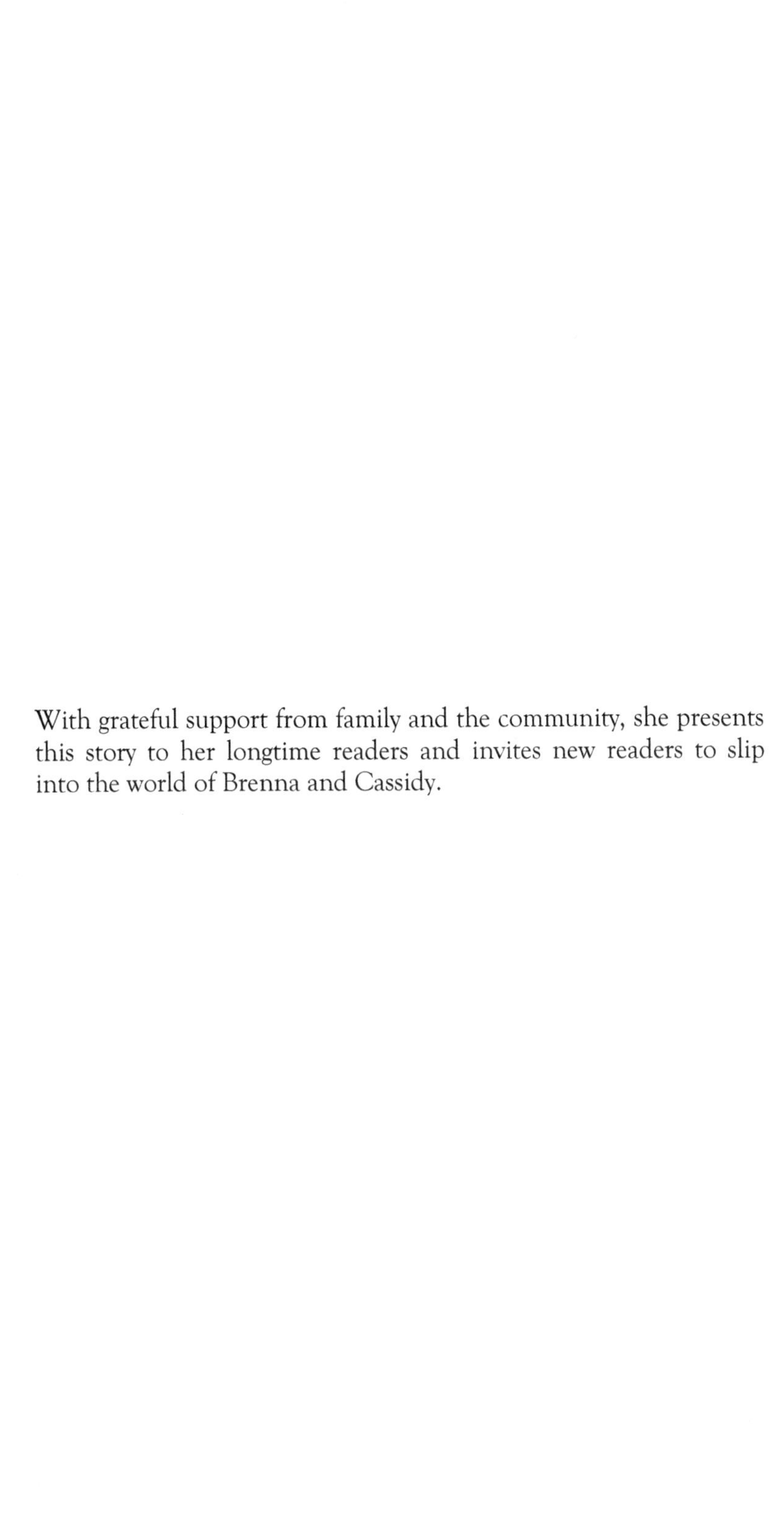

With grateful support from family and the community, she presents this story to her longtime readers and invites new readers to slip into the world of Brenna and Cassidy.

PROLOGUE

BRENNA LANIGAN pulled up to the curb just outside the entrance to Pacific Heights High School. It being just after seven in the morning, she was not the only parent delivering her sons to the new semester.

"What time tonight?" she asked as she stretched her right arm over the space between the front two seats and looked squarely at Thomas, next to her in the front passenger seat. At age seventeen, he was beginning to chisel and thicken in the chest. James, a little rounder and softer at fifteen, was pulling his book bag together in the back seat. Both were turning away from her already, their doors open.

She grabbed Thomas' shoulder before he could get out of range. He didn't look back as he answered, "No need. I've got orientation with FIRE. I'll catch the city bus when it's over."

She released his shoulder. "James?" she directed to where he stood outside the vehicle.

"I've got stuff planned with friends," he answered.

"Will I see either of you for dinner?" she asked. Thomas paused, but without turning back to look at her, he shook his head. She glanced at James and saw that he was looking at her, though she couldn't interpret his dour expression.

"I'm making Chicago deep dish," she offered. "All the toppings you like."

James shrugged. "Sorry, Mom. I won't be in 'til curfew."

"Thomas?"

"That's a big meal. We having company?" Thomas hazarded a glance toward her. His eyebrows drew together briefly, betraying his anxiety, before he assumed a bland expression.

Brenna had been thinking of inviting her new lover, Cassidy Hyland, and her son Ryan. She missed the blond woman terribly. The last time they had all been together, Cassidy had come over for New Year's Eve. Thomas and James had gone off to the Palisades neighborhood park, reluctantly taking Ryan with them. At the time, it had been wonderful, giving Cassidy and Brenna time alone together. But any ground she thought had been gained in her sons' adjustment to her new relationship was short lived. Up before dawn most days, both boys then stayed gone all day for the remainder of their holiday.

Any time Cassidy's name came up, Thomas and James acted as if they didn't hear a word Brenna said, and the last time she'd tried to talk to them about it, she'd ending up getting upset. The school driveway was no place for a scene, so Brenna reluctantly said, "It'll be just the three of us."

After a moment Thomas said, "I should be home by six."

"Thank you. James?"

Something near the building caught his eye, and his response was hurried. "I'll reheat. Catch you later."

He slammed the back door and she watched as he ran to catch up with someone. She decided his objective was a girl, despite the black leather jacket that hid most of her upper body. The jeans were just a little too snug on shapely legs to belong to a young adult male.

She turned to see Thomas walking away more sedately, but no less intent on some point in the flow of students entering the front entrance of the school building.

A horn honked behind her and Brenna reluctantly turned her attention to guiding the SUV away from the curb and into the flow of traffic exiting the school grounds. Safely in the flow of vehicles on her way back to her Pacific Palisades neighborhood, she turned her thoughts to the continuing problem of what to do with her sons' clearly expressed discontent with her new relationship.

Stopping at the grocer's for a short list of items, she wandered aimlessly, the dawdling giving her time to think. It had been a week since New Year's. It would be another week before she returned to work on the Pinnacle Pictures lot where she portrayed Commander

Susan Jakes on the science fiction series Time Trails. She had already cleaned her home top to bottom—refreshing drawer liners and shelf paper, cleaning out the refrigerator, and running the self-cleaning cycle on the oven which had been used heavily during the holiday season just past.

Unless she went against their not so subtly expressed wishes, this cold shoulder from Thomas and James would mean another week without seeing Cassidy.

Brenna hadn't given a second thought to going weeks without seeing either her first husband, Tom, or her second, Kevin. She had attributed that to their mutual understanding of conflicting schedules, or knowing their responsibilities had been as busy and demanding as hers.

She knew now that didn't actually account for her diffidence to being apart from her spouses. Her new relationship made her feel so different, and not just because of the obvious difference that her lover was a woman. She called Cassidy nearly every night, just to hear the sound of her voice, to share a thought or two, or find out about her day.

Brenna was forty-one, with an anything but sheltered history of lovemaking—from a series of affairs to two marriages—but for the first time she understood the physical craving that went with truly being in love, a craving that went beyond physical pleasure to emotional completion. She didn't understand how she could have ever settled for anything less, except perhaps because she had never known there was supposed to be anything more.

In the aisle that held magazines in addition to groceries, she studied the industry periodicals and her attention was snared by a cover with two semi-nude women kissing in a lovers' clinch. Curiosity piqued, she studied others nearby and made a selection. Picking up a travel magazine showcasing the Oregon portion of the Rocky Mountains for weekend getaways, she wondered how Cassidy might react to another invitation to go camping. Or, Brenna thought, maybe we can do something a little more indulgent, a little more romantic, just the two of us. Her face flushed at the thought.

In the checkout line, Brenna found herself looking at the other patrons. Did she ever respond to another woman with the same quickened heartbeat, the same catch in her breath, the same visceral, mind-stuttering desire that she did whenever she looked at, or even thought about Cassidy Hyland?

Watching the brunette ahead of her in line interacting with the cashier, how her hands moved from her wallet to her purse, Brenna listened to her voice—a quick patter...no easiness to it. The woman was close to her own age, laugh lines not quite defined at the corners of her eyes. Brenna assessed her emotions and found nothing beyond polite awareness, similar to when she had first met Rachelle Cheron when they were both reading for the Time Trails roles. Abruptly the woman turned to look at her and Brenna ducked her gaze to the tabloid rack.

The man monitoring self-checkout came to bag her groceries as she stepped up to pay the cashier. Brenna let him help, taking some time to consider her reaction to him as well.

He appeared older, probably having taken the job to supplement a retirement income. He chatted about the local news, his voice pleasant but unremarkable. When he offered to push her cart outside, she met his eyes and noted they were a vague brown. She smiled politely and declined. "Thank you, I can manage."

The interaction apparently dazzled him, because he smiled wider. He reached for the cart again, but she shook her head. "I've got it."

"Come see us again," he said after a moment, and she detected the hopefulness in his voice.

After placing her groceries in her trunk, Brenna climbed into the driver's seat and started the engine. She brushed the central console, surprised at the strength of her memory of Cassidy's hand caressing hers as it had rested there.

Once home, she unpacked the few groceries and put them away. Standing at her desk, she glanced through the mail and saw a reminder that the Satellite Awards were in two weeks, and she sighed at the reminder that she still had not acquired a gown for the occasion. That made her wonder whether Cassidy would like to go shopping with her. Just the chance to see her lover again propelled Brenna back to her car and she sped north toward Cassidy's home in Altadena.

CHAPTER ONE

THERE WAS a click of her bedroom door and the rustle of feet crossing the floor, and the blonde under the covers rolled onto her back. She opened her eyes to the sight of Ryan, her five year old son, leaping onto her bed. His "Good morning, Mommy!" made her ears ring a little as his body fell into her open arms. Inhaling, she detected more than the scent of his hair. Startled, she looked toward the door. It smelled like...

"Breakfast." Her lover of only a few weeks used her elbow to push open the door on her way into the bedroom bearing a tray laden with filled glasses, mugs, and plates. "Well, brunch, maybe," Brenna corrected, as she set the tray down on the bedside table. "It's almost ten, Cass."

Cassidy could see toast with a pale jam, coffee, and glasses of a red fruit punch. She looked at Brenna again and smiled as the other woman stepped out of her shoes—face partially obscured by a loose fall of auburn—and sat on the queen-sized bed next to her. The bedsprings creaked under the additional weight.

"Thank you," Cassidy said as darkening blue eyes caressed her face, coming closer. She reached out with both hands and tugged on the open collar of Brenna's light blue cambric shirt, encouraging her lover closer. "When did you get here?" Though they had spoken almost every night, discussing the impasse Brenna had come to with her sons, Cassidy hadn't seen Brenna since New Year's Day. Cassidy eagerly searched the beautiful features to see what, if anything, was changed, as well as to gain some insight into her present mood and the reason for the unannounced, but welcome visit. "Is everything all right?"

Brenna's eyes shone as she quirked a smile and leaned in. "It is now." The edge to Brenna's voice was husky, brushing warmth against Cassidy's ear. "I arrived just a little while ago."

When Cassidy tasted Brenna's lips, she discovered the jam on the toast was orange marmalade, and devoured her first morning kiss in over a week.

Brenna's lips were soft, supple, and little moans issued from the duo as their connection deepened. Ryan squirmed against Cassidy and dampened her rising arousal. She pulled back. "I missed you."

Brenna's gaze never shifted as she caressed Cassidy's cheek. "God, I missed you too."

Ryan interrupted impatiently, "Are you hungry, Mommy? Miss Lanigan made you breakfast for bed."

Watching Ryan's expectant smile grow, Cassidy blinked. She was ravenous, but not for food. Gazing at her lover, Cassidy knew Brenna was feeling the same swirl of emotion.

"I already fed Ryan," Brenna explained.

"She made me scrambled eggs in a sandwich," Ryan supplied.

"So you let her in this morning?" Cassidy asked. "You know you're not supposed to let people in when I'm not awake."

"But Miss Lanigan's not a stranger."

Brenna's smile faltered. "It's my fault. I should have called first. I'm sorry."

Cassidy reached out and caressed Brenna's cheek. Her son's opinion of Brenna was important to their continuing relationship. Ryan was right; Brenna was not a stranger. Finally, she said, "It's all right." Ryan flung his arms around her neck, hugging tightly. Over her son's head, Cassidy said to Brenna, "I'll give you my spare key."

Brenna grasped her hand and leaned forward, pressing her lips to Cassidy's temple. "Thanks."

Disengaging Ryan, Cassidy then watched as he got down from the bed and in the way only her son could, crept to the door, leaning over his legs and thumping away like an elephant. He shut the door with a loud thud behind him. Brenna, who had watched the whole thing, laughed out loud, rolling back onto the pillows with Cassidy. "What a charmer he's going to be, Cass."

"I bet he planned that whole entry with you," Cassidy replied, having learned a little about what could happen when the two people she loved most put their heads together.

Brenna snagged a piece of toast and passed it to Cassidy with a glass of juice. "He really wanted to go along with the surprise. I'm sorry that his letting me in was against the rules."

Cassidy sipped the cranberry-apple juice and took a small bite of the toast, truly moved by the gesture. "This is wonderful, Bren," she said with real appreciation.

"I hope it's not too inconvenient. After I... Well, I got Thomas and James off to school then I decided to come see you."

Cassidy held out the toast and Brenna took a bite. Watching Brenna chew, that delicious mouth twitching slightly, the muscles moving in her throat as she swallowed, Cassidy had to tamp down a flash of lust. Quickly she took another bite of the marmalade and toast, her taste buds tingling with the sensory satisfaction. Clearing her mouth with a sip of juice, she arranged the pillows so she and Brenna could lean back, legs stretched out side by side. "I can't recall the last time I had breakfast in bed."

"I'd like to do it more often," Brenna said, taking up a mug of coffee from the tray.

Cassidy lifted her own mug while she considered how to answer. She inhaled the scent of the deep rich roast, laced with cream the way she liked. She could do this more often as well, but there were considerations. "We'll be back to work next week," she said.

"I know," Brenna leaned against Cassidy's shoulder and picked up another piece of toast from the tray, "but our situation won't have changed. You'll still have your place, and I'll still have mine, and we'll still go our separate ways most nights."

Cassidy's nose nuzzled against the fine hair that smelled of fresh peaches. "You switched shampoos," she murmured.

"I did. Do you like it?"

"Marvelous." Cassidy kissed the crown and the fine silky strands tickled her lips. "We're together now," she said by way of answer to the last question hanging in the air.

"But Ryan's outside."

"So snuggle with me while we finish your wonderful breakfast in bed."

Brenna settled against Cassidy's shoulder as she lifted her coffee mug to her lips again. "I can definitely do that."

Deciding they couldn't leave Ryan to his own devices for too long, as soon as Cassidy finished eating, Brenna led the way from the bedroom carrying the breakfast tray. Cassidy, pulling the belt of her robe secure, was a step behind her. "Ryan!" Cassidy called out.

The sliding glass door to the back porch was open. While Brenna went to the sink to deposit the tray, Cassidy went to the open door and called, "Ryan! Time to come inside!"

The blond boy suddenly raced into view, a barking Ranger leaping and running at his side. The taxidermy animal they had acquired several months earlier was once again their toy. Cassidy sighed. "Come inside, please."

"Why don't we take Ryan and Ranger for a walk?" Brenna asked.

"Where?"

"You've got a neighborhood park."

"Yeah, but—"

"I don't want to go home yet," Brenna admitted.

Cassidy looked back over her shoulder, her nervousness manifested by the teeth worrying at her bottom lip. "All right."

"Are you tired?"

"No. I... It's... We don't really want to be caught by cameras."

Brenna shook her head. "Neighborhood park, not the local mall. Furthermore, it's your neighborhood, not mine."

"There's always a chance."

"Is it your parents? Cass, your parents are in Missouri. What can they do?"

Brenna was right, the chances were slim, but Cassidy had a distinctly unsettled feeling. And, while her parents might disapprove, they were more than a thousand miles away. She made her decision looking down into Ryan's expectant face as he slammed into her legs coming through the doorway. "All right. Let's go to the park." Wrapping his arms around her legs, he kissed her left thigh.

Brenna gently peeled Ryan off Cassidy and sent her lover to her room with a kiss. "Dress casual. We'll be waiting."

Cassidy returned wearing jeans and a long-sleeved aquamarine flannel pullover, her hair brushed and pulled back in a ponytail at the nape of her neck. Brenna grasped her right hand and Ryan's left, and led the way to the street.

Halfway to the corner, Cassidy spotted Lou Talbot in his driveway, poking under the open hood of the family car. She gave a friendly wave as his gaze rose to them. "Good morning."

"Hmph."

"Friendly sort," Brenna commented as they walked on. "That's Gwen's husband, Lou Talbot. You met Gwen."

"She's married to him?" Brenna shook her head.

After walking two blocks of sidewalk, Brenna and Cassidy entered the park through a high arched gateway. A path encircled the park's central feature—a duck and fish pond, large enough that there was a small dock out over the water on the far side. A walking path, a biking path, and an exercise path all separately circled the pond.

"It's about two and a half miles, three including the walk back to my house," Cassidy revealed. "So here you have my morning gym." She pointed at the equipment along the exercise path. "You remember; I told you about it during Ryan's birthday party back in October."

Joggers flashed by them, and a man in tight shorts but with a bare chest was hoisting his meaty frame on the chin-up bar. Brenna smiled. "Clearly it's a popular place."

"When Gwen showed me through the neighborhood, I knew I wanted to be right here."

"You said that you stayed with her and Lou when you came out from St. Louis to do small parts."

"It was a strain. At first I thought it was all me, traveling so much, not sitting still, always just getting on or just getting off a plane. But Lou... Well, I made a good bit of money from the vampire role, so I thought about renting something. Gwen liked having me around, so she showed me a few rentals in the neighborhood. When I was finalizing my divorce and knew I would stay, I talked the rental agent into letting me buy the house I'm in now."

Ryan ran for a children's jungle gym and they watched for a while as he threw himself over and under the various posts and poles.

People milled about, but it wasn't crowded. On the weekends, Brenna imagined this was a popular place for the neighborhood families. She could see the vendors Cassidy had mentioned, and picnic tables, in the grass by the dock. A grandfather and grandson—their apparent age difference making her assume the relationship—were seated, feet dangling over the water, straight poles with lines dropped in search of a fish's nibble. "This is wonderful," she concluded.

"Probably the best feature of the neighborhood," Cassidy agreed. "And not a reporter in sight."

"You don't like large crushes, formal events, do you?"

"I like my privacy. I don't hate the events, but I guess I'm still more the girl from the St. Louis suburbs." They walked along the path while Ryan ran around them.

"Is that guiding your choices after Time Trails?"

"Maybe. I haven't fielded a lot of offers."

"If you're staying here, I probably shouldn't go to England." Brenna paused. "Unless you'd like to come along." She found herself eagerly considering the idea. A little seclusion, just their families, time alone.

"Terry mentioned his theater," Cassidy replied.

"Or we could do that."

"But you should take the British part if you want it."

Unwilling to leave Cassidy for the length of time it would take to film that movie, Brenna grudgingly allowed, "I'll think about it."

"With Thomas graduating, you've only got James at home."

"If I can get him to adjust to us." Brenna was melancholy. She was dreaming dreams with someone who really mattered to her, and her sons, who mattered as well, were less than happy about it, despite their forced words to the contrary when she confronted them.

Cassidy caught Brenna's mood shift. "Have they said anything more about it?"

"No, that's just it. They aren't saying anything." Brenna sighed. "Thomas told me once he liked being someone I could confide in. But now, he's more scarce even than James, who just seems to disappear and reappear, without explanation."

She inhaled and exhaled the fresh air, finding the pine, palm, and pond scents calming.

"It probably feels to them as if you've been keeping secrets from them. You're different, and they don't know how to react to that."

"Am I different?" Brenna considered that. Inside she felt happier than she could recall in any other time in her life. She guessed maybe it showed outwardly in ways she wasn't aware of. "I guess I am a little different, but I'm still their mother."

"I've seen them with you. I think they'll come around."

Cassidy and Brenna leaned together on the bench, gazes intent on Ryan, minds mulling over Thomas and James, ears attuned to each other's quiet heartbeats.

"It's really quite nice."

"Weekday mornings the vendor has sausage and egg rolls, and coffee. He brings out hot dogs by noon."

"So we're just in time."

As if on cue, the vendor, with his supply of hot dogs, rolled his wheeled cart past them, and Ryan's attention was immediately drawn by the aroma of food.

The trio walked over to a picnic table near the dock, and Brenna sat with Ryan while Cassidy collected three hot dogs. When she returned to the table, she found Brenna and Ryan with their heads bent close, her son whispering to her lover. "Am I interrupting?"

Brenna lifted her head and smiled widely. "Not at all. I was just listening to Ryan showing how high he can count."

"What was he counting?"

"Ducks."

"How high did you get?" Cassidy asked, sitting down and distributing the hot dogs in their white crenellated carriers.

"I got to fifteen."

"Very good."

All of them were silent for a few minutes, consuming the foot long hot dogs. Ryan saved the heel of the bun. "May I go feed the ducks?" he asked when he'd finished the rest of his hot dog.

"Yes. Wait, though. Someone should go down to the water with you."

Brenna swallowed her final bite. "I say we both go."

"All right." Cassidy stood and Brenna took her hand. Ryan took his mother's other hand, holding the piece of bun in his right.

About three feet from the water's edge, Cassidy tugged Ryan to a stop. "Close enough. Try reaching the ducks paddling this way."

Ryan tore the bun into pieces and threw a handful of crumbs, most of which landed on the ground in front of him as they caught the air and fluttered down.

The ducks were undeterred. Long used to being unafraid of humans, they waddled out of the water, long necks stretching this way and that, black beaks snapping up the bits. Ryan had to back up and quickly throw away the remainder as a larger duck realized Ryan was the source of the bounty, and lifted his beak in search of more.

Brenna snatched Ryan out of harm's way. Startled by the larger person, the ducks squawked in alarm and quickly waddled away.

Cassidy wrapped her arms around Brenna and Ryan, and laughed away her anxiety. Brenna had been closer and had taken care of the situation without a moment's thought or outward alarm, but Cassidy's heart had been in her throat when she realized what was happening.

"Thank you."

"You're welcome. I think it's time to go home, though." Brenna nodded at Ryan snuggling against her chest. "I think someone's tired."

"It's nap time." Cassidy took Ryan from Brenna and the women walked back with more speed and purpose in their stride than during the slow amble to the park. In ten minutes they were back inside Cassidy's home and pulling Ryan's shoes off as he drooped sleepily on the edge of his bed.

As she and Cassidy retired to the couch and snuggled together, Brenna realized it was almost one-thirty. "All things considered," she observed aloud, "it's been a wonderful day."

"Anytime you want to come over, just come," Cassidy said.

The breath whispering through her hair sent tingles of pleasure down Brenna's spine which then lodged warmly in her abdomen. She squirmed in response and lifted her head, knowing she needed to go instead of dallying here. For now.

"I've got to get my sons adjusted. I'd like to have you and Ryan over to my place again, especially when the weather warms up and I open the pool."

"Now that school's back in session, the sense that your boys have their own things to do may help."

"I hope so." Brenna's breath sighed against Cassidy's collarbone. "I want everything with you. It's been a long time since I felt as if I had a friend and a lover in the same person. I want to wake up with you every morning. I can't do that until Thomas and James understand that their silent treatment, or even outright anger, is not going to change my mind."

"Thomas' and James' opinions matter, Bren. I wouldn't want them not to." Cassidy wrapped her arms around her lover, letting their curves fit together.

"I won't let Thomas or James push us apart."

"All right. So, what now?"

"What would you say to going in to work together on Monday?"

"Are you serious?"

"Thomas and James can get themselves to school. I'm sure they'd prefer it. I'll come here, and take you and Ryan in my car."

"I've got Ryan's car seat."

"I'll move it to my car," Brenna suggested. "It's not a major display, but it's a half hour drive back and forth, time that we could be together."

Cassidy grasped Brenna's hands earnestly. "Not yet. It's too soon. Let's try smaller things first."

Brenna was reluctant to agree. "Why?"

"Do you really want your sons inundated by the press before they are comfortable? And what about the détente you reached with Kevin?"

Brenna sat up. "It isn't fair that we have to hide."

"No, it's not," Cassidy agreed. When Brenna got up from the couch, Cassidy followed. "Are you all right?"

"I haven't even left yet, and I miss you already." Brenna snuggled into Cassidy's embrace.

As she wrapped her arms around her lover, Cassidy couldn't help thinking the same thing. Putting other people's feelings first, when she'd been used to ignoring her own for so long, was frustrating.

"I'll be waiting when you get to the set Monday."

"Maybe I can find more time to get away this week."

"Take some time with Thomas and James. Maybe they just need a little attention from Mom."

"Maybe." Brenna's lips turned down at the corners. "I offered to make Chicago deep dish tonight, their favorite. I finally got Thomas to promise to be home. James, who knows where he'll be."

"It will work out, Bren."

"Promise?"

"I promise." They shared one last lingering kiss before they reached the front door.

CHAPTER TWO

CASSIDY SMILED as she and Ryan entered the surroundings of the Time Trails soundstage on the Pinnacle Studios lot. The whole of it—with crew people scrambling thither and yon, unrolling cables, testing boom mikes, everyone smiling—provided a wonderful sense of familiarity.

Sean Durham, Time Trail's Jeremy Dewitt, gave her a wave, his sandy blond hair pinned under a blue baseball cap flipped backward on his head.

"Good morning," she offered.

"Sure is." He tapped the end of a ball point pen against the neon orange clipboard in his left hand. "Hey, brought the little man today. Did you have a good break?" He dropped his foot from a director's sling chair and approached her.

Cassidy nodded. "Did you?"

"Went to see some family out of state," he said. In the next moment they were both distracted by the door opening behind him.

Rachelle Cheron, Time Trail's Luria Dewitt, entered the soundstage through a door held by her companion. Rachelle was walking backward and elaborating on a story, hands flowing rapidly through the air. Brenna, Time Trail's Commander Susan Jakes, brushed her fingers through her short-styled auburn hair. Her blue eyes twinkled as they caught Cassidy's gaze past Rachelle's head.

"...and he didn't believe me!" Rachelle finished.

"I can't imagine why your brother didn't believe you," Brenna commiserated, though her tone was amused. She shifted her eyes away from Chelle and the melancholy gray became suffused with passionate blue.

Rachelle spun around. The cocoa-skinned woman was clearly agitated, her dark skin unable to hide the high color in her cheeks. "Oh, hey, Sean, Cass." Without preamble, the small woman threw her arms around Sean's neck and kissed him soundly.

He returned the affection. "Your brother didn't believe you about what?" he asked.

"That Rose's school had already taught her the basic colors, numbers, and was beginning on letters."

"I thought your brother had kids," Sean said.

"He apparently pays no attention at all to their education," Rachelle huffed.

"So, tell me everything." Sean slipped an arm around the diminutive woman and led her away, Chelle launching anew into her story.

For Cassidy, the conversation quickly faded into the general din as she feasted on Brenna's appearance. A warm smile and gleaming blue eyes hinted at the fiery and passionate nature Cassidy knew was hidden within. Today Brenna wore a maroon wool pullover, the white cambric shirt underneath visible at her wrists and collar. Drawn to Brenna's hands, Cassidy watched them move forward, reaching toward her, and then awkwardly try to hide away in the tight pockets of the name brand denim jeans. Following the arm back up to Brenna's face, she broke the silence as their gazes entwined. "I... Hi." Brenna's smile made Cassidy's stomach flip.

"Good morning."

Cassidy's heart raced at the warm tone, its smoky resonances blocking out all other sound.

"Good morning," she returned with more assurance. Brenna's hand slid over Cassidy's forearm, just below the three-quarter sleeve of Cassidy's pale blue, stretch cotton blouse. The contact caused a tingling deep in Cassidy's chest.

"How are you?"

Cassidy let Brenna take Ryan from her arms, amused briefly by the startled grunt the woman made as Ryan's full weight settled against her.

"Why don't we take Ryan to Karen's together?" Brenna suggested.

"I'd like that," she replied.

As they crossed through the soundstage area, Cassidy stuck close to Brenna's side. She wanted to reach out, put her hand on Brenna's back, but each time she came close, a rigger, or other tech, appeared from somewhere.

Once they stepped outside, Cassidy holding the door for Brenna, she rested one hand on Brenna's back and the other on Ryan's, and leaned in very close. "I've been waiting for you."

Brenna's scent, warm and spicy, assailed her. Helpless to resist, she nuzzled Brenna's hair, feeling the woman lean into her. Looking around and finding themselves in shadows and alone, she nudged Brenna's back, causing the woman to lift her chin to see what Cassidy wanted. Perfectly positioned, she thought. She smiled and brought her lips to Brenna's, intending a chaste and quick kiss.

Brenna's moan made her throb, and Cassidy reached for Brenna's shoulder to turn the woman more fully into her body. With Ryan nestled against both their shoulders, she wrapped her arms around the two people she loved most.

When they parted, Cassidy stroked Brenna's hair lightly.

"I missed you so much," Brenna murmured. "I should have found more time away. One day since New Year's wasn't nearly enough time together."

"We will work all this out," Cassidy promised.

Ryan lifted his head and looked at Brenna. "Did you miss me?"

"I missed you too," Brenna answered him seriously, sincerity clear in her voice.

With Ryan awake, Brenna stood him on his feet. He put himself squarely between the two woman, taking hold of a hand from each. "Where are we going?"

"To see Miss Karen," Cassidy replied.

He grinned and bounced their arms with his excited arm swinging. They let go of his hands, linking their own, as he ran around them, up and down the sidewalk, as the trio picked up the pace to the child care trailer.

Cassidy wanted Brenna next to her but the other woman hung back as Ryan ran ahead inside the trailer, leaving her standing on the stoop talking with Karen Grinaldi, the studio's tutor and caregiver.

"Anything special I should know?"

"No." Cassidy shook her head, but then a glance at Brenna gave her an idea. "Wait, yes. I'd like to make sure that Brenna can come pick him up, if need be."

"So you want to list her as an alternate?"

Out of the corner of her eye, Cassidy saw Brenna start up the steps, looking upset. "Yes, I would. We work odd hours. It might come in useful."

"Well, step inside here and we'll sign the paperwork."

"Thank you." Cassidy held the door for Brenna and put a light hand on her back to encourage her ahead, following Karen inside the trailer.

Brenna said, "I... shouldn't."

Cassidy shook her head. "Most nights we'll leave about the same time, but there could be late calls. For either of us."

Karen fished in her desk for the proper form, coming up with it quickly. "Are you rooming together?"

Brenna looked at Cassidy. "I... no. But..." She hesitated. "You're sure?"

"Yes." Cassidy watched as Brenna mulled over the situation, pleased to see how seriously she was taking it.

"It won't happen a lot, I'm sure," Brenna said aloud, clearly convincing herself that this was a small thing.

"It would make me feel a lot easier, knowing he's with you." Cassidy waited for her answer.

"I guess it's all right," Brenna finally said slowly, her words sounding more confident with each syllable.

Karen smiled. "Then sign and print your name and contact information right here." She pointed to a place on the form.

Brenna said nothing more until they were outside the trailer headed back to the set. "Cass, was that a wise idea?"

Cassidy leaned close and held Brenna captive with her gaze. "It makes me feel pretty wonderful."

"Me too," Brenna answered in a low whisper, their hands overlapping on the door panel as Cassidy reached for it.

Cassidy held the door as they reentered the soundstage. "It's a very early day today. Would you like to do something after work tonight?" she whispered.

Brenna's shiver of pleasure did not go unnoticed and Cassidy smiled.

"Your place, or mine?"

"Mine," Cassidy said, and it sounded more like she was claiming Brenna rather than simply stating her preference of location for their third official date.

Will Chapman, Time Trail's Mark Raycreek, drew the attention of both women as they stepped out from the shadowed corner where they had been speaking. "Are you ready to get to work?"

"Ready," Brenna answered with a smile. Trailing behind Will, each woman grabbed a bottle of filtered water as they passed the small catering table.

"Bren. Cass." Already seated, Rich Paulson grinned at Cassidy and Brenna as they appeared around the edge of the set wall. "Looks like vacation was good to you."

Cassidy blushed. A quick glance to her right saw Brenna was doing the same. Smiling brightly back at Rich, Cassidy nodded. "Ryan and I stayed in town for most of it."

Rich puzzled, "No family?"

Cassidy felt Brenna's reassuring touch on her back as the woman passed behind her to get to her seat. Cassidy wrapped her hands around the back of her own chair. Catching Brenna's nod out of the corner of her eye, Cassidy turned back to Rich with a steadier gaze. "A little."

"Something the matter?" Rich asked.

"No. We hadn't spent a holiday here in the city before, is all. What did you and Linda do?"

"We spent a week in the Pocono mountains," he said. "Perfect snuggling weather."

Recalling the breakfast in bed Brenna had brought her as a surprise, Cassidy smiled. "Yes, it was."

"Cass?"

Cassidy blinked, embarrassed she had "checked out" on her colleague. As she was debating what to say next, she felt a large presence move behind her. Cassidy stepped aside as Will Chapman brushed past. He seemed quite distracted.

"Is there news on your sister, Will?" she asked politely.

Uncharacteristically, he grinned widely and expansively spread his arms. "I'm an uncle! Christmas Day. Seven pounds eight ounces."

"Congratulations! Boy or girl?" Rachelle asked.

"Oh? Um..." Will was clearly flustered as several others in the cast pounded his back congenially. "It's a girl. My sister's doing great, too."

"That is good news." Brenna took her seat.

Cassidy watched as something intangible passed between Brenna and Will, then Brenna dipped her chin in acknowledgment of something and Will took his seat next to her with only a light brush of his hand over hers. Cassidy flashed back to Brenna's revelation that the two had a brief affair little more than eighteen months ago.

Forcing her mind from the disturbing thought, Cassidy was sitting down when she heard Brenna's voice again, this time filled with great warmth and surprise.

"Max! Brady?"

Cassidy glanced at Brenna and saw her face light up. Unable to resist, Cassidy turned around to study the two men, new faces to her, now standing in the doorway.

"Good to see you again, Bren." The older man, dark-haired and redwood-tall, quickly circled the table and enfolded Brenna in a bear hug as she came to her feet.

"No one told me you were in this one, Max."

"When I won the casting call, I asked them to keep it quiet so I could surprise you."

Cassidy noticed how Brenna patted him affectionately before she turned to the younger man, also dark-haired but leaner in build. His facial features were similar to Max's. He stepped up to Brenna, who had to look up about six inches to meet his gaze. Brenna's next words caught Cassidy off guard again.

"My God, you're your father twenty years ago. James and Thomas would love to see you." Brenna wrapped both arms around Brady's neck, hugging him while kissing his cheek. "You both have to come to the house." Turning to Max, she asked, "Did Mary come with you?"

Max shook his head. "I'm afraid I'm at the mercy of the commissary or take-out this time. Mary's with her mother on a cruise in the South Pacific."

Brenna could not seem to take her eyes from Max very long, nor from Brady next to him. She asked after Brady's studies, surprised to hear this wasn't a lark, but that he had chosen to go into acting. "My old man has so much fun at it," he finished, "I thought I'd check it out."

"Do you like it?" Cassidy asked.

Brenna beamed at her as Brady turned to answer Cassidy's question. "I've only done a few roles. Dad's helped pick them out, and advised me a couple of times, but overall, yes, I do."

Max and Brady circled the table shaking hands, trading greetings and introductions. The social conversation ended as the director and the episode's writer appeared. It was Cassidy's turn to be startled, though not in a good way. "Cameron?"

Cameron Palassis, one of the studio's writers, had been moved off the series early in December. She had ended her intimate relationship with him at the same time.

The last time she had seen him, he had pawed her in public and made them both a spectacle at the studio holiday party. Now he did not look at her. Instead he kept a guarded expression trained on Will Chapman and Terry Brown, who both stood as he had entered the room.

Either ignoring the standoff, or oblivious to it, director Jackson Tierson pulled out the chair at the head of the table. "Let's start."

The cast settled around the table to begin reading through the newest script. Across the table, Cassidy found Brenna's gaze, watched her smile fade into an uncertain frown as she looked at Max before following the page as Terry's voice started on the opening line.

```
    Chris:   Lieutenant, I thought I was taking
the point position.
    Susan: Heatherly was spotted this time. I'm
going.
    Chris:   Creighton?
    Creighton: The commander is joining us.
    Chris:   Right.
    There is a Vortex effect and briefly everyone
vanishes from sight. Raycreek is standing aside
with a smile. Luria at the console reacts to a
bad reading.
    Luria:    Interference at the reception site.
I'm going to reverse the stream, bring them back.
    Raycreek: You will not, Lieutenant. Wait for
the recall signal.
    A console light begins flashing.
    Luria:   Damn it!
    Luria performs the recall protocol. The
Vortex effect is radically different and when it
clears, there are four people on the platform:
Chris, Creighton, Susan Jakes (prime) and Susan
Jakes (Alt), who is considerably older.
```

Max let out a low whistle. "Two of you," he said to Brenna. "Yum."

"And you won't get either one," she teased.

"Damn," he said with a laugh.

Cassidy's stomach flip-flopped as Brenna laughed along with him. It was good to see her lover happy, but she was surprised at her own spurt of jealousy. She wondered who, exactly, Max was.

"So, wanna do some blocking?" Max asked.

"Cass?" Brenna looked at her.

"I'm just going to my trailer to work on my lines." She wondered whether Brenna would come with her. After all, it had been a week since they'd been together.

However, Brenna didn't pick up on her unspoken invitation, or was declining, since she looked up at Max and then answered, "All right. I'll see you when we're done."

Cassidy watched in surprise as Brenna put her hand on Max's offered elbow and walked away. All the while, she tried to tell herself that Max was obviously an old friend, and Brenna probably wanted to spend time catching up. It didn't cure the ache, but it did galvanize Cassidy into moving off in the other direction.

CHAPTER THREE

A REPORTER stopped Cassidy outside, requesting "a few minutes". Taking him at his word, she led him to her trailer steps, sat down, and gave a simple interview.

Finally she entered her trailer to get some memorization done. Just nearing the end, she heard her stomach rumble, suggesting she find some lunch, Cassidy heard a knock at the door. She hoped it would be Brenna.

Cassidy definitely wanted them to do something together off set, like get something to eat, just not too far away. Maybe with some clothes shopping afterwards. And then they could come back to the lot and pick up Ryan from Miss Karen.

However, the visitor at her door proved to be a Peter Murray, who said he was with the Virginia Dispatch newspaper.

"Ms. Hyland?" he asked.

"Yes?"

"I'd like to ask you some questions about the series and the final wrap. Do you have a few minutes?"

Hoping it would be only a few minutes, she didn't invite him inside. Leaning against the railing alongside her trailer steps, she said, "All right."

He started off by asking whether she had been enjoying the work. She answered by rote until a question came out of the blue.

"Do you have a favorite designer shop in the mall?"

Since she had just been thinking about clothes, she wondered whether she had said something out loud. Cassidy gave him her full attention. "Excuse me?"

"I was picking up gifts for my kids at the mall, and I spotted you at the food court."

"Me?"

"You are quite recognizable." He gestured toward the set. "So is she."

"Lanigan?"

"Yes. This is her, right?" He held out a small photograph. It had been taken at the food court at the mall when they all were there the day after Christmas. Centered in the frame, she and Brenna were leaning over a table, passing out food. "Who are the kids, yours or hers?"

"The two teens are hers," she supplied evenly, knowing lying would be stupid. She began thinking of ways to convince him to give her the picture—and the negatives. "The youngest is mine." She hadn't even seen a flash go off. Well, she reasoned, I was distracted. At least it wasn't when they had their heads bent together, quietly discussing Thomas and James.

"Ms. Hyland, the general belief is that the two of you hardly speak. I'd like the scoop if that's changed."

"Working hard together creates friendships in the toughest situations, Mr. Murray." She vaguely recalled Brenna saying something similar months ago.

"So you were just Christmas shopping together?"

"Yes," she answered. "Mind if I show her the photo?"

He stepped back from her outstretched hand. "That's all I needed," he said hastily. "Thank you for your time."

Cassidy watched him leave then, feeling a presence, spoke to the shadow behind her left shoulder. "I was waiting for the right moment to get the picture," she said. She did not have to turn to see the hard look Brenna had shot the reporter go slack.

"Picture? All I saw was your face go pale—"

"How can you tell under the makeup?"

"You're not wearing any, and neither am I." Brenna's expression turned tender as her voice became softer, private. "I learned to pay attention. I care."

"I'm sorry. I didn't mean to snap." There was silence as their eyes met. Cassidy swallowed. "I was thinking about doing something with you, now I'm not so sure."

"Why?"

"I didn't get the pictures from him."

Brenna raised an eyebrow in query. "Pictures of...?"

"Us at the mall with the kids."

"We can explain that easily, right?"

"But how many more are out there?" Cassidy fretted.

"Would it really harm anything to be seen out shopping together? Or having dinner?"

"Bren..."

"Why don't we go out after work? It might be fun. Nothing intimate, just shopping, a little dinner. Someplace nearby." Brenna shook her head, her hair in such disarray around her features that when she looked up, she had to brush the locks behind an ear to see Cassidy.

"Why don't we go back to the set, work on some walk throughs, and then call it a day?"

"I'd like that."

"You need to meet Max," Brenna said.

"Do I?" Cassidy asked, hoping her jealousy wasn't evident in her voice.

"He's got a wicked sense of humor."

Cassidy smiled at Brenna's gaze, all for her. "All right. Let's go."

Hours later, Cassidy understood a little of what Max was to Brenna. They'd been walking through several different scenes, and though Brenna hadn't memorized her lines, her interactions based on Max's cues were spot on, and he had the uncanny ability to pull spontaneity from Brenna. Out of the corner of her eye, Cassidy saw someone walk through carrying a coat. It made her think of the time. Looking at her watch, she said, "It's after four."

Immediately Brenna stopped talking to Max. Cassidy resisted the desire to smile broadly as Brenna turned to her. "You ready?"

"Been ready," Cassidy answered.

Brenna said to Max, "I'll catch you for dinner another night. I've got a date."

"Really?"

Brenna couldn't contain her pleasure. "Yes."

Cassidy saw the surprise on his face, but if Brenna was unconcerned about his reaction, she decided she could be as well. She casually followed Brenna out of the soundstage.

Once they were outside, Cassidy pulled out her cell phone and dialed Karen Grinaldi, letting the caregiver watching Ryan know they would be off the studio lot for a few hours. Karen assured her everything would be fine, and Ryan would be waiting for them whenever they were finished.

CHAPTER FOUR

"I DO. I think it's a good script." Cassidy lifted her glass of chardonnay to her lips. A light smile touched the bow-shaped lips and the candlelight from the small tea light between them on the table flickered in the darkening blue. Cassidy blushed. In a low voice, she commented, "You're staring."

Brenna shrugged. "You're beautiful."

Brenna's voice was pitched just as soft, but its huskiness rolled over Cassidy with palpable effect as her groin convulsed.

They had found this little jazz place only a few blocks from the studio and after their afternoon spent perusing shops without anyone interrupting their time together, Cassidy had begun to relax. No one seemed to be following them. She was still concerned about Mr. Peter Murray and those like him, but it was hard to worry when Brenna seemed so happy.

The musical interlude from the band made their words private, even if their looks and touches couldn't be. "When you talk like that," Cassidy said, "this is the perfect setting."

"What do you mean?"

"Your voice, it makes me... actually made me from the very beginning, think of smoky jazz clubs."

"You'd be the torch singer," Brenna corrected. "God, when I recall 'Hold Tight'..."

"You liked that?"

"Loved it. I think I half fell in love with you. The looks you gave me didn't help."

"I liked the song too."

"It felt like you were singing to me. I checked to be sure you hadn't rewritten the lyrics."

"I hadn't, but I felt something then too," Cassidy admitted.

Brenna shook her head and Cassidy found herself watching the firelight dance among the brown and red strands of her hair. Apparently she was quiet and thoughtful too long, as Brenna broke the silence.

"Cass?"

"Yes?"

"Something wrong?" Brenna asked with concern.

"No, everything is right." She started to reach across the table to clasp Brenna's hand resting just to the outside of her wine glass, but stopped. Looking up again, she added, "I'm glad we decided to do this."

Brenna nodded. "Me too."

The music stopped and there was a commotion as the vocalist headlining the evening at the tiny jazz club took the stage after her break. Cassidy shifted her chair around the table so she could watch the performer; it was no coincidence that it also gave her an excuse to sit closer to Brenna. She caught Brenna's smile and returned it as their hands joined under the table.

The floor before the stage slowly filled with couples as the sultry voice began with a danceable jazz standard. "I wish we dared dance." Brenna's breath brushed over Cassidy's throat as she spoke close and very low to be unheard by others.

"Should we finish our drinks and go?"

"Not just yet. It's still early. Maybe after this set."

Leaning back a little, Cassidy saw Brenna move closer, then freeze. Slowly Brenna moved again. She lifted her left hand awkwardly between them and shifted a lock of her own hair as if she was putting it back in place, though it hadn't moved. Cassidy realized that Brenna had just barely stopped herself from resting her head against Cassidy's shoulder.

"More wine?" Brenna asked, reaching forward to fill her glass from the bottle in an ice bucket at the table.

"If I have any more, I won't be responsible for my actions."

Brenna groaned as Cassidy accompanied her words by easing her right arm onto Brenna's lower back. She looked around quickly then let out a breath, hopeful the low lighting was keeping their intimacy unnoticed.

Cassidy leaned back and sipped on her wine, letting the music and the ambiance wash over her. Brenna's weight gradually eased against her body.

A small frenzy erupted at the entrance, drawing their attention as well as everyone else's as a couple popular with the paparazzi entered. The club's security quickly stymied the press, but the flashes continued from outside for several minutes.

Brenna moved away, and with a sidelong glance, Cassidy could see that Brenna had drawn in on herself. She herself was also concerned about the possibility of them being caught in the attention. "Do you want to go?" she asked.

Biting her lip so long that Cassidy wanted to kiss it and make it better, Brenna finally nodded.

"I'll go get the car," Brenna said.

"I'll pay the tab and meet you across the street at the garage in about five minutes."

Brenna stood quickly and ducked past a waiter walking by their table. The next sighting Cassidy had, Brenna was beside the short corridor leading to the rest rooms. She was able to track her to the front door, approaching it from the opposite site of the club. Cassidy shook her head and discreetly waved down the next waitperson. "I'd like my check, please." The young brunette nodded and disappeared briefly. When she reappeared, she wore a small frown. "There are two dinners here."

"Yes. Thank you." Cassidy did not explain, simply handing over her credit card.

A slight frown still marring her features, the waitperson stepped away, returning in a few minutes with the credit slip. Cassidy signed the slip and withdrew a few bills as she put the credit card in her wallet. She handed the money to the young woman. "Thank you for a pleasant evening."

"You're welcome."

Cassidy made her way outside with only a brief stop at the front door by a reporter who noticed her despite his tracking of the other couple inside. "Have a nice evening, Miss Hyland?"

"Very nice. Always excellent service," she added, though this was the first time she had been to this club, which was why she and Brenna had chosen it.

As she gained her bearings, looking up and down the street,

another question came.

"Out on your own this evening?"

Past the flash of his camera, for which she automatically froze, Cassidy spotted Brenna's Mountaineer about a block away. "Yes, of course. Good night."

The hasty retreat unfortunately drew more attention as the single reporter started after her and his flurry of motion drew other eyes. She quickly crossed to the other side of the street, hoping to lose herself in the shadows between the streetlights before crossing back to meet up with Brenna.

The Mountaineer was stopped at a light and Cassidy wondered if Brenna could see that she was being followed. When the light changed, the SUV went on through instead of turning down the street toward her. Cassidy exhaled as her heart rate increased. It would be up to her to catch up to her ride.

She ducked into the parking garage, searching through the darkness for the way to the other street exit. Crowd noises and shouted questions behind her drew her gaze backward. The security guard for the garage, meaty and fit for the job, looked small against the wall of surging reporters. Cassidy ducked around a support post and found her solitary way to the other exit.

The SUV door was already open, Brenna leaning toward the passenger seat.

"Everything all right?" Brenna asked with a frown.

Her question turned Cassidy around from looking over her shoulder.

"Yes." Cassidy pulled herself quickly into the vehicle and shut the door. "Let's go."

Brenna's hand on hers gradually slowed her heart rate as the SUV moved them further and further away from the scene.

Brenna had also nearly relaxed by the time she pulled the SUV into the Pinnacle Studios lot. The gate guard nodded them through, and she parked outside of the pool of illumination provided by a light pole.

While in the dimly lit restaurant, she had relaxed, with Cassidy's encouragement. Now Brenna was stiff, withdrawn, as she had been when she caught sight of the one reporter looking past the other couple he had come to track. The look on his face was as if he was mentally poring through an album of celebrity images, and she had looked quickly to be sure that Cassidy was mostly in shadow.

Cassidy's touch had relaxed her, but the enjoyment had gone from their time together.

Though they were alone now, Cassidy did not take her hand as they walked through the dark lot. "Do you think we've got a problem?" Brenna asked.

Cassidy did take her hand then, which made Brenna smile.

"I don't want our relationship splashed through the papers as something tawdry. Maybe we should work with our agencies to generate some positive press before it becomes a negative issue."

Brenna sighed and briefly rested her head against Cassidy's shoulder, jostling with its movement as they walked. "If I could get the divorce decree done tomorrow, I would."

"In an ideal world," Cassidy lamented.

"I'll bug my lawyer to see what she can do to hurry things up."

Their conversation stopped as they entered the child care trailer and found Karen sitting reading a magazine while Ryan slept soundly on a cot. Cassidy gingerly picked him up, and Brenna took his backpack from Karen.

Once outside, Cassidy spoke more quietly, as she asked, "Have you spoken with Kevin recently?"

Brenna swallowed. She had, and the conversation had not gone comfortably. "He's hurting, but... he's got his daughters to consider, as well as his campaign hopes. I don't want to hurt Ellie or Marie, either, so I've spoken with them."

"How are they taking it?"

"Marie—she's older—says that she knows a girl in her classes who likes girls, and in class, they've talked about homosexual relationships."

Cassidy winced. "It sounds like a 'but' is coming."

"But she says it's weird because I 'don't wear fatigues or dress like a boy'." Brenna sounded as aghast as her expression suggested.

Cassidy chuckled. "Clearly high school is not filled with 'lipstick lesbians'." Brenna looked disturbed. "What's wrong?"

"I never thought there would be a 'type' I was expected to be."

"So, what Marie said bothered you? Don't worry, Bren." Cassidy adjusted Ryan in her arms and leaned in to kiss her. "It's not like I have expectations of it all, either. I fell in love with you exactly as you are."

"And when the press asks, which you know they will?"

"How much did you say to them about your relationship with Kevin?"

"They never really asked me. Kevin talked about it. I did the usual pre-wedding spreads in Celebrity Monthly and People."

"Publicity." Cassidy nodded. "I guess we have to think about it, but..." She frowned. "I'm not really interested in 'coming out' and playing some political angle. What we have means a lot to me, and it's private."

"We don't want it tainted, or misconstrued."

"Exactly." When they reached her car in the parking lot, Cassidy put Ryan in his seat in the back.

Cassidy started to lower herself into her driver's seat, then stopped. "Bren?"

"Yes?" She leaned on the frame of the open door.

"I'll see you tomorrow?"

Brenna was disappointed that their conversation was at an end. "Yeah."

Cassidy's leaned across the car door and nuzzled Brenna's cheek. "I'm just not ready yet to share you with the rest of the world."

"Oh." As she stepped back, Brenna's blush was evident, even in the low parking lot lighting. "I'll see you tomorrow."

Brenna fought against the melancholy which welled up as she watched Cassidy drive away. She quickly went to her own vehicle and followed Cassidy's car out of the lot, turning right when Cassidy turned left. She didn't see the vehicle which turned and followed her to the outskirts of her Pacific Palisades neighborhood, turning off its lights in the parking lot of a darkened corner store.

CHAPTER FIVE

THE NEXT morning Cassidy woke to the insistent ringing of the telephone. Glancing at the clock, she saw that there were still ten minutes before her alarm was supposed to sound. Rubbing her eyes, she glanced at the caller ID and quickly picked up. "Bren? Something wrong?"

"We're in the papers."

Brenna sounded flustered.

Cassidy sat up, brushing her hair from her face with one hand while adjusting the phone against her ear with the other. "What?"

"Entertainment wrap up. That reporter with the photos must've been with EW."

"He said he was with the Virginia Dispatch."

"That lying sack of—"

"Whoa!" Cassidy cut into Brenna's vehement outburst. "We don't know that. What exactly does the caption say?" She wished she could read over Brenna's shoulder; her own copy of the LA Times was still on her front stoop.

"'Not known for their close association, Brenna Lanigan and Cassidy Hyland were both seen at the opening night of Suede's tour stop at Jazzy Jay's. According to the wait staff, the couple shared a check, ducking out separately during the uproar surrounding the arrival of current hot-n-heavy couple, Jeff Masters and Gail Oberlain.'"

"That doesn't sound too bad. We might get a few questions on press day about it, but truthfully, we can say we're friends and we went out for a break after work."

She could not see Brenna's face, but envisioned the half smile at her response:

"Nothing more than friends?"

Cassidy chuckled. "We don't have to say any more."

"All right. I'll practice my straight face."

That made Cassidy laugh outright. "See you in an hour on set?"

"Are you bringing Ryan again today?"

"Yes."

"I'll see you in an hour then. Love you."

Cass heard the sound of a blown kiss through the phone and offered one in return.

"Love you, too."

"What's up with you and her?" Max asked Brenna as she responded yet again to a wave from the blonde passing through the soundstage.

She erased her expressive smile and turned back to Max. "What's up?"

"I know we haven't worked together in a while, but I seem to remember you being a little more focused at work."

Brenna considered for a moment and then decided it would be a good opportunity to share a little of how much better she felt about her life in general with a long-time, close friend. "Max, I'm a lot happier now than I have been on a set in a long while. The work's not any easier, but it's more fun."

"Like at the beginning?"

"Something like that, I guess. But now I know what I'm doing, so the shine's off of the business and more on the... relationships I am building."

Max's brow furrowed. "Isn't Time Trails about to finish up?"

"Yes. These are good people. Did you know..." She trailed off, thinking that she didn't want to mention Cassidy first. "Terry Brown has a playhouse in La Jolla. He's invited me to join up."

"Plays? So you're thinking of leaving the small screen behind?"

"I don't know about full time. I've also got a movie in England in April."

"A movie? You haven't been this busy since Thomas and James were very young."

Brenna noticed Cassidy standing at the edge of a temporary wall. "Why don't we go to lunch and we'll catch up?"

"Am I going to get a home-cooked meal?"

"Nope. Commissary." She smiled, stood, and waved Cassidy over. "Do you mind if Cass joins us?"

"I... well..." Max hesitated and then shrugged. "I guess not."

Brenna was already moving to catch Cassidy's attention. "Cass, will you join us for lunch?" she called.

Cassidy turned, and for a moment her features registered surprise. "All right."

Brenna watched Cassidy's appraisal of Max as he stood to his full height. He was an imposing man, dark hair and thick, and he was assessing Cassidy right back.

Brenna stepped between them, reasoning that she wasn't jealous, but unable to articulate why the mutual study bothered her. "Let's go."

Cassidy's gaze dropped to meet hers and the quick sure smile eased the knot which had started to form in her stomach. "How long have you known Bren?" Cassidy asked Max.

"More than twenty years," he replied. Brenna caught Cassidy's surprised glance at her. Brenna's unease started up again until Max gleefully added, "So, how many dirty secrets do you want to know?" She turned in time to catch his wink.

Cassidy laughed out loud, and Max offered them each an arm. While Cassidy took the left with alacrity, Brenna was slower to take his right. She caught Max's eye and lowered her brow. His smile did nothing to assure he understood her unspoken plea.

Max is a lovely man, Cassidy thought, as she laughed at another story of a prank he had played on Brenna when he took her out for her first legal drink.

"She wanted a Long Island Iced Tea, having heard they contained several varieties of alcohol. I had the waiter bring plain tea, sweetened. I kept telling her if the drink was properly made, a person shouldn't taste the alcohol, which is true. She drank three rounds before she realized she wasn't anywhere near tipsy."

He rubbed his shoulder. "Still hurts when it rains," he said with mild accusation, but a broad smile.

"When I finally had a real Long Island, I actually couldn't tell the difference, but I had watched the bartender make it."

Stifling a chortle, Max bit into the deli turkey sandwich. "In another life, Bren, you were definitely a teetotaler."

"I snuck alcohol at home a few times before I was legal," Cassidy admitted. Brenna's gaze held hers for a moment with a gentle smile. "My father would have killed me if he knew."

"So what's your choice these days?" Max asked.

"Wine, or Irish coffee," Cassidy answered.

"Did you introduce her?" Max asked Brenna.

"No," Brenna replied with a smile. "Just something we found we have in common."

Cassidy nodded. Catching sight of a clock, she realized abruptly she had better go. "Wow. I didn't realize how long we've been at this. This has been very interesting, but I think I'd better go see how Ryan's doing, and get back to Terry for rehearsals."

"I'm going to send Max to his hotel in another hour, and then I'll come and watch," Brenna said as Cassidy stood up.

"All right."

"Come on, Bren, not even a single home-cooked meal?" Max sighed.

"You should take Max home, Bren, and catch up. I'll see you tomorrow."

Brenna nodded, but Cassidy could tell that Brenna was bothered by their separation. Frustrated by her inability to communicate openly with Bren, Cassidy left quickly.

"Max, let's go." Brenna stood as soon as Cassidy was out of sight. "The sooner we get the blocking done, the sooner we can get going."

He hadn't risen. "Bren, are you upset that I'm here?"

"Of course not. It was a surprise, but it's good to see you."

"You forget how well I know you. What's wrong?"

Retrenching, Brenna realized she had to take Max home. "Max, it's all right. I'm sorry. It is good to see you, and I'll take you and Brady home to see James and Thomas tonight."

"You'd rather she came along, though."

Brenna glanced toward the door through which Cassidy had gone. "She's the newest member of the ensemble."

"Bren, I read entertainment news too. She was your 'date' the other day, right?"

He didn't make the motion, but she heard the quotation marks in his pause over the word.

She sighed. She couldn't lie to him. "Max, will you accept that I can't discuss this here?"

He stood. "Will we eventually?"

Brenna looked away again, thinking about how to talk to Max, her oldest friend, about her newest lover. He had been with her through some of the toughest times of her life, but she still had no idea what he would think. Eventually, she just didn't answer his question. "Let's go finish our blocking." She led the way back to the soundstage, where they spent the rest of the afternoon.

Will and Sean were working with Brady, Max's son, when Cassidy arrived back at the set. "How's it going?" she asked, as Sean stepped back from a position pretending to hold a weapon.

"The bad guys have been apprehended," he said with a broad smile.

"Need any help from me?" she asked, picking up her script from a nearby navy blue canvas chair.

Will thumped Brady on the back. "Well, 'Heatherly Junior' here seems to like the ladies."

She circled around, smiling as Brady's gaze followed her. "Divide and conquer?" she said pointedly to Sean.

Sean laughed. "All right. Let's stage this thing again."

The four separated to their marks for the beginning of the scene, and the walk-through began, allowing her to put real life from her mind for a little while as she inhabited Chris Hanssen's life and times.

CHAPTER SIX

BRENNA CLEARED the table while the four males sat around it talking. Thomas and James had both come home in time for the late dinner she'd put together for Max, Brady, and herself. She had sheepishly told Max that she wasn't sure what her sons were planning for the evening, but she had made enough for everyone in case they did show.

Thomas was in the process of explaining the FIRE program to Max, who listened and asked about a variety of conservation topics. Brady had fallen into conversation with James, who seemed more open with him than Brenna had seen her son with any of his peers in a while. They talked of art shows and something called a CAP project, which apparently had to do with public school art programs partnering with galleries.

Each time Brenna had injected a comment, her sons would nod, but seldom responded, so she had decided to vacate the room.

She looked at the phone several times as she passed between the dining table and the sink, and after washing the last dish, she retreated to her bedroom and called Cassidy.

The phone rang twice before Cassidy picked up.

"Hello?"

"It's Bren. How did the rest of your day go?"

"Quietly. Ryan and I got home about twenty-five minutes ago. I just put him in the tub. How's dinner with Max and Brady?"

"They're enjoying conversation with Thomas and James." Brenna settled on her bed and stretched out her legs. She reached for the neighboring pillow and hugged it against her lap. It was a poor substitute for Cassidy's head there, but a firm comfort as they talked.

Cassidy must have heard the resignation in her voice. "Is it going well?"

"Now that I'm out of the way, I think it is."

"Bren, I'm sorry."

Brenna exhaled. "I'm sorry, too. I don't know that Max senses anything wrong. He hasn't seen the boys since they were in grade school."

"Before Time Trails then. Max seems like a fun guy. Did you ever date?"

Brenna detected the undercurrent. "It... No, he's just known me a long time."

"Would he be surprised, do you think?"

"Surprised? About us? At least."

"So that's why you were off at lunch," Cassidy probed.

"No, I was off at lunch because he was giving you a very deliberate once-over. Didn't you notice?"

Cassidy's laugh was light through the phone, and it made Brenna smile.

"I was too busy tamping down butterflies every time you looked at me."

"So, I'll see you at work tomorrow?"

"See you."

"Love you, Cass."

"Love you, too, Bren. Good night."

"Sleep well."

Brenna rejoined Max after Thomas and James turned in for the night, taking Brady with them to set up the game room space for sleeping. "Anything for you?" she asked Max, going into the refrigerator for fruit juice.

"A little straight talk," he replied.

He joined her in the kitchen, standing in the middle of the entry arch, leaning against the wall, arms crossed over his chest as he considered her.

"All right. What do you want to know?"

"Will you tell me about you and Cassidy?"

She leaned against the counter, crossing her arms over her chest in imitation. "It's a long story."

"Then why don't we go out to the pool deck? It's a nice night, and we can sit as long as we need to without any interruptions."

Brenna exhaled. He had never let her get away with anything for very long. "All right."

Out on the deck, she sat in the bench swing and he settled in next to her, leaned back and put his arm across the back of the bench. Brenna leaned forward, starting the swing rocking. She remembered sitting there with Kevin, just like that, when her own recognition of her irrevocably changed feelings had finally dawned on her.

"You haven't asked about Kevin," she said.

Something on the side table had drawn his attention but now he turned back. "The politician you married?"

"Yes. He... I... We're not going to be married much longer."

"So you're getting a divorce." He nodded at some silent thought. "Doesn't surprise me."

"It doesn't?"

"Brenna, I... When you are excited about something, you always share it with me and Mary." He looked down at his feet then back up at her. "I knew something was up when I read about your marriage in the paper instead of hearing about it from you."

"I'm sorry. I apologize."

"I'm not upset about that. I am upset that it took you a year to realize he was wrong for you."

"Just a little longer than that," she admitted. "It's not his fault, though."

"So he was a good guy?"

"Yes. I just wasn't suited to him."

"You're more suited..." He seemed hesitant to make the leap of logic.

"To Cassidy. She and I began an intimate relationship a little more than a month ago." She braced herself for any number of possible negative reactions.

"I don't think I've ever known you to have feelings for a woman before."

His observation wasn't particularly negative, just unexpected. She relaxed marginally. "I haven't."

"She's quite a bit younger, isn't she?"

"She's thirty-two. Her son Ryan is five."

"Does she have a history?"

Brenna knew what he meant. "A youthful episode. She says she never gave it much meaning."

"She seduced you?"

Brenna smiled. "No."

"So you..."

Brenna took some time to put her thoughts into a semblance of order, brushing her hands together and recalling the nuances of her emotions in Cassidy's presence, in her arms, when they made love. She slowly sat up.

"Max, I love who I am when I'm with her. She... I am totally me, and whatever I think, feel, do... She's... I don't know how, and I sometimes wonder why, after I treated her so badly, she can even stand to look at me. But when I do... her eyes never let me go. There's a connection I can't deny; I don't want to deny."

"I have known you through some of the highest ups and lowest downs of your life, Bren." He put a big gentle hand on her shoulder. "It didn't occur to me that a woman would ever capture your heart. You seemed to find pleasure rather freely with men."

Brenna considered her relationships and an even deeper recognition occurred. "Max, I never felt this level of completion with any of them. It's that ... my soul is happy, I think."

Max's lips curled into a smile. "You've never said that about any relationship." He squeezed her shoulder. "I guess I'm happy for you. Do you think it will last?"

Sighing, Brenna lifted one hand and ticked off potential barriers with the fingers of the other. "If we can get Thomas and James to relax, complete my divorce from Kevin, survive the press storm when our relationship inevitably becomes known. I also want to reconcile Cassidy and her parents..."

Max's chuckle filled the air as her voice trailed away. "Brenna, you are as bull-headed as they come. I have no doubt you will make it all happen."

"God, I hope you're right."

Impishly he said, "And when it's all over, I have no doubt you will be grand marshal at a Pride Parade somewhere."

Brenna's eyes widened, then she closed them and covered her face with her hands. "You think I'm going to grandstand."

"You never do anything halfway."

"Cassidy wants to keep us as quiet as possible for as long as possible. I don't want to unintentionally do something until she's comfortable."

"Then I'd say you should do your research discreetly." He looked at the small table again and picked up the dog eared copy of Curve magazine. "The store where you bought this, anyone could talk."

Brenna groaned and took the magazine from him. "I picked it up on my last trip to the grocer's."

Cassidy was just readying herself for bed when the phone rang. She didn't recognize the Caller ID, but it was a local call. With a sigh, she picked it up. "Hello?" The line was silent, then a click indicated the caller had hung up. Puzzled, she replaced the receiver and shook her head, lying back and closing her eyes.

CHAPTER SEVEN

CASSIDY WALKED onto the set in full costume and makeup and saw Bren and Max, with Brady between them, chuckling as they came in through the doors she knew led from the parking lot. "Hi," she called.

Max dipped his head in her direction and smiled. Brady blushed, clearly caught up by his hormones as he looked at her. Cassidy, however, was most pleased with Brenna's expression. A flush crept up her throat, and she swallowed several times. *Hormonal rushes aren't just for teenage boys*, Cassidy thought with a smile.

Finally Brenna summoned a "Hi." Max swatted Brenna playfully on the back of the head and she yelped, "Hey!"

Brady ducked past Cassidy and she saw him stop to chat with Sean and Chelle.

Cassidy approached Brenna and Max, and just caught the tail end of what Max was whispering.

"...a hormonal teen."

"Who? Brady? Don't worry; I'm used to it," Cassidy said with a chuckle.

"No," Max replied. "Bren here had her tongue practically on the floor. If the two of you want to keep it under the gossips' radar, you'd better be more circumspect."

Cassidy's humor instantly changed into concern. "Bren?"

"We had a long talk last night."

"Brady seems okay with it," Cassidy said with a puzzled frown.

"He wasn't there. Max waited to browbeat me until after the boys were in their rooms for the night."

"Oh." Cassidy lifted her gaze back to Max. "She seemed to think you might be surprised."

"In this business? When every fifth person I've worked with is gay? Please." He turned away from her and abruptly stopped speaking. Cassidy turned around to find Jackie Gabby, the episode's second unit assistant director.

The young woman tapped her clipboard with the side of her pen. "Mr. Brightman, we need you over at Set C for the battle baton choreography."

"Right." Max excused himself.

Jackie paused before turning away. "Ms. Lanigan?"

"I'll be right there, Jackie."

"Yes, ma'am."

Cassidy felt Brenna brush against her as she moved, presumably to watch Jackie walk away. "Another day apart," Cassidy replied.

"Let's try a slightly different outing tonight."

"What?"

"Let's take everyone to Terry's playhouse."

"So that's why he's not here today."

"No, it's what he's doing when he's not here." Brenna smiled and Cassidy shivered, from that, and the sensation of Brenna's fingertips across the back of her own hand. "I'm done here at four. The play starts at eight."

"You want to take Max, Brady, Ryan, Thomas, and James to a play out of town?"

"James and Thomas won't come. Ryan will enjoy it, and Max will be a less annoying cover than a publicist, so I can spend some time with you. And," she nodded, "yes, it's a bonus that it's out of town."

Cassidy laughed. How could she refuse? "All right. And maybe if we can get everyone used to seeing us together, you can accompany me to the opening of Vampyra."

Brenna shrugged. "How long have we got?"

"Opening is in three weeks."

"A vampire movie on Valentine's Day?" Brenna's quick distasteful twist of her lips made Cassidy laugh again. "I don't know about that."

"Would you rather we go to a chick flick romance?"

Brenna's expression turned to one of consideration and Cassidy ended the conversation before Brenna could say something which might be overheard. "Better get to your set."

"All right. I'll see you later."

Cassidy walked toward her own set call as Brenna walked in the opposite direction.

As soon as she had shut the door to her trailer, Cassidy flopped onto her couch. With a groan, she pulled off her shoes and lifted her feet in the air over her head, grasping one in each hand to massage them. When her cell phone rang, she considered ignoring it, but then thought maybe it was Karen Grinaldi with something about Ryan. She quickly rolled to her side and grabbed the phone from the desk. "Hello?"

She heard a click as the line closed. Shutting her phone, she waited a few seconds to see if the voice mail chime sounded. When it didn't, she looked at the caller ID. *Mitch? What is he doing calling?*

She wondered if she should call him right back. Part of her quickly said no; another part was curious about what he might feel the need to say to her; and another part was wary. In the end, she decided she didn't need the aggravation and did not return his call.

After work, the group of playgoers piled into Brenna's Mountaineer. With Brenna following directions as Cassidy read them, Los Angeles was soon left behind. The winding route put them on a two-lane road which turned around a mountain and entered foothills just off the Pacific Coast Highway. Vineyards, some old and clearly no longer cultivated, and others with rangy young vines, closely bordered the roadway on either side.

The road was relatively free of other cars. However, as they rounded a turn, a sports car behind them gunned its engine and passed, despite the double yellow lane lines.

Brenna jerked the wheel as the sports car cut back into the lane far too closely, only to speed away before she could get a good look at the vehicle in the headlights of the Mountaineer. She flashed her brights angrily at him, and pulled off onto the very narrow shoulder.

Taking a deep breath, she looked at each of the other occupants. "Everyone all right?"

There was a chorus of "fine" and "yes", while "what the hell was that?" came from Max. Brenna shot him a dirty look for using that language in front of Ryan.

Cautiously, Brenna pulled back onto the road and continued. Finally the sign for the playhouse diverted them onto a dirt road which they bumped over, much to Ryan's laughing delight but to the sorrow of everyone else's tailbones.

The art crowd seemed to be the only type of patron present. At least no one looks to be a reporter, Cassidy thought as she ruefully rubbed a sore shoulder from the jostling she had taken in the SUV.

Brenna approached, leading Ryan. "Sorry about the ride."

"No. It wasn't your driving. What was wrong with that idiot?"

"I have no idea. He seemed in a rather pointless hurry." Brenna looked around and grasped Cassidy's hand. "I'm glad we're here, though. I like the place."

"Does Terry know we're coming?"

"No. I purposely didn't tell him. I didn't want to draw attention to us."

"He'll see us, though."

"Yeah, and he'll figure out we want to be quiet about this."

Cassidy nodded. "Shall we go find our seats?"

Brenna took hold of Ryan's hand and turned around. "Max, get lost, will ya?"

"What? Who me? Such a big, lovable guy?" He smiled, lifted his arms and shoulders in a shrug and ambled off, throwing one arm around his son's shoulder.

Cassidy put her arm around Brenna's waist and laughed. "I think I really, really like Max," she said.

"We've been friends a long time."

"What would you have done if he hadn't been accepting of our relationship?" Cassidy asked.

Brenna looked momentarily upset at the prospect. "I was worried about it." She smiled. "But it didn't happen."

Cassidy remembered her own thoughts after the holiday gala. "I keep waiting for the other shoe to drop."

Brenna, who was leading the way through to the audience area, paused. "What?"

"I mean, we've had small, easily explainable mentions in the paper; your sons have a problem with it, but mostly because they just don't want to 'see' it. My parents have expressed their disapproval. You've had a long time friend not really blink. All pretty benign reactions. I can't help feeling that we're living on borrowed time."

Brenna slipped her free arm around Cassidy's back. "Let's just enjoy the show."

Cassidy admittedly felt better because of the cozy squeeze.

"All right."

After the play, Terry Brown walked up to them through the mingling theatergoers. "I thought I saw you two. Glad you could make it." He looked at Ryan clinging tiredly to Brenna's legs. "Did you bring the whole crowd?"

"Mine don't want to be seen in public with me right now," Brenna admitted. She was casually brushing her fingers through Ryan's hair as she sipped on a bottled water which Cassidy had purchased from the snack table.

"So it's just the three of you?"

When Terry's eyes fell on Cassidy, she shrugged. "We came out with Brenna's friends."

"Max is being a good friend?"

"Yes," Brenna acknowledged.

"Good." He grasped Cassidy's hand. "I'd really like you to think about coming here after Time Trails finishes."

"It's become a lot more complicated than when you asked me five months ago, Terry."

He laughed. "So, maybe I can get two for the price of one?"

Brenna nodded slowly. "It would be a good way to keep roots here when I have to go to England."

"As long as we haven't been driven underground by the press before then," Cassidy said.

Terry was confused. "What?"

"Cass thinks the other shoe's going to drop soon."

Surprisingly, Terry was on Cassidy's side. "You don't think so?" he asked Brenna.

"The only people whose opinions matter to me have already expressed their feelings. We'll work it out. That will be it."

Terry looked at Cassidy. "You don't see it that way?"

Cassidy thought there was more than a little wishful thinking in Brenna's assertion. "Terry, I..." She didn't want to argue with Brenna in front of Terry, and she couldn't really put her finger on why it all felt just too tenuous to believe. She gave a half-hearted shrug but fell silent. Brenna continued rubbing Ryan's hair.

"So, you want to hang out here for a while?" Terry asked. "I can promise there's no media. We're practically invisible to them."

Cassidy commiserated. "I'm sorry to hear that. It was an excellent play." Terry shrugged. "We probably shouldn't stay any longer tonight, either." She looked down as Ryan shifted to her legs from Brenna's, rubbing his face against her pant leg. "I think we should get Ryan home to bed." Brenna started to crouch to collect Ryan, but Cassidy scooped him up first. "It's all right, I've got him."

"Cass?"

"Good night, Terry."

"Good night, Cass, Bren."

Brenna followed Cassidy to the entry doors. "Hold on. We've got to get Max and Brady."

Shaking her head, Cassidy stopped walking. "I'm sorry."

"Are you mad at me?"

What Cassidy felt wasn't anger. "No. I'm... I thought we'd be more of the same mind about keeping things quiet, I guess."

"So you're disappointed in me?"

Whether they saw eye to eye or not, Brenna clearly didn't want to upset Cassidy. "I'm as tired as Ryan," Cassidy admitted. "Maybe I'm being just overly emotional."

"Good thing I'm driving, then. I remember worrying over you in the parking lot after you had that argument with Cameron."

"You did?" Cassidy watched as Brenna turned aside, waving at the air. She looked to see that Brenna had spotted Max. The man tapped his son on the shoulder and they joined the two women at the door.

"Going home?"

"Ryan's tired," Brenna said dispiritedly.

Max gave her an understanding smile. "All right. Let's go."

Brenna took Max and Brady by their hotel first. Once they were alone in the car with Ryan asleep in the back, Brenna asked, "So..." She hesitated. "My place is closer."

Cassidy looked over the seat to Ryan asleep in the back. "Bren, I..."

"No, I'm sorry I upset you. Please let me make it up to you?"

Cassidy asked, "What about Thomas and James?"

"It's nearly midnight. They're home, and asleep."

"Are you sure?"

"Cass, they aren't going to get used to us spending time together if we let them keep us apart." She reached across the center console and squeezed Cassidy's thigh.

"But I don't have a change of clothes for tomorrow."

"I seem to remember a sweatshirt in your size."

Out of objections, Cassidy reluctantly acquiesced. "All right. But I'll have to change as soon as we get to the set."

Brenna made the turn onto the highway headed south. "Done."

The house lights were off when they arrived. Brenna unlocked the door, flipping the switch for the foyer as she stepped back and let Cassidy enter ahead of her, carrying Ryan. "Come on, we'll tuck him into the guest bed and then get some sleep ourselves," she whispered.

Leaving the foyer light on to illuminate their way down the corridor, Brenna leaned in to flip on the light in game room. "No, leave it off," Cassidy whispered. "It'll be easier to keep Ryan asleep."

Navigating by the light of a nightlight in the wall, Brenna flipped open the futon and put on sheets from the storage drawer beneath. She fetched a blanket from a closet. Turning back, she saw Cassidy efficiently stripping her son to his underwear. His eyes were closed and he moved like a rag doll, obviously asleep on his feet. Soon Cassidy had tucked him between the sheets and stepped back. Brenna arranged the blanket over him. Standing in the doorway, she held Cassidy as they watched Ryan breathing easily.

Cassidy's head drifted against Brenna's. "Come on, time for you," Brenna said, guiding the woman out of the room and the few feet to her bedroom.

After closing the door, they turned on a bedside lamp. Cassidy automatically started to strip, and Brenna just watched her for a moment, marveling at her beauty. She was far too tired, and they had to get up far too early for Brenna to do anything about her arousal, but she loved watching the shadows and light flowing across Cassidy's curves as she moved.

She went to her closet to look for something for Cassidy to wear, inhaling sharply as a naked Cassidy pressed up against her back. "We don't need anything," Cassidy said.

"I was just thinking we don't have time for me to ravish you," Brenna said, turning around. She let Cassidy unbutton and remove her blouse.

"So, how about I ravish you?" Cassidy's whisper trailed off and her hot breath brushed Brenna's skin as it was uncovered by Cassidy removing the rest of her clothing.

Brenna stepped out of her shoes and pants as Cassidy instructed.

"I'd like that."

"I know."

Their body heat alone was enough to keep them warm as they slid between the sheets together, naked. Brenna stroked every bit of skin she could reach as they entangled themselves, feet over ankles, knees between thighs, bellies and breasts pressed together.

Cassidy's hands stroked up and down Brenna's back until she cupped Brenna's buttocks, pulling her up slightly.

"Mmm, good." Cassidy's murmur brushed Brenna's temple with warm breath. Her movements slowed, then stopped.

Brenna drew her head back and chuckled softly, brushing Cassidy's hair from her cheeks. "Sweet dreams." She kissed Cassidy's breastbone and snuggled back into her lover's arms, joining her in sleep.

CHAPTER EIGHT

THE NEXT morning, leaving Cassidy warmly wrapped in her sheets, Brenna pulled on a robe and stepped out of her bedroom. She checked on Ryan, who was still sleeping soundly.

Coming out of the game room, she met Thomas walking out of his room, a radio still playing inside. "Good morning," she said.

"Morning," he replied. "When did you get in last night?"

"Around midnight."

He looked at the door to the game room. "Ryan's here," he guessed.

"Yes."

"So she's sleeping in your room?"

"Of course." She put her hand out. "Come on, Thomas, please. Cassidy is important to me."

"I don't want to deal with this right now."

"When?" she demanded.

"Mom, why don't you understand that I can't?"

"Because you aren't talking to me," she replied with exasperation. "You and James—"

"What have I done now?" James appeared at his door, rubbing his hand over his head and face sleepily.

Her second son's appearance forestalled Brenna's response to his question. "What are you doing sleeping in your clothes?"

He looked down at himself. "I, uh, fell asleep as soon as I got home."

"What time was that?" She saw him cast a look at Thomas. "What's going on?"

"Come on." Thomas shoved James down the hall in front of him. "We'll make our own breakfast, Mom. You'd better get ready for the set. See you around."

Brenna grasped his shoulder. "Stop. What's going on? What time did you get home last night?"

"About eleven-thirty," Thomas answered. James said nothing.

"James?"

"Eleven-thirty."

She had the distinct impression he was lying. "I told you we were going out to the playhouse. Knowing I wouldn't be home, did you go somewhere, as well?"

It was Thomas who answered. "We made it in before curfew."

"That wasn't what I asked." She pointedly directed her gaze. "James?"

"I hung out with some friends."

Cassidy appeared in her bedroom doorway, and Brenna watched both Thomas and James eye the blond woman then quickly push past.

"Gotta go."

Brenna leaned against the door jamb. "Well, I guess I wasn't going to get any more anyway."

"Problem?"

"I think Thomas and, or James broke curfew last night," Brenna said, "but I don't have any proof."

"And my appearance ended the interrogation. I'm sorry."

"Don't be. Come on. We'll get dressed. Maybe I can try again over breakfast."

"When do you have to report to the set?" Cassidy asked, stroking Brenna's arm as she embraced her on her trailer sofa. They had dropped Ryan at the childcare trailer and retreated here for some private time.

Looking at the small digital clock on Cassidy's desk, Brenna settled a hand atop Cassidy's, which was lying across her stomach. "Not until eight."

"We have a whole hour together?" Cassidy asked. "No demands, no kids, no colleagues, no reporters?" She sighed happily and bent to inhale the scent of Brenna's hair. "Alone at last."

Brenna kissed their laced fingers. "I love spending quiet time with you," she said. "It's amazing."

Cassidy's hand slipped away from Brenna's arm and down her side to her hip, stroking suggestively close to Brenna's crotch. "And here I was thinking we were in the same bed this morning and I completely missed out on some serious groping because someone had to get up and see why her sons missed curfew."

Laughing, Brenna turned slightly and Cassidy eagerly kissed the offered lips. "Mmmmm....oh," Brenna murmured. "So you really want to make love now?"

"I never thought I'd be randy enough to do something like this, but I can't imagine anyone else I'd rather be the first I do it with. I have been wanting to get into your pants for hours," Cassidy's words sounded dramatic but they were a true expression of her desire, nearly constant, for her lover.

"Ah, I get to be your first." Brenna chuckled, lifting herself up over Cassidy and straddling her thighs. Cassidy rested her hands against Brenna's hips, holding her easily as they fanned each other's arousal with deep, long kisses, tasting lips and tongues. Between kisses, they bared each other's skin and indulged in heated exploration.

Cassidy lay nude but warm under a blanket, and dazedly happy on the couch in her trailer. Brenna had just left to go to the set for her call. Cassidy's call wasn't until later, and they decided she should stay and relax until she was officially due on the set.

Initially there to change from the borrowed clothes to the spare things she kept in her trailer, Cassidy had finished what she had barely started the night before. She curled her knuckles against her lips, still able to smell Brenna's scent on them.

The next time she saw Brenna, they would both have to be in character, but the interlude had been sustaining, and thoroughly fulfilling.

She was surprised at their creativity. The trailer couch was narrow. It should have been impossible to pleasure each other, but they had found a way. Shared oral sex had been the most intoxicating experience. They were both so new to their intimacy, it was as much an exploration of the tastes as it was of touches that would please. Even as Brenna requested a particular touch, she ushered Cassidy toward climax as well. Brenna's way of making love had Cassidy feeling, for the first time, the difference between being someone's prize and being a treasure.

She could still feel Brenna's breath, hands, and tongue moving over her skin. As she had shuddered in release, crying out that she was falling apart, Brenna's strong, soft embrace held Cassidy together, and the rich husky voice whispered over and over again how much she was cherished, showing her a mutual lovemaking unlike the possessive, forceful way every man had ever touched her.

Rubbing her thigh where Brenna had nipped her when she orgasmed, Cassidy recalled experiencing the moment when Brenna let herself go, and her orgasm washed over Cassidy's fingers while her nails pricked into Cassidy's legs and her mouth closed over Cassidy's thigh to muffle the sounds of her ecstasy. In the aftermath ensconced on the sofa, wine-red lips soothed over the faint marks, but Cassidy relished their presence. The tenderness of her breasts and the wetness renewing itself between her thighs just at the thought of Brenna's touch felt wonderful.

Finally sitting up and going to the bathroom to clean up, Cassidy delighted in the flavors on her lips as she licked them. Combing her fingers through her hair to smooth it, she studied herself in the mirror with bemusement. A satisfaction that had been too long missing curled her lips; color accentuated her cheeks; and barely submerged passion still had her pupils wide. She lifted her fingers to her nose, again inhaling the scent of Brenna's sweat and sex.

She sighed. She wouldn't see Brenna again until after she had lunch with Ryan and reported to the set for a short filming session.

The phone rang. She checked the Caller ID and recognized it as an on-set number. It had to be Brenna calling from a set phone. They'd had such a hard time parting. Invitingly, she answered, "Hello."

"Love that whisper of want there, Cass."

Her blood instantly turned to ice. "Mitch?" Why is he calling now? "What do you want?"

"Seems you're a mighty popular person. Made the news lately."

"What do you want?"

"Been interesting reading. Seems you're done with that writer fellow. Moved on to someone else."

"I've made some friends in the cast," she replied.

"Your friend," he said snidely, "what's her name? Brenna Lanigan, right?"

"The papers are wrong, Mitch. She's just a friend."

"You've been staying at her house. You weren't home the other night. She's a lesbian. I won't have my son raised by lesbians."

She wasn't going to get into a discussion with Mitch. He didn't need to know Brenna's re-orientation was a new thing. "The custody has already been decided, Mitch. That won't change. This is California."

"I came here to talk to you about that."

"You're here at the studio?" she said. "Come by the house later."

"I don't want to wait. I went by Gwen and Lou's place and they said you started bringing Ryan here with you, so I thought I'd come for a visit."

"It's not your visitation time. You don't have that choice." Cassidy's knees quivered, but she was proud of herself.

"Damn you've gotten pushy. Certainly not the good girl I trained you up to be. Why don't you come to where I am with Ryan, and I'll tell you all about it before I take him away from all the fancy Hollywood queers."

Flabbergasted at his words and his cool threats, her breath rasped harshly through the phone. "You are not taking Ryan anywhere."

"Oh, but I've already got Ryan. How about we pick you up and have a nice family lunch?"

"You can't have Ryan," she insisted, panic chasing the calm from her voice. "I'll call the cops, Mitch. That's kidnapping."

"Why don't you come and say goodbye? We'll be leaving in a few minutes."

"Don't move!" Cassidy shouted into the phone and slammed it down on its cradle, shaking and angry. *God, he's got Ryan. No! No.* She tried to think. *He has to be bluffing. Ryan is safe with Mrs. Grinaldi.* She picked up the phone and dialed the extension in the tutor's trailer. It rang three times then a fourth without an answer. Her heart raced when the number of rings reached ten. *Oh God!* She burst out of her trailer and hurried toward trailer 14.

CHAPTER NINE

MITCH HYLAND grinned as he hung up at the pay phone just outside of the Time Trails soundstage. *You are a genius, my man,* he congratulated himself as he turned around and saw his ex-wife exit one of the trailers. Run scared, sweetheart. It'll all be over soon. With care for the distance between them and remaining out of sight, he followed Cassidy, knowing full well that she would go directly to wherever she had Ryan, to assure herself of his safety. Then, and only then would she draw others into a search for him.

He had planned on that.

He had been surprised to hear the news about Cassidy's new choice in lovers, but then again, she had always been too adventurous for her own good. It had attracted him at first, and after years of molding her, he had thought her completely his, bound to him by their son.

She stupidly clung to her acting, though, first taking up a guest role on some limited series. He should have put a stop to that. However, she had sweetly made love to him, just as he liked, and addled his brain. From there, these Time Trails people had seen her and enticed her away from him. If I had only followed her here in the beginning. When she told him about the open-ended offer they'd made, he had punished her for even considering leaving their son.

Mitch had underestimated the writer. He frowned, trying to

recall the name. Palassis. He wondered briefly if the man was around somewhere. They certainly had a score to settle for taking his family from him.

Mitch considered the woman he had seen on the set. Brenna Lanigan. That lowly, tiny woman now stood in his way too. With her lesbian seduction of his wife, she had disrupted his plans to pull Cassidy back when the series was over and she was out of work and desperately in need of protection again.

Getting on the lot had been surprisingly easy. He had thought the restraining order Palassis had taken out might still be in effect; he had even planned for that contingency. However, the guards had let him pass without even noting his name. Not surprising, considering the hundreds of people they must check through every day.

The tour forming up had readily taken him in, and the group passed through many areas of the lot. When he saw the first sign for the Time Trails soundstages, he waited, then broke from the group, wending his way through unfamiliar equipment and corridors. What a mess, he had thought derisively. His wife deserved to not work in such squalor.

Ahead, on the path, Cassidy reappeared from a small trailer. Since no one had come outside with her, he suspected where she had led him. Now that she had brought him to Ryan, it was time for him to make his move, and he stepped out from the bushes, whistling Dixie.

"Mitch!"

"Hi, sweetheart," he drawled, hands tucked in his pockets, presenting the non-threatening posture that so often made her drop her guard. He kept his eyes on her hands, watching the cell phone attached to her hip.

"Stay back!" She circled just out of reach of an easy lunge.

Come on, baby. Trust me like I know you can. Her body moved fluidly, despite the fear he could see widening her eyes.

"Where's Ryan?" Cassidy growled.

Ryan wasn't in the trailer? Interesting. He could use that information to his advantage. "In the car. I came back to get you. Let's 'do lunch'. Isn't that how these Hollywood types say it?"

She shook her head. "No!"

Her rejection of his invitation infuriated him.

"Really?" He lunged, catching her off-guard with a feint and able to get around behind her, grabbing both shoulders and pulling them tightly toward her back. "You want to see Ryan again, you'll cooperate."

He started dragging her toward the trailer nearby, but she screamed and surprised him by tripping him up. As she wrenched herself from his grasp, he stumbled as he tried to regain his footing.

"Bitch!"

"I'm not going!" she screamed, and she surprised him with a fist into his throat.

He grabbed her arm, but it slipped until he only had her wrist. He heard it crack as he twisted and wrenched hard. Her face turned white and she screamed in pain.

Pulling the wrist again he twisted harder. The agonized sound she made filled him with pleasure. "Now are you going to come quietly? I have to save you from the queers. You know I do," he cajoled.

With a scream, she yanked herself free. As he reached for her again, she ducked away but he tackled her and they fell against the paved walk with a thud. She grunted and rolled under him. Terror filled her eyes as he settled his weight on top of her.

"Let's go," he ordered brusquely, standing up and grabbing her injured wrist. He didn't care if it was separated or broken; he dragged her up the steps and into the trailer.

During a break in the filming with Max, Brenna looked over and saw Mrs. Grinaldi leading Ryan through the soundstages. Filled with an uneasy flash of concern, she asked, "What is it?"

"When Ms. Hyland didn't come to pick up Ryan for lunch, I thought she must be here with you."

"She isn't," Brenna offered, carefully keeping the alarm from her voice. Cassidy wouldn't leave the set without Ryan, her little voice told her emphatically. And she would feel terribly guilty if their tryst had made Cassidy miss lunch with her son. Brenna crouched at the edge of the soundstage and spoke to Ryan. "Why don't we go and see if your mom fell asleep in her trailer?"

"Okay."

Coming up behind Max, Will noted the looks of concern. "Something up?"

"Cassidy didn't pick up Ryan for lunch."

Will pursed his lips. "I saw Cameron earlier. Do you think they got into an argument?"

"Maybe." Brenna stood up. "I'm going to go looking for her."

"I'll be right behind you," Will said. "Just let me tell the director where we're going."

"Right." Brenna grasped Ryan's hand and strode ahead of Max and Karen toward the row of trailers.

Stumbling as her ex-husband pushed her, Cassidy tried to think past the pain radiating through her fingers and up into her left elbow. In an odd sort of disassociation, she tried to flex her wrist, able to ignore Mitch as the agony became her focus.

"Fucking bitch! Ignore me? Damn you!"

The epithet-filled outburst was accompanied by a backhand knocking Cassidy's head up and aside. The blow made her jaw ache and her ear ring so badly she forgot about her wrist as she stumbled again, this time into a low desk and child-sized chair.

Grabbing the chair as she fell, Cassidy thrust it into Mitch's body when he came after her. With a quick inhalation, she used her undamaged arm to haul herself a few feet away before trying to get her legs under her and stand.

"Where did all this fight come from?" he asked, tossing the chair against the wall. "Do you have any idea how mad this makes me?"

Cassidy lurched against a bookcase, unable to silence the agonized scream which bubbled up when her wrist struck the wood. "Mitch, leave me alone. You don't want to do this!"

"What the hell do you know about what I want?" He smashed his body into hers. The force of his forearm against her chest knocked the wind from her lungs and she gagged and sagged, his weight the only thing holding her up as she fought for breath.

"You are mine! Ryan is mine!" He punctuated each pronouncement with his fists.

Gasping as she pushed, trying to force some space between them, she yelled at him, "Ryan will hate you!" As he pressed forward, she threw herself to the side and slammed her head into his face.

"My boy loves me."

"I'll tell him everything!"

Heedless of the chairs, Mitch lunged through the debris, eyes wild. "The hell you will!"

Oops, wrong thing to say. She got behind the tutor's large desk, circling it as he stalked around the other side.

"Always hiding behind something, or someone, aren't you?" he sneered at her. "Do you hide behind your lesbian friend?"

"No!" Cassidy did not want to let him get on the subject of Brenna. She could take him belittling her, even his physical attacks, but if he turned his venom on Brenna, Cassidy was not certain she wouldn't end up dead trying to make him regret the words. "She has nothing to do with this! Ryan's custody is between you and me!"

"I told you I will not have a lesbian raising my son."

He turned his back, as if to make for the door.

His feint drew her out. Cassidy threw herself after him and caught his lower torso, and they went down in a tangle. His hands wrapped around her head and she struggled to remain conscious as he slammed it against the floor.

Brenna! She conjured the woman in her mind's eye. Soft auburn hair curling around smooth tan features flushed with love, mouth whispering 'I love you', blue eyes sparkling with desire. It kept the mental cobwebs at bay as she fought to get free.

"Wait here, Ryan." Brenna let go of his hand and hurried up the steps to Cassidy's trailer door. Rapping twice, she called inside, "Cassidy, it's Brenna." She pressed her ear to the surface, listening for sound inside though she realized her heart was racing almost too hard to hear anything. She stepped back and knocked harder. "Cass!"

Sweeping the assembled group below with her gaze, she caught Will's eye. He frowned and nodded, and Brenna yanked open the door.

The lights inside were off. She reached for the switch and illuminated the space. It was tidy. She looked into the open door of the bathroom at the back. "Cass?"

She laid a worried hand against the sofa cushion. It was cool to the touch. Cassidy had not been there for some time. *Where are you?*

She hurriedly exited the trailer, reporting, "She's not here."

Terry turned to Mrs. Grinaldi. "Maybe she went to pick up Ryan and just missed you?"

"That's possible," the tutor considered, but no one felt reassured.

"Let's go," Brenna ordered briskly.

Terry pulled out his cell phone as they walked hurriedly along the path. "What's Cassidy's cell number?" he asked.

Brenna quickly gave it without slowing her pace. "What's up?"

"Just thought I'd try the line. Pinnacle's a big place."

"What if she's not wearing her phone?" Brenna asked worriedly.

"You didn't see it in her trailer, did you?" Brenna shook her head. "Then let's just try it." Terry pressed the 'send' button and put the device to his ear. "It's ringing."

CHAPTER TEN

CASSIDY'S HEAD felt like lead balls were rolling around inside. When she swallowed, she tasted blood in her mouth and smelled the coppery stuff filling her nose. Pinned under two fallen toy shelves, she could not recall anything about the last few minutes. Frantically she looked around the devastated classroom.

Agony ripped through her and she retched, trying to turn over. One toy shelf moved, freeing her left leg. Automatically she said, "Thank you."

"Much better." Mitch scowled and yanked her to her feet.

His face was bruised around the nose. She guessed she had managed to break his nose with one of her attempts at head-butting him.

"Now let's talk custody."

The pain in her chest was excruciating. Breathing shallowly, she shook her head. "You will never get Ryan!" She shook her head again, groaning at the sensation of her brain sloshing around in her skull. "Ever!"

A dull ringing sounded in her ears. *The cell phone!* She had forgotten she was wearing it.

She fumbled the tiny phone from her hip, lost it, and watched it slide across the floor, making a scraping sound against the linoleum. Diving after it, she took her eyes from Mitch.

Something struck her leg and she turned to see Mitch wielding a short, dark blue baseball bat.

"He's mine!" he snarled.

The solid wooden bat aimed for her chest.

Raising her arms defensively, she felt the bat land against her forearms instead. Winding up again, Mitch swung for her head. She ducked but felt the swoosh of air as the weapon passed over her. Inhaling sharply, she dove after the electronic lifeline.

Mitch grabbed her leg and her body slammed into the floor, breaths wheezing agonizingly from her lungs. The phone continued to ring. One chance. God, help me. Her knee twisted and gave a sickening pop as she lunged from Mitch's unrelenting grasp. With her other foot, she kicked him in the head. Her hand wrapped around the cell phone.

Just as she pressed the 'talk' button, Mitch brought the bat down against her hand, crushing it and the phone. Bits of metal and plastic drove into her tightened fingers and she screamed.

He hauled her up and threw her against the wall. "Who was that?"

Clawing at his face, she screamed, "I don't know!" Her fingers left a red trail across his cheek.

"You better hope they don't look for you." He raised his fist. "Especially your lesbian lover. All she'll find is a dead body!"

A fever ripped through Cassidy. The cell phone had been her last chance at summoning help. She was on her own, alone, the only thing standing between her manic ex-husband and Ryan. It's him or me, she realized. Watching as he edged toward her, Cassidy propelled herself off of the wall and had a momentary glimpse of Mitch's wide eyes before she landed against him. The surprise took him down more than her weight. She clawed at his face as his flailing arms tried to block her way.

He pushed at her. She pushed back. Her fingers dug into his cheeks and she heard his howl with feral satisfaction. The only way she was going to get out of this was if he died first. It was up to her to save Ryan. She forced her hands into fists and smashed them into his face. His head snapped up and back, and his skull made a loud crack against the floor. She howled in animalistic delight as her prey struggled. She drove her fists again and again into his face, his arms, his upper body, landing punches solidly. The bones under her fingers crackled like paper. She snarled as Mitch reared up.

"What the—"

Clutching his face with her fingers clawlike, she felt the skin shred. She plowed her knee into his groin. As he hunched over, she bashed her fists to the back of his head and brought her knee up against his face.

I will kill you! You will die! Her vision became red; her breathing suddenly seemed easier. Mitch fell to his knees before her. When she kicked him in the head, he dropped to the floor face first.

She followed him to the ground, all fists and claws. *Die!*

"Bitch!"

His fist closed over her jaw. As she wrenched herself away, she distantly she heard the bones separate.

Terry frowned. "I had a connection, then the line went dead," he puzzled.

Brenna was still trying to figure out what he meant when there was a thud against a wall somewhere close by, then another, followed by a scream of such raging volume and pitch that it sounded like an animal. Brenna leaped into action.

"The childcare trailer!" Releasing Ryan's hand, she ordered, "Stay!" and was up the stairs to the trailer before anyone else could take another breath.

Behind her she heard Terry yell, "Call 911!" She looked back to see him and Chapman bounding up the steps behind her. There was no guessing exactly what they would find, but Brenna feared Cassidy was in real trouble.

Will reached the door Brenna had flung wide. "Bren!"

Brenna ran headlong toward a hulking man wielding a baseball bat while Cassidy cowered on the floor, her blond hair streaked with dark patches and matted with fresh blood. Her face was a mass of black and blue, and blood. *So much blood!* With surprising strength, Cassidy shoved a desk at her attacker.

The man wasn't Cameron. Blond and muscular, there was something in the shape of his face that made Brenna think of Ryan. It had to be Cassidy's ex-husband.

She yelled, "Mitch Hyland!" and green eyes swung toward her, gashes bleeding sluggishly in his cheeks and forehead.

The bat in his hands continued its downward path toward Cassidy's head, and Brenna lunged to intercept his attack. She hit Mitch's legs with the full force of her lunging body, striking sideways at his knees. Mitch, the bat, and Brenna all hit the floor inches from Cassidy's head.

"Run!" Brenna encouraged as she wrestled for possession of the bat. Her hands met Cassidy's, and she saw a wild, sightless glaze in her lover's eyes, one of which was nearly swollen shut. Cassidy's lips drew back, her jaw opened, and Brenna only just got out of the way as the woman's teeth closed on Mitch's forearm.

Startled, Mitch reared up, and Brenna had her chance. Her hands closed around the bat and she looked down wild-eyed, seeing Mitch as if in the distance beneath her. She tried to swing the bat but caught a table's edge instead, jarring the muscles and bones in her shoulders, neck, and back.

Mitch lurched up and threw her off.

"The Security team is here."

The sound behind Brenna was almost unintelligible. Immediately on her feet, she advanced on Mitch, still carrying the bat, ignoring the pain shooting down her back. Mitch's attention was on her. Hopefully Cassidy could catch her breath and somehow move away.

Mitch moved to her left; Brenna followed, guarding Cassidy. People swarmed around her to the right and left. Mitch looked away from her, eyeing the newcomers with panic. Her lips drew back in a snarl as she spied the bleeding bite mark Cassidy had inflicted on his arm.

Mitch lunged for Brenna, but the security guards, wielding nightsticks, wrestled him into submission between them.

She heard the door open again and spun around to assess a new attack. Instantly she identified the tutor Grinaldi. "No! Stay with Ryan!"

Mitch took advantage of the men's slackened holds and burst free. His momentum took him at top speed toward Cassidy, who was just beginning to rise shakily to her feet.

"Cass!" Brenna yelled, rushing forward.

Mitch's head and shoulders collided with Cassidy's chest. Everyone in the room heard the sickening crunch of ribs breaking. Cassidy's screams went silent. She coughed up an alarming amount of blood as she sank to the floor, head lolling.

Brenna tried to go over Mitch to reach Cassidy, but his forearm slammed against her head, bringing her down and blinding her for a terrifying instant. She scrambled on the floor, blinking to clear her vision. Her fingers miraculously closed around the bat, her nails biting into the wood.

Through narrowing vision, Brenna saw Mitch struggling between the two security guards who were pulling him away. Mitch's head snapped back as one of the men landed an upper cut. Brenna growled and launched herself at Mitch, bat raised over her head. She unleashed a scream with her swing. "Aiiiiieee!" Again the bat jarred in her arms as it failed to reach her quarry. She screamed in frustration, struggling to free her arms from a muscled grip.

"Bren! Brenna! Stop!"

She struggled wildly as the bat was stripped from her hands, and her thrashing hands curled into claws.

"Bren!"

Her head hit something. "Shit!" The arms around her adjusted and she broke their hold, only to find herself in other arms.

"Bren." This voice was calm. "It's over. He's down. You're safe. Cassidy is safe."

She screamed and the haze slowly cleared as the arms gradually loosened.

"Oh...God..." Brenna's knees buckled and she fell to the floor beside Cassidy. "Oh... God... Cass..."

Tenderly she brushed aside the blood-matted hair to examine the blue, black, and purple face. With shaking fingers she checked the pale throat for a pulse.

There was a faint flutter under her fingertips. She tried to carefully rearrange the still body, feeling the heat and softness in Cassidy's ribs. Moving the torn blouse aside, she found mottled bruises covering most of Cassidy's chest and stomach.

"Ambulance! We need an ambulance!" Turning around, she kept a hand supporting Cassidy's wrist and hand with its puffy fingers and blue knuckles; it looked broken.

"Already called." A security guard fastened handcuffs on Mitch and shoved his prisoner toward the other officers, then approached Brenna. "What the hell happened here?"

"He," Brenna spat, "is her ex-husband." She stroked Cassidy's face and hair. "Howinthehell did he get on site?" Fury warred with worry that deepened the longer Cassidy remained unconscious. There was a disturbingly soft, spongy area on the right side of Cassidy's head. She bent close to the blond hair and nuzzled close, hiding her tears.

Will appeared at the officer's shoulder. "Bren, the EMTs are here."

"I don't think she can be moved," Brenna worried.

"We'll take it from here." A medical technician carrying a kit came around the other side of the overturned table. He moved it aside and surveyed Cassidy, then reached for her limp hand in Brenna's. Brenna did not move and did not release the hand.

"Ma'am, I really need her hand."

"Her, her wrist, I think it's broken."

"Hand, too, I'm guessing," he considered, pressing gingerly around the knuckles. Brenna felt the blood drain from her face. "Ma'am, listen, we'll get her fixed up. It's what we do." He patted her shoulder and she eyed his hand, disconnected from the sensation.

"Bren?" Will's voice sounded behind her then his hands were on her shoulders.

She jerked her gaze to Cassidy. Pulling away from Will, she leaned over and pressed her lips to Cassidy's forehead, then whispered fiercely, "You'll be all right. I love you."

A flash of light drew her eyes to the side. Terry Brown wrestled a camera from a reporter who had somehow gained entrance to the small trailer in the confusion.

He protested, "I've got a valid pass!"

"Then have some respect," Chapman barked.

"Who is it?"

"Cassidy Hyland," Brenna informed him sharply. Shaking as she stood, she looked down at Cassidy, hugging herself in an attempt to hold herself together.

"Who's he?"

Brenna spun to Mitch Hyland, seated in a chair, handcuffed and being treated for his broken nose and the cuts on his face. "Don't you treat him!" She rushed over and batted the medic's hand away. "He tried to kill her!"

Strong hands grabbed her shoulders and she couldn't shake them off.

"Let me go!" She covered her face, crying her pent up anguish. "Let me go!" She fought harder.

Arms wrapped around her chest and she struggled to breathe. She spun away, gaining her freedom and falling to the floor. The position put her next to Cassidy.

Cassidy had been moved onto her back and an apparatus supported her head and neck. The medic held her right arm in his lap, swabbing something over her inner forearm. Then he pulled out a syringe, removed the plastic covering and tapped the needle clear.

"What is that?" Brenna demanded. He didn't answer and Brenna watched the injection. The plunger tube was removed and another tube inserted, this one connected to a bag of fluid. Saline solution, she realized.

"You need to move now, ma'am. We need to get her onto a backboard."

Brenna stood up, still shaking. As the haze left her, she saw Will staring at her.

A loud thunk behind her made her spin. The second EMT had set down the backboard. Her heart pounded in her throat as she considered the paralysis Cassidy could suffer if anything went wrong. Brenna covered her mouth to stop the helpless sounds from escaping as she watched them secure Cassidy and the board to the gurney with straps.

"Time to go," one said to the other.

"We'll clear the way." Brenna's rough voice was unfamiliar to her own ears. "Will and Terry, help me." She grabbed the reporter and shoved him out ahead of her. Stepping outside, she was blinded by flashbulbs and bludgeoned by questions.

"Who was hurt?"

"What do the medics say?"

The medics bearing Cassidy behind her, Brenna tried to descend and clear a path. Someone jostled her; she shoved back. "Get the hell out of the way!"

"You're covered in blood. Were you hurt as well?"

"It's not me I'm worried about," she barked. "Now leave us alone." She hovered as the medical personnel lifted the gurney into the back of the waiting ambulance.

At the doors, Brenna grabbed an arm and demanded, "Why is she still unconscious?"

"She suffered several major traumas. Actually, being unconscious is the best thing for her."

"She's... It's not a coma, is it?"

"Her pupils are reactive."

Brenna had no idea what that meant, but the ambulance engine roared once and the EMT pulled away from her before she could ask.

"Gotta roll," he said with an apologetic shrug.

"What hospital?" She grabbed the outer bar to haul herself into the back.

"Get down," he ordered. "Pasadena General."

Brenna shouted the information back to Will Chapman and then tried to follow the paramedic into the rear of the ambulance with Cassidy. Someone behind her grabbed her shoulder.

"No, ma'am," a male voice said firmly.

She turned furiously. "I'm going."

"She's critical, ma'am. They can't take you in this one." The policeman looked her up and down. "Are you hurt?" His gaze paused at her face and a frown furrowed his brow. He reached up and touched her cheek.

Ducking away from his touch, Brenna tried again to mount the truck. He held her back and she began to panic; she could hear the ambulance had just changed gears. "I'm fine."

"Nasty shiner. You sure you don't need treatment?"

She looked at him. Something in the way he said "sure" suggested there might be a way around the regulations, and she waited.

"If I get an ice pack," he said with a smile, "maybe they'll take you up front."

A monitor going off accompanied a rough command from inside. "I need help here."

"Help her," she begged, while the police officer looked at the medic for his call.

The man growled under his breath, but rummaged in his bag and handed her a chemical ice pack. "You take that up front with you. The hospital can check you when we get there."

He was already half inside a second after handing her the cold bag. Just before he slammed the door, she caught a glimpse of Cassidy's face as it was obscured by a hand-pump and mask. Brenna hurried to the front of the truck and banged on the door.

"Let me in!"

The third man up front behind the wheel leaned over and pushed the door open. "What the hell?"

"They said I'm to ride up front with you," she said, as business-like, I-do-this-all-the-time as she could manage.

"Well, get in. We gotta get outta here."

Brenna exhaled quickly and pulled herself into the high seat.

"Seatbelt," he ordered. She complied just as the ambulance followed a police cruiser out through the back gate.

"How long?"

"Depends. Five to eight minutes." He grabbed the radio microphone and barked into it, "Pasadena General, this is Rescue 1-8. We're transporting a beating victim. ETA in five."

A disembodied voice confirmed. "Roger, 1-8. ETA in five. Already in communication."

"Great." Putting down the microphone, he concentrated on driving.

Brenna turned to look into the back, straining against the thick distortion, finding it nearly impossible to see through the window separating the cab from the back compartment.

"Friend of yours?"

"I... uh, yeah. She's a friend."

"What's your name?"

"Brenna."

He concentrated on a turn for a second, the ambulance siren on as he moved against the traffic signals through an intersection. "What's your friend's name?"

Brenna continued trying to look into the back. "What are they doing?" she asked.

"Stabilizing her." He asked again, "What's her name?"

"Cassidy."

"How's your head?" he asked. "Need the ice pack anymore?"

Brenna looked at the bag resting on her lap. Her face did throb. Sheepishly she put the ice bag against her face. "I'll be fine. What's going to happen?"

There was a faint sound from the back. Brenna looked quickly to make out Cassidy struggling with the paramedics before being restrained. Her own panic resurged. "What's going on back there?"

The driving paramedic tapped the window with his fist, then the radio next to him crackled and he picked up the mouthpiece. "Can you give us a status on our patient? Lady up here wants to know."

"Briefly conscious. She wanted to know where someone named Ryan is."

The driver looked at Brenna. "That's her son," she answered. "Tell her he's safe with Karen."

"Will do," answered the paramedic from the back. "What's our ETA, Chaz?"

"Less than one."

"I've got Trauma on the other line. PG's scrambled the heart surgery team."

"Got it." The driver switched the radio. "PG this is Rescue 1-8. ETA update, pulling through the drive now."

To Brenna's relief, the last turn they screeched around was just beyond a sign declaring "Pasadena City General".

"You'll need to pull around to the dock. You've apparently got hot cargo there, Chaz. Reporters have already hit the place."

"Got it." He circled around past the drive leading to the large overhang labeled "Emergency" and took a service drive to the west wall where a loading dock was hidden by a line of bushes.

Brenna's mouth was too dry to speak as he put the vehicle into park and leaped out. She unbelted and reached for the door.

"No!" The driver's sharp voice froze Brenna in her tracks. "Let the doctors get her going inside. You take yourself around to the ER and check in." Leaving Brenna to stare after him, he turned to help his partner unload the gurney from the back of the ambulance.

Chapter Eleven

When James came out of the game room, he found his brother stalking around the living room and punching numbers into the phone. Every few seconds he would stop and stare at the television. "Yes? Pasadena General? ... I need word on a patient, Cassidy Hyland." Thomas slammed a hand into the wall, rattling the pictures. "What the hell do you mean you don't have her? I just saw the damn news report!"

"What news report?" James asked.

"Shut up!" Thomas barked at him, then returned his attention to the phone.

James turned back to the TV. "Special Report?" He sat down. "What's going on?"

A reporter on site had a microphone and was recapping the breaking story. "At approximately one p.m. today, domestic violence claimed a very public victim."

Tape rolled. A melee scene filled the screen and the camera zoomed in.

"Shit, that's Mom!" James recognized their mother, and grabbed the air fruitlessly for his brother, still stalking, still on the phone, and apparently still on hold, cursing steadily. "Who's that she's leaning over?"

"On the busy Pinnacle Studio lot, an ex-husband took his former wife on a journey of terror."

As James watched the tape continue, his mother moved aside, revealing the victim.

"Popular star, Cassidy Hyland, Time Trails' sexy rebel officer, Chris Hanssen, was severely beaten in a trailer on the Pinnacle lot, allegedly by ex-husband Mitch Hyland."

James inhaled. "Man, she's really messed up."

"As her costars hovered helplessly, Ms. Hyland was transported to Pasadena City General Hospital, apparently unconscious, possibly comatose, as a result of her injuries."

The tape followed the woman being carried on a backboard then loaded on a gurney. Next to her, James also saw his mother, spattered with blood. Over his shoulder, James heard Thomas gasp.

James watched his mother climb aboard the ambulance, using forceful language he had never heard from her. He called over his shoulder, "Mom'll be there at the hospital too."

"Mom? Shit, what the fuck happened over there?"

"Ms. Hyland's ex, apparently." As Thomas headed toward the door, James called, "Where are you going?"

"To the hospital."

"In what? Mom's got the car."

Thomas kicked the wall. "Shit!"

"You couldn't do anything if you did go." James grabbed his arm. "Mom will call."

"They said Cassidy is comatose!"

"They said she might be."

Thomas sank to the sofa, dropping his head in his hands. James grabbed his shoulder, feeling it shake as his brother gave in to his emotions. Watching the TV, James wondered how their mother was doing.

He had just known there would be trouble eventually, but he hadn't figured it would be this bad.

The gurney legs snapped down noisily and Brenna followed as they wheeled through a supply corridor. A nurse approached and grasped Brenna's arm as she tried to follow the gurney into the exam room.

"Do you know the patient?" When Brenna nodded, the nurse said, "Follow me."

"But—"

"We need some information from you."

Brenna sighed. "This won't delay her treatment, will it?"

"The trauma team will stabilize her. After that, we'll see."

Brenna was ushered through a doorway and emerged at the end of a large waiting room.

She was settled on a chair in a small room just off that, looking at a woman perched before a computer and holding out a clipboard. Brenna automatically took it, and the nurse left before she could ask another question.

"Patient's name, date of birth, home address, insurance, and any known allergies. Please."

The request was issued in a monotone, as if she said these words dozens of times an hour. Which no doubt she did. Brenna blinked, putting aside the ice pack and studying the clipboard. "I'll do my best."

"Insurance card?"

"No. Everything's back at the set," Brenna explained, indicating her attire. She was still in her own costume from filming.

The secretary's eyes widened then narrowed with realization. "God, you're the two they've been looking for." She nodded out into the waiting room that could be seen through the small window in the door. "They have been pounding my door every twenty seconds to find out when you were coming in."

Brenna briefly recalled throwing one reporter to the ground back at the trailer. How long could her energy hold out against a room full? From the growing commotion just outside the door, it sounded as if she was about to find out. Groaning, she looked pleadingly at the secretary. "Couldn't we just ignore them?"

"If you can do it, I can do it," the woman said with a conspiratorial grin, turning back to the computer.

They worked through the necessary information, as much as Brenna could provide, while the reporters hovered just outside, snapping pictures through the security-threaded glass.

Brenna hoped all they got was glare from the glass. "Please tell me there's another way out of here. A tunnel under your desk would be fine."

"Nothing so devious, but there is a back door to the exam room bathroom. We can get you out that way." She nodded toward a slender door on the opposite wall, mostly invisible because of an angled bookcase.

"I'd really appreciate it. I need to get back to see her as soon as possible."

"What happened?"

"I won't know everything until she wakes up, but we found her ex-husband attacking her in an empty trailer on the studio lot. We tried to break it up."

"You got caught in the middle, I see." Brenna nodded, starting to return the ice pack to her cheek when she realized it was no longer cold and set it on the desk. "Well. So... how did you get nominated to come along? Usually a studio grip brings the workman comp paperwork."

"There was no way I was not coming," Brenna stated emphatically. "Please, can we go back? I need to see her." For all her politeness, she was nearing the end of her rope.

The secretary nodded. "Give me the studio number so we can get her file from them. We'll also need a next of kin..."

"She will make it," Brenna insisted firmly.

"But only next of kin can make her medical treatment decisions... unless we find a health care proxy in her documents, or a living will?"

Brenna frowned. She didn't know whether Cassidy had either of those documents, but she knew that in any event, her name was not on them. She swallowed and nodded. "I... I'll see what I can do."

Finally, the secretary led Brenna into the antiseptic white and green hallway behind the office. Behind her there was a burst of clatter against the secretary's door. She sighed. *God, I want to get out of here!* She closed her eyes and amended, *but only if Cassidy's coming with me.*

"Here's the nurses station. Let's find out what room your friend is in." The secretary leaned over the desk and spoke to the nurse sitting there going through the clipboards. "I've got to get back to the office. What do you want me to tell the reporters?" she asked Brenna.

"To go away. Barring that, give them the number for the studio's PR office." Brenna sighed. She grabbed the back of a prescription pad and wrote two numbers. "The first is for HR. They've probably got Cassidy's medical file. She was in last year, I think, for a sprained ankle during a publicity event." The secretary nodded. "The second is the studio's PR." The secretary nodded more enthusiastically. "Thank you for everything."

"She's in exam room 8." The station nurse pointed then handed her a pad. "If you'll just sign in, you can meet with the doctor."

Brenna breathed a sigh of relief and signed the form. At last. "Thank you."

Taking back the sheet, the nurse asked, "What's your relationship to the patient?"

After a thoughtful pause, Brenna answered, "I'm her lover." Ignoring the gaping reaction, she turned on her heel and strode down the hall.

Pushing the door open to room 8, Brenna stepped inside, her eyes quickly locating the bed. The room was crowded with equipment, but she only had eyes for the woman looking small and hooked up to most of it.

An oxygen machine rasped to one side, the accordion pump hissing as it compressed and expanded, feeding Cassidy oxygen through a tube wrapped around her cheeks and under her nose. The heart monitor beeped slowly but steadily.

Stepping closer, Brenna laid her hand gently across the sheet-covered chest, feeling the reassuring rise and fall. A tube fed out from under the sheet, flowing with a murky liquid. She was not sure whether it was good stuff going in, or bad stuff coming out.

She lifted Cassidy's bandaged right hand and kissed the fingertips just peeking out beyond the edge. "Can you open your eyes for me? Please?" There was no response to her touch, not even a flutter of eyelids. She bent close. "Please get well."

"She's not going to be well for some time."

Exhaling, Brenna turned. "Doctor?" She was face to face with a man of Asian descent, in a green smock wearing a stethoscope around his neck. He was about her height, giving her a clear view of the fact that he was not smiling.

"What do you know?" She had not meant for the question to sound like a challenge. She amended, more softly, "So far."

He examined a few readouts and made some notations, all the while leaving Brenna hanging for the answer to her question. "Your friend here—"

"Her name's Cassidy. Cassidy Hyland."

"Well, Ms. Hyland suffered several separated ribs. When the x-rays come back, we'll know how many are broken. There's at least one. It punctured and collapsed her left lung." Brenna looked at Cassidy in alarm. "We've already reinflated the lung," the doctor assured her.

He checked the tape sliding out of the heart monitor and

frowned. Brenna noticed the expression. "What's wrong?"

"There's some pressure buildup around her heart. She may have pericardial bleeding. Or it could just be fluid build up. The lab has several samples, so we'll know shortly what we're dealing with."

"What can you do?" Brenna forced herself to remain more composed than she felt, but she had to work hard to focus on the doctor instead of the limp hand she cradled in her own.

"We'll have to relieve the pressure. That will involve surgery. I'm scheduling an O.R. with our cardiac surgeon as soon as she's stabilized." He flipped through a printout he had brought with him. "You signed her in?"

"Yes."

"Is there any family we can contact for the admissions paperwork and the permission to do surgery?"

"No one is local. Her family's in Missouri." Brenna added, "She has a five year old son. Her ex-husband did this to her, so I guess that leaves me."

"Do you have a medical power of attorney to act as her health guardian?" She shook her head. "Are you a relative?" She shook her head again. "Then who are you?"

"I'm... We're involved, though it's only recently, you see, but—"

"I'm sorry, you're going to have to leave."

"What?"

"I need to discuss Ms. Hyland's medical condition with someone who can authorize the treatments. Her injuries are extensive and severe. We need to determine—"

"You need to heal her!" Brenna interrupted emphatically.

"Within the guidelines of her wishes and those of her family, yes." He left the rest unsaid, but Brenna heard it in her head, and wanted to scream. You're not family.

"How long before surgery will be absolutely necessary?"

"Her blood pressure is still too low. Probably by morning, unless she goes into respiratory failure before then. We're moving her up to CCU as soon as I can get someone to authorize her admittance."

"Who can do that?"

"Her insurance company. Or her employer."

Brenna felt the tendrils of hope. "Where's a phone I can use? Local call."

"You can use one at the nurses station but then you'll have to return to the waiting room. You can't stay back here." She started to protest and he reiterated firmly, "You can't stay here."

Turning to look at Cassidy's face, she kissed tenderly alongside a bandage covering most of her injured jaw. "I'll be back; I promise." Maybe the studio could authorize her to act in their stead. There has to be something that can be done so that I can stay with you, she thought. Because I am not leaving you alone.

Back at the nurses station, Brenna made her call as the duty nurse hovered. "Human Resources. ... Yes. This is Brenna Lanigan. Tell them I'm— ... Yes, that's right. Pasadena General. ... They need to admit Cassidy." She grabbed a pen and a piece of paper. "Right." She wrote quickly. "No, they don't know everything that's wrong yet, but she's in trouble. ... I guess you should. Ask Victor Branch to handle it. I'll... do this." She frowned then hung up.

The doctor reappeared. "Well?"

"I've got your authorization here." She waved the paper at him. "Personnel already faxed her file. There's no living will."

He nodded. "We're not there. Yet." He went on, "Family?"

"The studio said they'd contact her parents." Brenna could not stop the dejection from entering her voice. "Another colleague is on his way over with her son, though."

"But you said he's five. He can't authorize anything."

Brenna was firm. "He needs to see his mother. He was there when she was put in the ambulance and whisked away from him."

The doctor frowned and strode away, and Brenna handed the authorization note to the nurse. "Please notify me when they move her. He probably won't think to do so."

The nurse nodded slowly. "Can I ask you a question?" Brenna nodded. "Are you and she really dating?" When Brenna nodded again, the nurse shook her head, wearing an expression of confusion. "You sure don't act like the others that come through."

"What others? Actors?"

"Nah, the gays. They wave those health proxies around like red flags."

Brenna inhaled and exhaled slowly. She needed a friend back here. "We haven't been seeing each other very long."

The nurse shrugged. "Haven't had your second date yet, huh?"

There was a hint of amusement in the voice and Brenna fumed.

"Thanks for nothing." She stalked away, leaving the exam area and emerging into a cacophony of light and sound. The press still crowded the waiting room. She couldn't even see the other patients waiting for emergency services.

"What's Ms. Hyland's condition?"

"Serious," she supplied with a growl.

"Is she being admitted, or released soon?"

"I just said serious!" she snapped. "What the hell does that suggest to you? Now get out of my way." She pushed through the throng, heading for an empty chair, but they followed.

"What was your role in the events that occurred?"

"I helped break up the fight."

"Who was her attacker? Her husband?"

"Her ex-husband. Can't you ask the police these questions?" She pushed past the empty chair and more of the reporters in exasperation.

"They say it was a domestic dispute. Jealousy?"

Brenna was still upset she had not known Mitch was in town. She had not fully understood the level of danger he posed to Cassidy. The question hit on that. "I found him standing over her with a baseball bat! She was barely conscious!"

Pushing her way through them again, she stumbled against a door, and noticed the universal sign for the ladies room. Thank God! She pushed inside and shoved the door closed, locking it before sliding down to the floor and huddling while reporters posed their questions loudly through the door.

Tears streaming down her cheeks as the tension finally overwhelmed her, Brenna prayed. She prayed for the reporters to go away. She prayed Cassidy would recover. She must have dozed because suddenly there was a sharp rap on the door and a thick male, authoritative voice demanded, "You have to leave the restroom, ma'am."

"Are the reporters gone?" she asked weakly.

"We've ordered them off the premises."

"Thank you," she breathed, rising to her feet. Unlocking the door, she stepped out and looked into the quiet waiting room. No one carried a writing pad, or a camera. She exhaled in relief.

"Are you Brenna Lanigan?" one officer asked her.

"Yes."

"Man here says he's a friend of yours and a patient inside. He has a little blond kid with him."

Brenna pushed through the throng of officers and spotted Terry Brown—God bless his familiar and friendly face—seated beside

Ryan Hyland. Both looked up as she rushed forward. She got a strong one-armed hug from Terry as she lifted Ryan and hugged him, pressing her face into his jean jacket. She kissed his hair and caressed his cheek.

"I thought you might need these as well." Terry held up two handbags.

"Her insurance card should go to the nurse in there. Also, we need to know if anyone in town is authorized to sign treatment forms."

"Just Pinnacle, I think."

Brenna frowned. "That's what I thought, too. The office is looking up her parents' number but that may not get her help."

"Why not?"

"Over Christmas, she had to leave their house of her own volition or be thrown out."

"What for?"

"They learned that she and I had become involved."

"Yes." He shrugged. "But what does that have to do with this?"

"I don't know. Maybe it doesn't have anything to do with it. But they're apparently the only ones who can authorize treatment, and they're not exactly on speaking terms."

"What was Mitch doing on the set? She used to have a restraining order against him."

"How did you know that?"

"Brenna, just because you didn't want to know anything about Cassidy when she first arrived, doesn't mean some of us didn't know something about her."

"So you knew she'd been abused in her marriage."

"It wasn't hard to decipher."

"Except for someone who was ignoring her with every fiber of my being."

"Now you're being hard on yourself for no reason."

"Damn it, I'm an idiot. Cassidy was afraid of our relationship getting out. Even when she couldn't put it into words why. Damn, I should have listened to her. She must have known that sonofabitch Mitch would pull something."

"Mr. Hyland has been transported to the police station," Terry reported evenly. "He struck two of the officers as well."

Brenna closed her eyes and offered up a silent 'thank you'. "He tried to kill her with a baseball bat," Brenna hissed softly, looking toward Ryan. "How can I tell that to Ryan?"

"You can't, until Cassidy advises you."

"She hasn't awakened since the ride over."

"It's that serious?"

She nodded. "They need to operate to relieve some pressure around her heart."

"What can I do?"

Fishing in her purse, Brenna came up with her car and house keys. "I'm going to call Thomas and then...Could you take Ryan to my house?"

"Your car is still at the studio." He looked her over. "And you're still in costume."

"I know. You can take the vest with you, but the rest will have to stay. I don't want my sons here; I want Ryan to stay with them. I'll catch a cab and retrieve my car later." She rubbed her cheeks in fatigue, wincing as she aggravated her bruised eyes. "But not until Ryan and I have seen Cassidy." She reached out and coaxed the boy off the chair to take her hand. "Ready?"

"Where is she?" Terry asked.

"Hopefully by now they've gotten her settled into CCU. I have no idea, though. I got thrown out of the exam room and then mobbed by the press out here."

"Productive afternoon," Terry offered dryly.

"What time is it?" She caught sight of a wall clock. "It's after five already. God, the boys will be frantic." She withdrew her change purse and headed for a pay phone booth along the front wall of the waiting room.

"I'm hungry," Ryan complained, snuggling into her lap as she dialed. "And I want to see Mommy."

"I know, sweetheart. I'll find you something to eat in a minute and we will see your Mom." She dialed.

"Who are you calling?" Ryan asked curiously.

"Thomas and James."

Ryan smiled, looking tired. She kissed his head and held him against her chest more firmly.

"Hello, Thomas. ... Yes, it's me. ... I'm okay."

Her elder son's voice was worried as he asked, "And Cassidy?"

"She's hurt very badly, but I don't know much more than that."

"It's been more than four hours," he commented anxiously.

"It's complicated," she said firmly. "Thomas, listen." He fell silent on the other end of the line. "I've got Terry Brown and Ryan here. After I take them in to see Cassidy, I want to send Ryan to you. I need to stay here."

"Do you want us to come there?"

"No, it's better if you don't... not yet."

Thomas fretted, "Is Cassidy going to be all right?"

"They're doing everything they can," she countered, knowing how little comfort those same words had brought her.

"I'm sorry. I'll watch Ryan. It's fine."

"I'll call you again in an hour. We'll have a better idea what's happening then."

"All right."

"Thomas?" She offered him as much reassurance as she could. "I don't know what the news stories said, but I don't want Ryan seeing any of the reports, all right? I'll try to explain something to him while I have him here. You're only responsible for making sure he gets some sleep. And keeping your chin up, all right?"

"Mmm hmm."

"Sweetheart, I love you. Thank you."

"I know, Mom. I... Yeah."

"Bye."

"Bye." Brenna hung up the phone, her son's farewell still echoing in her ear. God, he sounded almost as bad as I feel. She stood, hefting Ryan in her arms. "Let's go see your Mom."

CHAPTER TWELVE

"...HER LOVER!" Brenna bit her lip. The nurse finally nodded and pointed.

Terry looked at Brenna as they walked away from the desk. "That... approach was effective."

"I can't seem to get anywhere without saying so," She cupped Ryan's hand and found a small joy in how easily the boy accepted her touch.

At the elevator she pressed the button to summon a car. T

Terry nodded. "A reality of the situation. How will Cass feel about that information getting out? It's certain the press will play it up."

Brenna sighed. "What will she think about me 'outing' us publicly? Yes, I know that's the term, Terry. Don't look at me like that. I never pictured myself in this situation, but I'm not naïve." She shook her head, stepping into the summoned car. "Cassidy didn't want it to come out abruptly. She sort of figured we'd get people used to us being friends first. I'd hoped to have my divorce final..."

"Will told me you finally broke it off with Shea."

"Will's definitely known for a while. Did he tell you?"

"We've discussed the situation."

"I don't know that I like that."

They stepped off on the fourth floor. A sign pointed the way to

CCU.

"You didn't want to see what you were doing to yourself or Cassidy, remember? You avoided her off camera. I'm surprised all it took was a birthday party to get you to open up."

"It was more than that, but I get your point." They had reached the nurses station. Brenna leaned over the counter and stated, "We'd like to see Cassidy Hyland."

One of the nurses sitting before the monitoring stations looked up. Must be the one assigned to Cassidy, Brenna thought.

Predictably, the woman asked, "Family?"

"This is her son, Ryan." She skirted actually having to lie.

"Right this way. I have to tell you she didn't take the transfer very well. Her fever spiked and the bleeding resumed. She had a mild heart attack." Brenna looked alarmed. "From the stress her body's going through. Her condition's been stabilized for now."

They stopped at the doorway to the heavily monitored room.

"She's the second bed. Now that you're here, we can get all the approvals done for surgery in the morning. The doctor didn't seem to think you'd get here this quickly."

"That's okay. How long can we stay?"

"A few minutes inside, but there's a lounge nearby." She offered one last piece of advice. "Be careful of the tubes, we had to intubate her. Can he keep his hands to himself?"

"I promise Ryan will be good." Brenna waited until the nurse left and Terry took up a sentry position.

When Brenna turned around, she found Ryan walking toward the curtain around the far bed. The first bed was empty.

"Mommy?" He pulled aside the curtain and Brenna stepped quickly to his side. Ryan looked up at the bed. "Wake up." He reached out and touched the bandaged hand that lay on the edge of the blankets. "Mommy." He nudged the hand. "Miss Lanigan, what's wrong with her?"

"She was hurt at work today. You saw us take her in the ambulance, right?"

He nodded. "I saw Daddy, too. He didn't come here. Policemen took him away."

"Yes, they did." Brenna exhaled to keep her voice even, trying not to reveal the anger she felt.

"Will Mommy wake up now that we're here so that we can go home?"

"Your mommy needs her sleep. You're going to come home

with me for a little while."

"Can't I stay here with her?"

"No, sweetheart, you can't. But we'll come back tomorrow, and every day until she's better. Is that okay?" Brenna moved alongside Cassidy's head and brushed her fingers over the lank blond hair. It still had much of the blood Brenna had first seen and she paused a moment to study the rust color on her own fingers. God, I'm sorry, Cass. The blood on Cassidy's face had been washed away; what remained visible was the bruises, though bad ones. Brenna touched one gingerly and felt the heat under the skin.

Ryan climbed up on a chair beside the bed and leaned over the railing to look down at his mother's face. "Her face is dirty," he said, reaching out to clean it.

Brenna gently but firmly kept his hand away.

"She's not dirty; those are bruises. Like when you fall down?"

He touched the oxygen tube tucked under his mother's nose. "What's this?"

"It helps her breathe." Brenna recalled the nurse's information about a heart attack and had to calm herself before she could speak again. "Don't touch."

Ryan cocked his head. "What's that noise?"

"Which one?" she asked.

"The beeping."

"The machine listening to her heart." Brenna pointed to the far side of the bed.

"Can I listen too?"

"I'm sorry but we have to be very gentle with your mom. She's delicate right now."

Ryan climbed down and found his mother's hand again, taking it more surely in his own. "Is this okay? I can hold her hand?" He looked at Brenna for permission. She granted it with a nod. "Mommy," he said, addressing her hand, "Miss Lanigan is going to take me home with her."

Brenna tucked her hand around Ryan and Cassidy's joined ones. "You just think about getting well. We'll be here."

At first Brenna thought she or Ryan had moved, then she felt the motion again. Cassidy's fingers flexed around her son's; her knuckles moved inside Brenna's palm.

"I love you, Mommy." Ryan leaned forward and kissed his mother's hand, his lips touching Brenna's fingers too. She closed her eyes and let the tears of relief come.

In the hospital cafeteria, Terry coaxed Brenna to nibble on an apple turnover along with her coffee. Beside her, Ryan devoured a hamburger and French fries.

"You should go home. You've already been here longer than six hours," he reasoned.

"I can't leave her alone."

"Actually, I wasn't thinking that. You need to settle Ryan. I can stay. I'll call you if something changes."

"I can't ask you to do that."

"You didn't. It shocked us all." He put a hand on her shoulder. "You're going to have enough people not offering help." He added with a quirk of his lips in a half-grin, "As a group, we might be able to frustrate the reporters before they can frustrate you."

Brenna sipped her coffee as she thought. It would help Ryan if she settled him rather than just sending him everywhere. "It was quite a run-around just for me to get to see her. If I leave, I might have to start the process all over again."

"We can be sure that doesn't happen."

"We?"

Terry picked up his cell phone and pressed the button along the side, initiating a long tone. The cafeteria doors behind Brenna swung wide, and she turned at the sound. Terry's wife, holding up her own cell phone, walked in at the head of a sizable crowd.

"What have you done?" Brenna recognized half the cast and crew from the set. Spouses seemed to make up the rest of the entourage. A cacophony of support flowed from the group as they surrounded her. Hands patted her shoulders, touched her back, gazes offered a mix of smiles and supportive determination.

Rachelle stepped forward bearing a bundle. "We suspended shooting." She put the bundle in Brenna's hands. "I went through your trailer. Thought you might like to change."

Brenna looked surprised as Rachelle enveloped her in a hug. Against her ear, Brenna heard Rachelle's soft, private words. "You've been in those all day, and frankly, I think Wardrobe would like a chance to get the blood out." As Rachelle stepped back, Brenna looked down at herself. *Cassidy's blood. Probably even some of Mitch's,* she thought with revulsion.

The reaction must have shown because Rachelle wrapped her up in a tight hug again. "God, I'm sorry this happened." She pulled back and brushed Brenna's tears from her cheeks. "But really, I don't know how else to handle this. It's kind of shocking."

"Which? That Mitch beat her up or that I'm involved with her?"

"Both, but... How could you let me find out like this?" Rachelle put her hands on her hips and feigned an injured look. "I knew you were finally relaxing around her, but this... I'm surprised."

A small smile tugged at Brenna's lips. "Cass took me by surprise too."

"Oh, I like that smile," Rachelle complimented. "Can we all go up and see her?"

Terry intervened. "I was just trying to convince Brenna to go home for a while."

"So Cass is doing better?"

Brenna shook her head. "She's in CCU. Only family can see her. She's going into surgery soon."

"Depending on what?"

"Whether the pressure around her heart gets better or worse."

"Her heart?"

"Yes." Brenna swallowed again, collecting herself. "The attack seems to have caused heart damage."

"God." Rachelle's hand covered her mouth and several others registered similar shock on their faces.

Brenna shook her head, turning to Terry. "I can't leave. I just can't."

"Then we'll stay in shifts with you," Rachelle suggested. "I'll take the first shift."

"I'm not going to be able to argue that point, am I?" Brenna sat down. Ryan scooted into her lap and she put her hand on his back. "We've got some pretty wonderful friends, hmm, Ryan?" He nodded against her chest. "All right. The doctor is probably on rounds somewhere. I'll find out what's happening and then decide what to do." She looked at her bundle of street clothes and added, "First, I think I'm going to change."

Terry and Sean Durham entertained Ryan while Rachelle accompanied Brenna to the restroom.

"So, I heard the reporters had you cornered in one of these earlier?"

"Yeah," Brenna answered from within a stall. She appeared a minute later, her costume over her arm, pulling her blouse's collar straight. Rachelle stepped forward from where she had been leaning on the sinks and helped. "Better?" Brenna asked with a weak smile.

"Much. It'll be a little easier for you to go incognito now." Rachelle took the uniform pieces. "Jacques'll drive me back to the studio and I'll deliver these. Do you want me to return with your car?"

Brenna nodded. "I need to get Ryan to my place."

"Terry will be happy to do that." Blinking at her reflection, Brenna acknowledged the help. Rachelle met her gaze in the mirror. "So, are you going to tell me everything?"

"I've told you all I know."

"Not about this. Well, I'm sure it will get back to this, but I meant about you and Cassidy, and Mitch... And don't you still have a husband?"

"You seem to be one of the few who didn't see it. I didn't see it," Brenna admitted. She leaned over the sink and splashed water on her face before answering. "But she's just... I've never met anyone like her." In her mind's eye, she could see the beautiful face studying her across a campfire in the middle of the mountains. "I've never met anyone with the intensity she has..." *All directed at me.* "The freedom she gives herself to just feel..." Brenna shook her head and tossed the paper towel in the trash. "She's mischievous and playful, unassuming and even shy."

"Shy? Cass?"

"It's all a front, Chelle. Since the beginning. Only Cameron knew, and he made sure no one else did. Remember how she didn't sit in any scenes?"

"That was blocking."

"That was planned that way because she was recovering from broken ribs Mitch gave her when she told him she'd gotten the contract to work with us."

"So she really was abused? God, that's awful."

"I didn't know for the longest time. We started... talking. Do you remember when she said she'd been camping with my charity group?"

"Yeah. What about it?"

"We... talked... and... well, that weekend it... it became something more than just friendship."

"Really? She was pretty happy the week after that."

"We just kept growing closer. After the gala, I asked Kevin for a divorce."

Rachelle blew out a deep breath and then asked hesitantly, "Is this something more than friendship? Sexual?" Brenna nodded. "That's a surprise."

"For me, too." Brenna blushed.

"The media isn't going to let this go."

"Maybe they will. It's not like we're the first they've ever seen."

"But you are the first where a man has tried to take his ex-wife apart bodily for being involved with another woman."

"Sensational," Brenna sighed sarcastically.

"Exactly."

CHAPTER THIRTEEN

BRENNA CALLED home again, as promised, to tell her sons Ryan was on his way with Terry Brown. Brown agreed to stay the night with the boys and return in the morning to the hospital with Ryan. While Rachelle and Jacques Cheron went to fetch Brenna's car, Sean Durham accompanied Brenna back to the fourth floor to find out what they could about the doctor's latest visit.

"She responded to Ryan, squeezed his hand," Brenna was explaining with pleasure as they entered the room where Cassidy had been assigned.

The dividing curtain was thrown back, revealing the second bed was empty, made up with fresh sheets. They quickly returned to the nurses station, where Brenna accosted the nurse at the desk, a different one from her earlier visit. "Where's Cassidy Hyland, 408?"

Looking at her charts, the nurse pulled the appropriate board. "Ms. Hyland went to surgery twenty minutes ago."

"Twenty minutes? Why didn't someone tell me?"

"Ma'am?" Scanning a list, she asked, "What's your name?"

"Lanigan. Brenna Lanigan. I came in with Cassidy this afternoon by ambulance."

The nurse shook her head. "The family issued a list of visitors. I don't see your name."

"The family issued a list? When?" Sean asked because Brenna was struck silent by the double blow. She stepped away from the desk white as a sheet.

"About an hour ago. Admissions dropped it off."

Brenna exhaled her question in a rush. "Does it say why Cassidy went into surgery?" Back to the matter at hand: news about Cassidy. She required it. Now.

The nurse returned to the chart. "Pericardial pressure. She had another Code Blue."

"But she was responsive when I was up here with her earlier with her son. She squeezed his hand."

"These cases can turn very quickly. I promise you she's under excellent care." The nurse picked up another clipboard. "Can I tell the family you stopped by?"

Brenna's eyes widened. Face Cassidy's family? "No. I... No." Brenna walked away from the desk.

Sean asked, "Is there any way she can see Cassidy? Just look at her?"

"Certainly not before she's out of surgery, but even then... CCU's policy is family only. She isn't a relative, is she?"

"As close as you can get. They've worked together sixteen hours a day for the last year and recently started a relationship."

"Perhaps she can speak with the family. Maybe they just overlooked her."

Brenna overheard and stormed over. "They didn't overlook me. They excluded me." Anger vibrated in her chest like a living thing as she lashed out. She shook her hand toward the empty room. "Her family wouldn't care if she dies!"

Anguished and astonished at her outburst in the face of the nurse's startled expression, Brenna moved away quickly and sat in a lone chair. Covering her face with her hands she cried.

Sean tried again. "There has to be something."

The nurse returned her attention to him, clearly consternated by Brenna's reaction. "Yes, um... I... Well, there's Patient Advocacy. They've been known to get domestic partners visitation rights when no other avenue was available."

"Are they open now?"

"There's always one rep on duty. The office is down next to the hospital chapel."

"Would you call down there when Cassidy returns from surgery?" He waved his hand to forestall her objection. "I know, there's regulations, but... one phone call can't hurt."

The nurse nodded, watching him walk to Brenna's side. He

grasped her shoulders and pulled her to her feet. "I think I know where we can wait." Brenna looked toward the nurses station and he assured her, "She'll call."

"Where?"

"Patient Advocacy."

"They can get me in to see her?"

"It's the only possible option to being on the family list. And..." He frowned. "Was that, um, true about her parents?"

Entering the elevator, Brenna sagged against the wall. "I don't know. I'm just scared I won't see her again. It's wrong to think they would let her die, but Cass says that her father was not at all understanding over Christmas. He hit her. She left their house and told me she won't go back."

Brenna stepped out on the first floor and they followed the signs to the advocacy office. Noticing the chapel signs, she thought about how she had prayed, sitting on the bathroom floor. "Sean, wait."

She looked into the small room softly lit with candlelight and a few halogens recessed in the ceiling. The far wall was dominated by a stained glass window, backlit by the night lighting outside.

She entered, feeling the softness of the place seep into her. It was very different from the rest of the hospital. Light refracted through the glass and she found herself watching it dance through the air. She stopped at a table of candles near the front, some already lit, watching the tiny flames.

Using memory as her guide, Brenna selected a votive candle and lit it, setting it among the others in the box. Memories flowed over her, a soothing balm to the stresses of the day, of doing this with her mother at her side when she was a little girl and a relative was ill. Now she knelt against the altar railing with more purpose than she had in those young, naïve years.

Through the litany of her memorized prayers, Brenna poured out her soul. In silent uncertainty, she questioned whether she even had a right to ask for intervention. She cried when Cassidy's face appeared in her mind's eye. She prayed earnestly Cassidy would be whole and healthy soon, alive with the love they had found together. I didn't look for it, but it found me. She found me.

Brenna had to believe she and Cassidy had been brought together for a reason. She thought of how Cassidy had fled her husband and joined Time Trails. Cameron, yes, had done that, but then he had thrown it away. Everyone, it seemed, had taken

Cassidy, used her, and thrown her away. Her husband, Cameron...

She examined her own life and its choices. Driven by acting, she had left her home and struggled through a young adulthood in New York City. She had found what she thought was love, only to have it thrown back in her face when it produced a child. Unable to do anything less, she had carried the baby and then given it up for adoption.

It seemed she had been searching ever since for another heart to hold, to promise to take care of, to love her as much as she loved them. Tom, she thought first. He had proved inconstant, unable to offer her support or accept hers. Her relationship with Kevin had merely been grasping at something she thought she was supposed to have.

Then came a birthday invitation tucked shyly in a mirror, and Brenna had awakened to the realization that her impression of another person had always been colored by circumstance, not by who they really were. When she finally got to know Cassidy, she found the woman behind the cool exterior, replacing fear with something deep and cherished.

Her mind filled with images of their times together. She remembered being enveloped in intensity staring back at her from behind the veil of character. Remembering their earliest talk off-camera made her smile. She blushed at remembering when she had flirted. *God, did I really do that?* The memory filled her mind:

Brenna presented two pairs of slippers.

"Go on. Blue cotton or Bullwinkle J. Moose?" Cassidy laughed and reached for the brown character slippers. "I figured you for a Bullwinkle fan," Brenna commented when Cassidy settled to the sofa to slip them on her feet.

"Really?" Cassidy sighed in relief as the thickly padded, one-size-fits-all interior hugged her achy feet.

"Really. Don't ask me how I knew. I just took one look at you and said, 'Bullwinkle.' But you can see I took the blue plain ones, just in case I was wrong."

"I find it odder that you would like Bullwinkle," Cassidy admitted.

Brenna shrugged. "I grew up with this earnest moose who seemed to mess everything up."

"But it usually came out right in the end."

"Serendipity." She smiled.

"Or his buddy Rocky," Cassidy chuckled.

She remembered now being struck silent by the laughter,

something heavy in her chest dislodging as genuine like shoved out wariness and replaced it.

Her mind skipped ahead to how much she had wanted to tear the store apart, helping Cassidy look for Ryan. She had also wanted to strangle the store manager for shattering Cassidy with his talk of kidnapping:

The manager asked one more thing before turning around to catch up the intercom microphone. "How long do you want to wait before we call the police and report a kidnapping?"

Cassidy's face went even paler at the blunt question. Supportively, Brenna wrapped her arm around Cassidy's waist. "Just make the announcement," she ordered sharply. The manager shrugged and turned around.

She remembered how good it had felt when Cassidy turned into her body, the feel of her hands on her hips, how that had broken every barrier she had ever established, shattering her need for distance from this woman like a stone wall being breached.

She remembered being absorbed in Cassidy's pain following Cameron and Will's fight:

Cassidy drew a ragged breath and Brenna could see some of the blond woman's composure slowly returning. Brenna helped her tug the inner top off her shoulders. "Thank you." With the intensity Cassidy had offered her, Brenna knew it was about more than the costume.

"You're welcome." She hoped Cassidy knew she meant more than just the costume too. She leaned away, picking up a loose t-shirt. "Here." With a quick pull, Cassidy's chest was covered again, falling to her sofa and tugging off the lower half of her costume. Brenna settled next to her and slumped forward, a defeated posture.

"Brenna, I'm really sorry."

"You don't have anything to apologize for. Cameron should. Hell, Will needs to make a trip to a confessional. I've come to realize something," she said quietly. "All you've ever done is your best. And I admire that."

Cassidy was silent; Brenna easily read her surprise.

"You do?"

"Yeah. I do." Brenna smiled gently and patted Cassidy's leg, only realizing as she felt the warm skin beneath her palm, that Cassidy hadn't yet finished dressing.

She remembered the entire camping trip, every minute—from watching Cassidy as they drove down the highway, to setting up the tents, to swimming in the spring together, and that mountain climb. She recalled the days afterward—being in a daze from feeling so much. Every look they shared conveyed so much emotion, much more than she thought she could handle. But damn, she'd come alive then. Like being reborn. Cassidy had felt it too. She remembered being so alive when they tried a simple 'popcorn and movie' evening and instead romped with passion on her bed. A laugh bubbled up, warming her insides and filling her with sunshine in the darkness.

Resolve and peace filled Brenna. She looked up at the stained glass images. Several of the panes together looked like hands reaching toward one another. She nodded in affirmation.

"Miss Lanigan?"

Brenna turned to see a spare man with brown hair and glasses wearing a dark suit and tie. She nodded. "Yes, I'm Brenna Lanigan."

"I'm Paul Heath with Patient Advocacy." He offered his hand. She took it, then withdrew. "Your friend said you might want to ask me some questions?"

She looked past Paul. "Where is Sean?"

"He said he had to go, but a Rachelle is waiting outside."

She nodded. "They're staying with me here in shifts. I don't know why. I can't get in to see her and her parents will be here in the morning and—"

He held up a hand. "Who is 'she' we're talking about?"

Brenna swallowed. "Cassidy Hyland. She's a patient in CCU."

She followed him out into the corridor. Rachelle put a hand on her shoulder as they all walked down the hall to Paul's office.

"You're involved with her?"

"I love her."

"Her parents don't approve and they left you off the list."

"Sean told you all that?"

He shook his head. "I've heard the story before." He sobered. "I've told the story before." Brenna's eyes widened, but he shook his head and returned to her. "Why don't you tell me your specifics?"

"Can you get her visitation?" Rachelle interjected. "Cass is in emergency surgery right now."

"I would like to be there for her," Brenna acknowledged.

"Now?" Paul questioned.

"Her ex-husband beat her with a baseball bat today." Brenna shuddered at the remembered horror.

Paul gave a low whistle. "She came out of the closet to him?"

Brenna shook her head. "I don't know. I don't think so, but he learned about it. About us."

"What makes you say that? Did you witness the fight?"

"No."

"How long have you and... Cass, you said? How long have you been involved?"

"You mean...?" Brenna looked at Rachelle whose eyes sparkled with interest waiting for the answer. "Sexually?"

Paul nodded. "Yes."

"I... About a month." Brenna studied her hands in her lap.

"This is your first relationship?"

"I've been married twice." Paul looked at her startled. "Oh, you mean of a ..." She blushed scarlet and sighed, "Yes. I...I didn't expect it."

"You're obviously struggling with identity issues at the same time. I can hook you up with a local support group, but we need to address your immediate problem." He smiled and took her hand. "Can't have such a promising start end prematurely."

Brenna sighed. "Is there anything you can do?"

"Have you at least seen her since she was admitted?"

"Once. I accompanied her in the ambulance. I haven't left the hospital since. I sent her son—he's five—to my home to stay with my sons. Another co-worker took him over."

"You've certainly tried to tend to her business for her." He nodded and jotted something down.

"Will that help?" Rachelle asked.

Paul answered, "It could be shown as concern beyond some mere physical relationship or desire for personal gain." He turned back to Brenna. "How did you find out you weren't on the approved list?"

"I went up to check on her and talk to the doctor. When she wasn't in the room, I went to the nurses station and found out she was in emergency surgery and that I wasn't privy to any further information."

"Until then your questions were reasonably accommodated?"

"I think so. I know there are rules for the patients' privacy, but..."

"But you think Cassidy needs you."

"I brought her son up to visit and I know—I know—she responded to him, to us."

"Her son has seen her already?"

"Yes. He needed it. He'd seen her taken to the hospital. I learned with my own sons that you don't keep them in the dark.

Give them an explanation, or show them something, and they'll deal with it."

Paul nodded again, making more notes. "Are her parents here in the hospital?"

"Not yet. They're due in the morning."

"Did you call them?"

"No. The studio did. I should be okay with that. They're her parents. But Cass said her father hit her when they argued at Christmas. I saw the bruises."

"I'll talk with them in the morning, but you have a pretty solid argument here for visitation. You have her son. What's his name?"

"Ryan," she answered with obvious warmth in her voice.

Paul smiled indulgently. "You've also tried to take care of other things. You filled out her paperwork when you arrived here, right?" Brenna nodded. "I think we can get you in to see her."

"Tonight?" Rachelle asked firmly. Brenna put a hand on her arm to quiet her. "No. Listen, you need to see her. She needs to see you. It will help."

Paul raised a hand. "I've heard enough for me to sign you in and let you spend the night up on the CCU floor."

"You're serious?" Brenna asked in astonishment. She really had not expected anything.

"You can take your friend here up with you." He patted her hands as her eyes went wide. "Give my best to Cassidy when she wakes up and sees you."

"I... I'll do that. Is it going to be all right to bring Ryan back in the morning?"

"He's her son. Even though you're acting only temporarily, you are watching out for him. Definitely make sure he continues to see his mother. It's important to his health as well as hers." He stood. "Come on."

Brenna stood, supported by Rachelle for a brief moment as she let the shock fade and the hope return. Paul held the door and led them out.

CHAPTER FOURTEEN

BRUSHING BACK her dark hair, Rachelle watched as Brenna paced around the empty bed in CCU room 408 yet again. The agitated woman ran her hands over the silent monitoring equipment then paused to look out the window and hug herself.

"There's still a news van out there. I'll bet that reporter knows more about her condition than I do," Brenna commented mirthlessly, forlornly grasping the edge of the curtain.

"Paul said you would be updated. The doctor will visit after the surgery."

"It's been almost three hours." Brenna circled back to the near side and flopped onto a chair tucked up by the headboard. Her arms splayed along the chair's arms and her head dropped dejectedly.

Paul had left them over an hour ago. Now, with the hour passing midnight, Brenna was agitated beyond anything Rachelle had seen on the set as they worked together. She had long since fallen silent on the story of the attack.

"Do you want to talk?" Rachelle invited.

Brenna rolled to a more normal sitting position but then leaned forward over her knees and covered her face. "I'm becoming unhinged, aren't I?"

"I have never seen you like this," Rachelle assessed frankly.

"I don't think I've ever felt this helpless before."

"So let's not talk about this. Let's look forward. What are your plans after Time Trails?"

"Cass and I haven't worked that out yet, but I have an offer to do a film in England. Terry's also got his playhouse. Somehow we'd like to work it out as a family."

Rachelle smiled. "You really see yourself as a 'family'?"

"More than I did with either of my husbands, Chelle."

"Have you ever been attracted to women?"

Brenna shook her head. "Not that I'm aware of."

"Did you get this idea from Luria kissing her in 'Brains and Brawn'?"

Brenna groaned. "That did shock the hell out of me. I barely remembered my next line."

"Cass was surprised too. Will had the idea; Sean liked it. I was game, so we blocked the scene that way. So, seeing her and me..."

"No jealousy. I didn't know what was what yet." Brenna looked at Rachelle with open curiosity. "How about you?"

"Nope. Like kissing a sibling. Stage kisses always are."

"Not for me."

"Not for Cass either, I think. I don't think she'd ever thought of kissing another woman."

"She has."

"Oh?"

"Just once, though, in college." Brenna paused.

"A little jealous?"

"Well, it did make our first time a little easier."

Rachelle laughed. "A little easier. Right."

"Can we change the topic?" Brenna was finding herself drifting into melancholy. Lovemaking was a nice topic, but not if her partner wasn't there to share it with her. "Catch me up on Rose? How is she doing?"

"Good. She wants to know what everything is, so she holds them out until we tell her then she repeats it. We have a little myna bird."

"Thomas was like that, always parroting. James, though... He seemed to wait forever. When he finally did talk, it was like he had a tape recorder. Everything was exact."

"How are they?" Rachelle asked.

"I hope they're at least trying to sleep. Thomas was very upset."

"Did they know about you and Cass before the news coverage today?"

Brenna exhaled. "Yes. Only since the holiday break, though. Thomas had developed a crush on Cass."

"So your son had a crush on your girlfriend."

"She wasn't... We weren't together yet." Brenna sat back and focused on some distant point in time.

"So, you opened up and became friends. That's easy enough to understand." Rachelle continued with open curiosity, "I just don't... What turned you on to her physically?"

Brenna responded sheepishly, "Her feet."

"Excuse me?" Rachelle choked on a startled laugh. "Her feet?"

Trying to find a way to explain, Brenna stood up and stepped away from the chair. "What part of your body hurts the most at the end of a shooting day; what's the absolute worst?"

Without hesitation, Rachelle responded, "My back. Playing Luria just kills my back." Looking up in bemusement, she asked, "What about you?"

"My feet. My calves. Jakes is a strider. When I turn her 'off', my first order of business is a foot massage, then I can actually drive home." Brenna sat down on the edge of the bed. "I caught Cassidy once, just collapsed in her trailer. I don't remember why I thought to follow her. She had her arm over her face. I remember I just grabbed her shoes off," Rachelle nodded, "and I massaged her feet."

Leaning back across the foot of the bed, Brenna sighed.

Staring at the ceiling, she added, "Cass looked at me and it wasn't 'have you lost your mind?' It was more like, 'Thank God, I could just kiss you.' I felt fire in my stomach, Chelle." Brenna's hands folded over her abdomen and she traced idly, obviously remembering. "My fingers tingled and my chest ached. And I wanted her."

Rachelle felt a rush of heat from Brenna's retelling, as if her friend had just told her how she and Cassidy made love. "God," she managed with a steadying breath, "was that the first kiss?"

"No. That came on our camping trip."

"The one Cassidy came back from all excited about mountain climbing?" Brenna smiled fondly as Rachelle asked, "Did she climb more than just the Sierra peaks?" Brenna blushed, but shook her head. "You didn't make love then?"

"No, but we both knew we would."

"Brenna, how did you, you know, know what to do?"

She shook her head. "Cass did. I didn't. When it first happened, instinct failed. I think we over thought the whole thing," she considered honestly.

"But you're together now?"

"The night she came back from her parents, neither of us thought very much at all. It was all feelings." She exhaled. "It was the most incredible experience. Never have I had this happen. Not with Tom and not with Kevin. Not even Will, though we had a lot of fun briefly. Lying there together..."

Rachelle's blush indicated she was envisioning the two women wrapped around one another. Brenna's voice was soft and awed as she continued.

"I didn't need to say anything, not a word, and she didn't either." Brenna inhaled raggedly and hugged herself. "I saw it in her face. Like I was reading her mind."

Brenna fell silent, rubbing her shoulders and thinking of that night, shaking from the mere memory of the emotions. There was a sound from down the hall—worn, badly oiled wheels rolling against linoleum. Bolting to her feet, Brenna ran to the doorway, Rachelle quickly at her side.

An intern in hospital greens pushed an occupied gurney toward them. A gauze cap covered his head, and a mask still hung around his throat. Pausing at the nurses station, he lifted the clipboard from the dangling IV stand, signed it and handed it across the counter. He spotted the women outside 408. "Hi," he said with a friendly smile. "Friends of the patient?"

The patient was covered chest to toes by a green sheet and a cotton blanket. The head was covered in white gauze. Brenna stepped close, reaching out hesitantly, but anxious to see for herself.

"Something like that," Rachelle answered. Brenna had finally given in to her need and was gingerly running a fingertip over Cassidy's bandaged cheek, so Rachelle asked, "How is she?"

The intern pushed along again, and Brenna followed. "The doctor'll be up here after he's cleaned up. She was in real trouble. We did a lot of work on her chest and her stomach. Whoever did this managed to bang her around pretty good. We had to reset her jaw, too, and put a steel pin in to stabilize it."

"What about her heart?" Brenna finally asked. Rachelle reached out a hand, cupping her shoulder.

"We drained off the fluid and that should stabilize on its own now. She's going to have to be very quiet for several days. Then there's all the healing she'll need for the broken ribs."

"How many were broken?" Rachelle asked.

"Three. A total of five were floating, though. She'll need intensive care for now. A regular room might be possible in a few days. She'll be recovering from this for a long time, though it doesn't look like there was any permanent spinal injury."

"Thank God," Brenna breathed. She pulled down the sheet and watched, holding her breath, as the intern moved Cassidy to the bed.

"She'll be under for a while longer, so don't worry. The doctor can tell you more about her post-op care when he gets here."

Brenna grasped his hands. "Thank you," she said earnestly, looking up into his face.

"Pretty special lady?"

"More than I can express."

He nodded and left.

Brenna immediately returned to Cassidy's bedside, leaning over the railing and staring down at the still face.

Rachelle came up along the other side of the bed. "Mitch broke her jaw?" she asked, noting the heavy bandaging and recalling the mention of a pin.

"I guess. God." Brenna's eyes trailed down Cassidy's chest. Rachelle watched as Brenna found the puffy blue and black left hand and cupped it in her own, tracing over the scrapes with her fingertips.

"Looks like she got in a few good hits on him herself," Rachelle said.

"She did. I saw his face. She's got one mean right hook."

Rachelle saw Brenna's frown. "What?"

"I'm going to find out when Mitch is scheduled to be arraigned," she said, a definite chill in her voice. "I want to testify. Mitch Hyland needs to stay behind bars. He could've killed Cass. He would have if we hadn't found them when we did."

Brenna's eyes watered as she brushed hair from Cassidy's temple. Much of it was trapped under bandages and Rachelle suspected some of it had been shaved away. Brenna leaned forward and pressed her lips to Cassidy's. The look on Brenna's face made Rachelle feel like she was intruding on a very private moment. She waited until the other woman straightened. "Well?"

"She looks better."

Rachelle took in what was visible of Cassidy's bruised face, though it was almost completely hidden behind the bandages covering her jaw. Next her gaze drifted to the cast-bound right wrist, and the heavy strapping around Cassidy's waist immobilizing her damaged ribs. And there was all the internal damage the intern had mentioned which she couldn't even see. "This is better? Jesus." She couldn't imagine much worse.

The skewed images began to fade from her mind and pain invaded. Cassidy groaned and opened her eyes. Curling on her side, or at least making the attempt, sparked agony, and her eyes widened. The dimly lit room took shape. She was lying on a bed. Overhead she made out the runner for a curtain and turned her head to find the source of a low hum. The monitor beeped periodically. She couldn't make out what was on the blurry green screen.

She swallowed; her mouth was dry and uncomfortable. The muscles in her face and throat also were not responding as she expected. Putting a hand to her face dumbfounded her as the dulled sensation of bandaged flesh met other bandages.

"Where am I?" she thought, but the sensation in her throat suggested she had spoken aloud.

"You're in Pasadena City General Hospital."

She turned toward the voice and found a woman wearing a white smock covered in flowers standing at the foot of her bed. She had a clipboard in her hand. "You're a nurse."

"Yes. I'm sorry my checking on you woke you up."

"What time is it?"

"Four-thirty in the morning. Your friend there finally fell asleep about half an hour ago, after the brunette left."

Cassidy's gaze followed the nod down to her left side. There was an arm across her abdomen, creating a dull pressure. The woman's right arm was bent under her face, the sight of which created a warm stir of familiarity. "She can't be comfortable," Cassidy remarked, moving her hand until it brushed the slack upturned cheek.

"She settled there and hasn't moved. I offered her the empty bed, but she wanted to be close by in case you woke up."

Carefully moving her bandaged hand, Cassidy let her fingertips absorb the sensation of fine hair as she stroked the sleeping woman's warm cheek. She is clearly someone I am very close to, she thought, recognizing the fullness in her chest as deep affection.

Fine lashes flickered against skin and eyelids fluttered open, revealing clear blue eyes that gradually focused on her. Cassidy's chest hurt with anxiety as she waited. "Hi," she offered uncertainly.

Almost as tangible as a warm blanket, the woman's husky reply soothingly wrapped around her. "Hi," the woman said as her lips curled into a tired but adoring smile. Then she sat up, reaching out a hand toward her.

Cassidy pressed back uneasily into the pillows. "Um." Warm fingers brushed over her forehead. A smile that made her insides melt held her attention.

"Cass? It's Bren. How are you feeling?"

A sense of trust replaced her hesitation, and of all the questions plaguing her, she asked only, "What happened to me?"

Brenna stood up and Cassidy let her gaze follow her up until the pain in her neck and back stopped the motion. She listened carefully as Brenna spoke.

"Would you mind if I turn on a light?"

"No. I mean, go ahead."

The light bar above her head flickered on and Cassidy studied Bren's back before she turned around again. The woman's face— such a beautiful, demurely featured face, Cassidy thought appreciatively—was suddenly alarmingly serious. "What do you remember?"

"From when?"

"Anything at all in the last twenty-four hours?"

Cassidy closed her eyes, willing something to float to the surface of her mind. She furrowed her brow, momentarily making her headache worse. A brown cartoon moose and a squirrel in an aviator's cap appeared, completely befuddling her. What are their names? She opened her eyes. "Why would I be seeing a pair of cartoon characters?"

Brenna met her expression with a confused one of her own. "Who?"

Searching her reluctant-to-respond brain, Cassidy puzzled, "A moose and a squirrel? The moose is... Bull... winkle? The squirrel is... Rocket?"

"Rocky," Brenna corrected softly. Cassidy could see tears glistening in the pale eyes. "Oh boy," Brenna worried.

"You haven't answered my question."

"What question?"

"What happened to me?"

Brenna sat down again. "You're in the hospital. Your ex-husband, Mitch... we found him beating you in the childcare trailer. I don't know what set him off."

"He..." Cassidy tried to think. "We were arguing... custody. He wanted to take Ryan away because I was dating a lesbian." She screwed up her features. "That doesn't sound right."

"We're dating, Cass."

"We are?" Cassidy shook her head. "You're a lesbian?"

Brenna cupped her cheek and kissed her lips. Cassidy suddenly had a flash of holding this woman down and kissing her in a darkened tent, the material of a sleeping bag against her legs. She smiled. "Seems you are."

Brenna laughed. "Actually, before you, I had no experience at all with women. You're the one who had a girl in college."

"I don't think so. My parents would have killed me."

"Maybe that's why it didn't last." Brenna fidgeted. "I need to tell you something."

"What is it?"

"Your parents are on their way here."

Cassidy frowned. *My parents are coming?* She felt a wave of nausea and closed her eyes, hoping it would pass, but the sensation only grew stronger. A face, fleshy and mottled red in rage, appeared in her mind, accompanied by physical pain, which suddenly constricted her chest, choking off her breath. She gasped.

With a firm touch, Brenna cupped her cheeks. "Shh! Shh, it's okay. Shhh."

The whispered reassurances gradually calmed Cassidy and the disruption in her breathing subsided, but the alarm had sounded when Cassidy's heart rate sped up and tripped the threshold on the monitor, so the nurse appeared.

Brenna looked back over her shoulder and said clearly, "She shows... signs... shhhh..." She interrupted herself to soothe Cassidy again. "She's disoriented, not sure of some things."

The nurse nodded. "I'll get the doctor."

"My... parents," Cassidy gasped, aware of tears painfully clogging her throat as she clung to Brenna. "I had an image of a very angry man."

Her lips against Cassidy's hair, Brenna asked, "Describe him?" Still shivering, Cassidy did. "Must be your father, as you last saw him. Your ex-husband, Mitch, doesn't look anything like that."

Cassidy felt another kiss against her temple.

The sensation of the hug and the kiss awakened another

memory. "Ryan?" She looked around. "Where's Ryan?" She had a sudden memory of being in a small office, wondering where Ryan was. Brenna had been with her.

Brenna exhaled and pulled back, meeting Cassidy's gaze. "This is probably going to sound like a stupid question, but... humor me?"

Instinct driving her, Cassidy agreed. "Yes."

"What's Ryan's connection to you?"

Cassidy blinked then answered with some assurance, "He's my son."

Brenna's smile was brilliant and Cassidy's heart lurched with pleasure.

"How old is he?"

"He's... five. He... His birthday was... several months ago, October 8th. I gave a party."

"Yes, you did." Brenna's smile softened and she cupped Cassidy's chin again. "Ryan is at my house for now. Terry Brown will be bringing him by later today."

"Why is Ryan staying with you?"

"You, um, didn't have anyone else to watch him. He gets along well with my sons and I thought it would be okay."

"We work together." Brenna nodded. Cassidy went on, grasping at facts as they occurred to her. "Terry Brown. He... works with us too." Cassidy had a scary flash of a dark-skinned man grasping her and yelling in her face. It left her vaguely unsettled, but not as much as the image of her father. "He's not usually scary."

"Not usually. You must be remembering filming a scene with us. I vividly remember one about six weeks ago that scared you."

"Filming?"

"You're an actor. So am I. We work together on a series called Time Trails."

Cassidy studied Brenna. A sensation of intimacy flowed through her as their eyes met. "And we're dating?"

"Yes. It hasn't been very long to wrap our heads around it."

"That was a nice kiss. I don't think I'd have forgotten for long."

Brenna blushed, but tried to explain. "Mitch's attack gave you a concussion. That's how it works sometimes."

"So that's why some things are hard to remember?"

Another voice answered, "You took some pretty hard blows to the head."

Cassidy and Brenna looked toward the end of the bed. Brenna straightened up and turned toward the doctor. "She does seem to be piecing things together."

"Does she remember anything about the incident that caused her injuries?" he asked. Brenna shook her head. "It will probably come back to her." He turned back to Cassidy, addressing her directly. "You'll have trouble for a little while. Your brain was severely bruised." He studied her chart. "What's your name?"

"Cassidy Hyland," Cassidy answered automatically. Seeing Brenna's surprise, she added, "That's good, right?"

The doctor nodded. "Good. Birthday?"

She hesitated, clearly searching her foggy memory. "February 18th, 1968."

"Excellent. Just the short term memory centers are affected, apparently." He put down the clipboard and pulled a scope out of his coat pocket. "I'm going to take a look inside your head."

For reassurance, Cassidy held Brenna's hand while the doctor examined her eyes and ears. "Do you have any ringing in your ears?"

"No."

"Any dark spots in your vision?"

"No."

Removing the pillow from behind her head, he helped Cassidy lie back flat. Again holding Brenna's hand, Cassidy grimaced at the prodding and gasped at one particular poke to her left ribcage. "It's going to be a good six weeks on those ribs," he said, "but your chest sounds are finally clear."

He checked the IV bag. "I'll have a different antibiotic switched into your drip. How's your stomach feel? Your chest?"

As he palpated those areas, she bit her lip to keep from making a sound, but she had to squeeze her eyes shut, and still tears dripped down her cheeks. At last he stopped probing her.

"You had a hemopneumothorax and lost a lot of blood. There was heavy damage to your liver and spleen. Surgery took care of some of it, but there's going to be a lot of drainage. You'll have another day or two on IV fluids, then start on a liquid diet. Maybe Saturday you'll be ready for something more substantial. If you're very good," he added with a smile. "We'll get you into a general room as soon as I'm sure there is no danger of blood clots."

"But she is getting better?" Brenna asked.

He addressed Cassidy. "You're conscious. Fairly self-aware. Your eyes are clear and alert. There are no indications the swelling around the base of your skull cut off anything vital and the swelling has gone down. A day or two more and I'll be able to make a better prognosis, but I'd cautiously project that full recovery is quite possible."

Cassidy squeezed Brenna's hand, exchanging a shy smile with the other woman when she turned. "Thank you, Doctor."

"I'll be back for my regular rounds at eight." When Cassidy nodded her understanding, he left.

Brenna exhaled in relief. "Thank God."

"You were worried about me."

"Yes, I was. I saw what Mitch did to you and it scared the hell out of me. I thought I might lose you."

Contentment filled Cassidy. Adrenaline reserves began to fade, leaving her exhausted. She blinked sleepily. Soft lips moved against hers then Brenna pulled back.

"Now maybe we can both get some sleep."

"Will you stay?"

"I won't go anywhere. And when you wake up, Ryan should be here."

CHAPTER FIFTEEN

"MAX!" ABOUT to step back into Cass's CCU room, Brenna had her hands on the shoulders of a small boy. She smiled at Max then restrained the boy. "Just a minute, Ryan."

Max Brightman met her halfway. Though there was a weary grayness to her blue eyes, she smiled warmly and hugged him with energy. "Quite a stir," he commented.

"Everything's going to be fine soon," she replied.

Terry Brown walked over. "How are things on the set?" he asked Max.

"Shooting has restarted. Front office is all over, keeping the press mostly at bay. They wanted a status report on Cass."

"It's been a long night," Brenna answered. "I should have sent a report with Rachelle when she left." She smiled then. "But Cass has shown improvement even since then. She woke up around four-thirty and the doctor thinks she'll make a full recovery over time."

"Encouraging," Max concluded.

Brenna shook her head.

"Very encouraging," she corrected with another smile. "I'm taking Ryan in to see her now." Brenna grasped Ryan's hand and stepped inside. Max started after her, only to feel a hand on his shoulder.

Terry shook his head. "They need time alone."

Max moved into the room but remained back, observing as

Brenna watched over the reunion between mother and son. His friend of nearly twenty years had one hand lightly on Ryan's back and the other on Cassidy's shoulder.

"Someone's here to see you," she said quietly.

Taking his cue from Brenna, Ryan also spoke softly. "Mommy?"

"Ryan, hi." The voice was very tired, but even so, Cassidy was very happy to see her son.

Max watched Brenna bend over the railing to lightly kiss her forehead. Over the years of friendship, Max had seen Brenna at many hospital bedsides, and in many relationships.

It was clear to him that this was different; Brenna was different. It was in the way she met Cassidy's gaze; there was a directness in her expression that he hadn't seen for anyone else. The younger woman's expression also was filled with pure devotion. There was no way he could see to interpret their connection other than that they were in love. While he had been flip with Brenna, he still hadn't been sure. He had even seen them at the play and been wary of believing it. But seeing Brenna with Ryan on her lap in the chair at the head of the bed, he finally believed. She was telling the boy about his mother's many bandages. Occasionally she kissed his cheek as she and Cassidy spoke.

"I'll take Ryan downstairs for breakfast while you sleep."

"You should... go to the studio," Cassidy replied, her voice washed out so Max had to read her lips to understand what she had said.

"When you're out of here, I'll go back to work. Not before," Brenna insisted. "Consider that incentive to get well, all right?"

"I really messed things up," Cassidy said sadly.

"No you didn't; Mitch did. I will make sure he pays for this as fully as possible."

The determination in Brenna's voice was to be expected, but not the underlying pain. Max had heard that specific mixture of determination and pain only once, back at the very beginning of their friendship.

"You will do no such thing."

A male voice accented from somewhere in the South or Midwest interrupted the quiet conversation. It came from almost on top of Max, and he stepped back to see a man and a woman standing in the doorway, both staring at the tableau around the bed.

Max watched Brenna stand up, set Ryan down by her legs, and turn to face the new visitors. She appeared to struggle a bit for composure before speaking. Still, her voice shook.

"Mr. and Mrs. Hockman." She nodded at each but her eyes darkened with anger and lingered on Cassidy's father. "I'm Brenna Lanigan. I've been with your daughter since the attack."

Max was taken aback by the amount of tension suddenly filling the room, and the very dark and dangerous look on the face of the older man. Before Max could speak, though, Cassidy's father barked, "You've been with her longer than that! It ends now. Get out of my daughter's room."

Brenna kept her eyes on Cassidy's father, even as she held her place at Cassidy's bedside. "Mr. Hockman," she began. She paused, reconsidering her deference. They were all adults, and the stakes were high. "I have permission to be here," she concluded firmly.

"Not from me! Get out!"

Behind her, a small hand clutched at her pants. Brenna glanced down at Ryan, who was wrapping himself around her leg and staring up at his grandfather with wide-eyed uncertainty. Soothing the boy with a gentle touch along the side of his face, she found it easier to steady her own nerves. "No."

"You are not in charge here. I left orders who was allowed in, and you are not on that list. I will not have you influencing Cassidy."

"She has the right, and the ability, to make her own choices," Brenna replied evenly.

"Not in this. Not when she's my daughter."

"Is that why you struck her and drove her from your home? Because you're afraid of what her choices say about you? No one should live through their children that way." Brenna stepped back. "No one should control their family through fear."

"Holiness is only attainable through fear of God."

"You are not God, Mr. Hockman, and neither is your former son-in-law. God does not beat people to death." She gestured toward the bed, drawing the Hockmans' attention to their daughter. She was sure that when they saw what Mitch had done, they would not remain steadfast in their condemnation of Cassidy.

"What happened?" Sylvia tentatively stepped closer. "Oh, dear sweet Lord..." She looked to Brenna questioningly. "Can I?"

"Sylvia!" Mr. Hockman—Gerry, Brenna mentally corrected—sent a warning glare toward his wife.

Brenna took another step back from the bedside and gestured

encouragement to Cassidy's mother. "Go ahead, Sylvia." She gambled by using the woman's first name. It got her a worried, uncertain look, but the woman did step forward, her gaze returning to Cassidy's face as she reached out and hesitantly touched the bandaged hand.

"Now you get out!" Gerry shouted, taking a step toward Brenna.

Brenna stood her ground and made herself very clear. "Lay a hand on me and you will not enjoy the consequences."

"Who did this to her?" Sylvia asked softly.

"I would have thought someone would have given you some of the details. Mitch did this to her. I arrived in time to stop him from doing worse." Sylvia frowned. "He's in jail awaiting a bond hearing. Didn't the studio explain when they called?"

"Gerry?"

Sylvia looked toward her husband and Brenna realized he had been the one to take the call.

She directed her remarks to Cassidy's father.

"Being selective with your facts, Gerry?"

He looked away. "She deserved it. No decent wife would want this acting more than she wanted her husband."

"No one deserves this." Brenna exhaled as she tried to keep her voice calm. "Damn it, no one!"

Cassidy awakened at the sound, and Brenna twisted quickly to stop her as she struggled to move.

"Cass, no." When Cass met her gaze with understanding and determination, it set Brenna's heart singing, despite the gravity of the situation. She adjusted the bed so Cassidy could face her father.

Cassidy exhaled carefully then begin to speak. "Would you prefer Mitch had killed me?" Sylvia's face went pale, but Gerry's hardened at his daughter's breathy, pain-filled voice. She caught her breath and went on. "Sorry to disappoint you..." She had to stop and collect herself, tears wetting her cheeks at the amount of effort it took just to speak. "...again." Cassidy dropped her head back against the pillows.

Brenna's tears threatened to fall as she squeezed Cassidy's shoulder, offering what support she could.

"Go... away," Cassidy wheezed as her energy failed.

Ryan reached up and prodded his mother's arm, plaintively calling out, "Mommy?" Cassidy did not respond.

Brenna felt Cassidy's tremors fade away as her eyes closed in exhaustion, and quickly checked the heart monitor for reassurance before turning back to Gerry.

Sylvia fell heavily into the bedside chair, covering her face with her hands. Gerry walked toward the bed and every muscle in Brenna's tensed as her body flooded with adrenaline. She took a step forward, placing herself between Cassidy and her father. Slowly, she straightened, tucking in the covers as Gerry stopped at the foot of the bed. He looked as unmoved as before, but Brenna thought perhaps there was a flicker of doubt in his lowered gaze. Perhaps if she left, gave them some time to think about what had happened between them, they would see what they had done was terribly wrong, regardless of their reasons for doing it.

"I'm taking Ryan down to the cafeteria for breakfast. Maybe by the time I return, you'll be ready to be reasonable."

She withstood the withering glare from Gerry with a neutral expression. Taking Ryan's hand, she noticed how he clung to her, watching his grandfather warily. She reassured him with a squeeze of his hand and led him out of the room.

In the corridor she went to the nurses station, greeting Cassidy's nurse with a terse smile. "She's sleeping, so we're going down to breakfast. Her parents are with her." Terry Brown reached her then. "Terry, would you stay please? I think Cassidy got through to them, but... Just watch out for her?" He nodded and she turned to go to the elevator. Max appeared alongside as they waited.

Wracked with tension, Brenna had forgotten he had briefly been in the CCU room with her, Cassidy, and Cassidy's parents. Now, she appreciated his quiet, steady presence. The elevator emptied into the lobby. One by one, milling reporters identified them and began circling.

Brenna held tight to Ryan, but probably need not have worried. Scared by the closing crowd shoving microphones in their faces and calling out questions, he clung to her.

She answered an update question with, "Her parents have arrived." She answered a status question with, "She's sleeping now." A few of the questions made her realize that her statement about their relationship had made it into entertainment press rooms around the country.

"When you return to shooting, will the characters be re-written to reflect your changed relationship with Ms. Hyland?"

She stared at the questioner. "Excuse me?"

"Will the writers put Jakes in a romance with Hanssen?"

"I have no idea what the writers plan. Now, if you'll excuse us." She pushed past the reporter, only to be faced by another.

"Ms. Lanigan, does this mean your character will be coming out of the closet and admitting she's gay?"

Brenna groaned. "What Jakes does is her business, and Pinnacle's, not mine! Excuse me."

She shoved past the rest and entered the cafeteria. With everyone jostling for the perfect angle to take pictures, the media crowd could not immediately follow them through the narrow doorway.

Max stood with them in line, his jaw flexing with anger. "You're not going to get a moment's peace."

"It'll blow over. The media will figure out what's real and what isn't, and eventually leave us all alone. This is just sensationalism," she rationalized. "A star is beaten up by her ex-husband and they immediately assume jealous rage. So they have to figure out who he was jealous of."

"You are the one he was jealous of."

"No. Mitch is a chronic abuser. If it wasn't about me, it probably was about custody, but it could have been about anything else. He created excuses to do what he wanted." Looking at her buttered toast and coffee, Brenna closed her eyes.

"All right. Do you need me to stick around?"

"You probably should get back to the set. I'm sorry your time here during the shoot couldn't have been more pleasant."

"It has been good to see you, Bren."

"I'm glad you were here."

He put his hand behind her head and kissed her temple. "Me, too." He got to his feet and she watched him walk away, pushing easily through the crowd of reporters because he simply did not interest them.

Turning back, she watched Ryan eating his scrambled eggs.

"Miss Lanigan?"

"Yes?"

"Will we go back to see Mommy?"

"After you've eaten," she assured him. He redoubled his efforts to eat quickly. "Slow down. You don't want to make yourself sick," she coaxed, pulling the fork away from his mouth and encouraging him to put it down for a moment. To give his body a chance to catch up with the food he'd already stuffed in it, she asked, "What would you like to get as a present for your Mom from the gift shop?"

"A toy motorcycle," he said with a smile.

"That sounds like it'd be more for you than for your Mom," she commented with a smile and a light ruffling of his hair. "How about some flowers, or a picture frame?"

"Who would be in the picture?"

"I still have your mother's purse. Why don't we find a picture of you to leave with her after you go?"

"I can't stay?"

"We should get someone to take you away from this mess. You don't like the reporters, and unfortunately they aren't going away."

"Why do reporters ask so many questions?"

"That's their job. But we can avoid them sometimes."

"Okay." Calmed by the quiet talk, Ryan returned to finishing his meal.

When the pair returned to CCU, Brenna carried a vase of carnations and Ryan carried a small box. When they emerged on the floor, Ryan immediately spotted his grandfather talking with the doctor and stepped behind Brenna's leg. "It's all right," she assured him. "Let's just go see your mom."

Sylvia stood at Cassidy's bedside, looking more concerned than when Brenna had left. An oxygen mask had been pulled over Cassidy's bruised features and a fresh bandage covered her throat. "What happened?" Brenna asked, putting the flowers down on the rolling table.

Her voice barely audible, Sylvia answered, "They argued. She complained... her chest hurt."

Afraid that Cassidy had had another heart attack, Brenna asked heatedly, "What did the doctor say?" Sylvia frowned, but Brenna urged, "She almost died while I watched, Sylvia. Please tell me!"

Cassidy's mother studied her, obviously conflicted. "Please?"

Perhaps it was a recognition that Brenna cared for Cassidy as much as she did, or just a way for Sylvia to reach out for support she needed. In any case, Sylvia finally nodded. "Her left lung had collapsed again. They revived her."

Brenna quickly went from alarm to relief. "Thank you," she breathed. Ryan climbed up onto the chair next to the table and opened the box, putting up the picture so his mother could see it when she woke. Brenna stepped back to let him work diligently on his own, arranging things as he wished.

Out of the corner of her eye, she saw Sylvia watching her with puzzlement.

Reaching out, Brenna offered, "Don't go. I don't want to be in conflict with you."

"But it's a sin," Sylvia whispered, clearly shocked.

"We're not that different," Brenna insisted.

"You're a—"

"I'm a mother, too," Brenna interrupted firmly.

"You're shameless!"

"No, I'm not. I'm very ashamed of how I treated Cassidy when she first joined our cast."

"Your series caused her divorce!" Sylvia charged.

Brenna shook her head. "It probably saved her life. She had been keeping it all inside. Only one person even listened to her, and it wasn't me. I ignored her, too. You wouldn't believe her when she said Mitch was awful. You and I, we both left her to twist alone, until she had nowhere to turn."

Sylvia looked stunned. "She always sounded so sure of her choices."

"If she had admitted her mistake in marrying Mitch, what would you have said?"

Sylvia's face froze then she frowned.

"How could you know?"

"Because I thought my mother would say terrible things when I made a horrible mistake as a young woman. Unlike Cassidy, I took the risk and told my mother. And she said the terrible, hurtful things that I thought she would. So I know it happens."

Brenna swallowed. The pain was still sharp. Years later, Brenna was sure her mother had ultimately showered her with love only because illness had taken away her memories of those earlier disappointments.

Feeling too vulnerable, Brenna walked away from Sylvia but could not leave the room. Cassidy needed her. Settling into another chair, she turned so Sylvia could not see her face.

"What the hell is going on in here?" Looking up, her muscles tensed, Brenna saw Gerry Hockman filling the doorway. "I told you to get out."

"Gerry," Sylvia called to him from Cassidy's bedside.

"What is it?" He sounded exasperated, but he crossed the room. Brenna suppressed an instinctive cringe as he passed her.

"What does the doctor say?" his wife asked.

"She can't be transported anywhere right now."

Brenna surged to her feet. "You can't be thinking—"

"She needs the best care."

"She'll get that here."

"She needs family around her."

"What about Ryan? He's her family, and he needs his mother."

"We're taking him with us."

"No, you're not!"

Gerry raised his fist at her. "You don't have any input here."

Damn, Brenna thought, taking a step backward. *There has to be some other option.*

Terry appeared, drawing all eyes to him at the doorway where he stood with a man at his side. Brenna recognized Paul Heath, who inclined his head toward her in silent greeting.

"Who the hell are you?" Gerry demanded.

"I'm Paul Heath, Patient Advocacy. I represent Ms. Hyland's and Ms. Lanigan's interests."

"You called in a lawyer?" Hockman asked her in shock.

"Not formally," she replied. "But I will."

"Since when do my rights as her father get questioned?"

"Ms. Hyland is an independent adult with her own rights. From what Mr. Brown told me, she had already conveyed her wishes that she not be removed from this hospital," Heath answered calmly.

Gerry frowned but did not say anything else inflammatory. Brenna hated thinking the only things he would respond to were legal threats. She also lamented the interruption, feeling she had almost connected with Sylvia, was almost able to appeal to a shared outrage at the violence, getting the woman to see her as something other than a rival for her daughter's affections.

Sylvia Hockman was weak, though, when faced with her husband. Brenna wondered if there was abuse there too, if only mental.

"What now?" Gerry asked, sounding more reasonable.

"We wait until Ms. Hyland wakes up, then we all hear what she has to say," Paul explained. "Or I call Security and no one sees her except her doctor and her nurse." He indicated the doorway. "There is a lounge on this floor where you can wait."

Brenna made the first move to follow the directive, taking Ryan into the corridor and looking for the lounge sign. Finding it to the right, across from the elevators, she led Cassidy's son to the leather-padded chairs in a small room with two round tables and a drink machine. Terry followed close behind, sitting beside her as Ryan curled up in her lap.

"Do you need me to stay?" he asked.

The question drew Brenna's eyes away from the doorway as Paul entered, followed by the Hockmans. Cassidy's parents took the opposite corner from Brenna and Ryan. Paul settled at one of the tables, flipping open his portfolio notebook and beginning to work in the silence.

Brenna considered Terry's question. With Paul there she felt less vulnerable to the wishes of the Hockmans. "You should go to the lot," she said. "Ryan and I will be fine. Cassidy'll wake up and this will all be settled. As soon as that happens, I can probably go in myself for a few hours."

"Are you sure? I can call someone else to stay with you."

"It will work itself out," Brenna insisted. "Go on."

Terry stood. He returned a nod from Paul Heath then left the lounge. A few moments later, the beep of the elevator's arrival signaled his departure. Wearily Brenna met the wary gazes of the Hockmans and then closed her eyes, feeling Ryan tuck himself up under her chin as she dozed.

CHAPTER SIXTEEN

THE DOOR to the lounge opened with a click. Brenna looked up from the table where she sat looking over Ryan's drawing efforts. She recognized Cassidy's nurse. The woman's smile made Brenna's heart lift in anticipation. She put her hand on Ryan's shoulder and kissed his head.

"She's awake. The doctor says she can see you now."

Brenna pushed her chair back and rose, sweeping her gaze to the other side of the visitor lounge. The Hockmans also rose from the corner they had staked out over two hours ago. Neither looked particularly relieved that Cassidy was awake. Sylvia had been crying quietly for a good portion of the wait. Brenna had heard her in the tense silence, but breaching the separation had been out of the question while Gerry was present.

Gerry, on the other hand, cast yet another angry glare her way, as he had most of the time in the lounge. When he returned his attention to his wife, it was to make her walk out ahead of him. Brenna turned away, helped Ryan to put the borrowed crayons back in the sturdy plastic box provided by the floor nurse, stalling for a moment before guiding him out to see his mother again.

The first thing she noticed was Cassidy lying flat on her back; even the pillow had been moved away.

Since Cassidy's parents stood alongside the head of the bed, Brenna moved Ryan and herself to the end. Paul Heath, whether he realized it or not, was the buffer between the two groups, standing at the lower corner.

Cassidy looked up at her parents. Anxiety shaped her features, drawing her eyes down before furrowing her brow when she met her father's stare. Brenna held her breath as Cassidy lifted her bandaged hand up, past the rail, toward her mother. "Mom."

Sylvia's reaction was a combination of fear and indecision. She started to reach for Cassidy's hand.

Gerry snatched Sylvia's hand away. The move so sudden, that Sylvia gasped. Cassidy cringed.

"If you want forgiveness, girl, you know how to get it." As Cassidy pulled her hand back and met his eyes, he added, "We're waiting."

Cassidy's lips trembled and her eyes went glassy. Twisting her gaze away, Cassidy next noticed Paul. "Who are you?"

"I'm Paul Heath. My job is to speak for patients' rights in situations like yours."

"Like mine?"

He nodded. "Yes. Your parents want to transfer you to another hospital."

"I told them I didn't want that," Cassidy reiterated. "I need to stay here."

"You need your family around you," Gerry said sharply.

Paul was not fazed. "As long as your wishes remain unwritten, Ms. Hyland, your parents are the authorities that the legal system will accept to speak on your behalf in the event of a catastrophe."

"What's a ca-taz-fee?" Ryan asked curiously.

Brenna patted his shoulder as he stood against her thigh. "Shhh, honey, I'll explain later." When she turned back, Cassidy was studying her and trying to lift her head to see Ryan better. She eventually stopped trying and lay back quietly, holding Brenna's gaze for a long, thoughtful moment.

Pinning Heath again, Cassidy asked, "What do I have to do?"

"There are two documents that offer assurances you will be cared for as you see fit." He waited as Cassidy's gaze returned to Brenna, the look now searching her, delving for something. Brenna swallowed.

"What are they?" Cassidy prompted.

"A Living Will and a Health Proxy." Paul waited for a response. "Would you like to discuss them?"

"She doesn't need to discuss them. She's going to come home

like a good girl."

Cassidy bridled at her father's assumption. In a voice more sharp than she probably intended, she asked for clarification. "The documents. What exactly would they do?"

She was tiring already, Brenna saw, leaving her head and neck carefully aligned, facing the ceiling instead of the lawyer.

"The first spells out the way you expect a hospital to proceed with your care. It can't cover all contingencies, though. The Health Proxy designates someone with the right to authorize your care in those instances the LW doesn't cover."

Cassidy closed her eyes and Brenna worried the strain was getting dangerous. "Maybe this should wait," she suggested softly. "You shouldn't do anything that might put extra stress on your heart."

Blue eyes filled with pain found Brenna. "No. I want this settled," Cassidy wheezed. "Do I have to complete both right now?" she asked Paul.

"No."

"I'd like to designate a proxy then," Cassidy said.

"No, Cassidy dear. Please. Give it some thought?" Sylvia asked.

"She's not fit to make these decisions right now, anyhow," Gerry challenged.

Paul had her chart in his hands. "Do you mind?" he asked Cassidy. She shook her head, just barely. "The doctor thinks she can be moved to a regular room by Monday. Her recovery is expected to be slow, but she's not been judged delirious or without clear judgment in any of her lucidity exams."

Brenna breathed a sigh of relief. "Then she's out of danger." Turning to Cassidy, she encouraged, "You don't need these things." She sensed what Cassidy wanted to do—cut her parents as they had cut her. *But does it have to happen right now?*

"There's no one I trust more than you, Bren. I want you to do this for me."

"Wait. No."

"It should be family!" Gerry argued.

"It doesn't have to be someone here right now, does it?" Brenna asked Paul earnestly. He shook his head. "Then pick someone not in the middle of this."

Cassidy shook her head. "I have no other family, Bren. Please?"

Brenna wavered. Cassidy, it seemed, was determined. Brenna was not family, not legally. But Cassidy's statement seemed to be enough for Paul Heath. She looked from the lawyer back to her beloved's face and worried at her bottom lip. Everyone looked at her intently, awaiting her decision.

She could see that Gerry wanted to kill her, figuratively at least, if not literally. Sylvia was afraid of her. When Cassidy gave a small nod, though, the world around Brenna collapsed to just those trusting blue eyes. Swallowing, Brenna nodded back. Her stomach twisted and her head hurt. She could not deny Cassidy her protection. Not now. "I'll do it."

Gerry threw up his hands explosively. "That's it?" He pointed at Brenna. "You're in charge because she says so? Your control is insidious, bitch!" He turned to see Paul withdrawing a pre-typed document from his portfolio. "I will fight this in court! You just see if I don't, you gay-loving bastard!"

Paul paused and looked askance at Gerry, and with utter calm said, "Yes, sir." He gave the older man a faint smile.

"Father, get out."

Brenna spun to see Cassidy, strain drawing her face in heavy lines, pushing herself up higher against the pillows.

"You can't mean that."

"I mean it. You didn't want to see me again until I'd changed my mind. I haven't. And I won't. I am done with you. Get out. Don't come back. The law is on my side."

Though Brenna clearly saw, as everyone else in the room surely did, Gerry Hockman wanted to strangle the first person he could lay his hands on, he managed to contain himself, only stalking from the room. Judiciously, both Brenna and Paul moved out of his way.

"Mom?" When Cassidy had her mother's attention, she continued. "There will be no courts, no lawyers." Sylvia remained at the bedside, searching her daughter's face. Cassidy looked back at her with a plea in her eyes.

"I understand." Eyes reflecting her hurt, Sylvia's gaze shifted to Brenna then drifted sadly over Ryan. Her body screaming resignation, Sylvia Hockman walked from the hospital room.

Paul spoke again, drawing Brenna and Cassidy to him from their individual thoughts. "Hmm. I thought maybe she might serve as the second witness." To Cassidy he said, "Are you ready to do this?"

"Yes."

"All right. I'll find the head of nursing." He left the formulaic document on the small rolling table. "In the meantime, read this."

Cassidy carefully reached for the paper and said, "Thank you."

He nodded briefly, tucked the rest of his papers together and quit the room.

For the longest time, as Cassidy lay quietly reading, the only sounds in the room were the swish of her oxygen pump and the regular echoing beep of the heart monitor. At the end of her bed, Brenna did not move.

Ryan fidgeted. "Mommy?"

Despite being unable to really see him, Cassidy heard and responded to the worry in his voice. "Ryan, come here." She saw Brenna's shoulder move as her hold on Ryan lingered until he tugged his hand free, coming up the window-side of the bed. Brenna's eyes followed Ryan's progress. Meeting Brenna's gaze when it reached her, Cassidy tried to ease Brenna's distress. "You too, Rocky."

Brenna blinked and offered her a puzzled look. "Huh?"

"Of the two of us, I'd definitely say you're the smart, short one," she explained.

"Oh. I thought maybe you meant the boxer," Brenna responded sheepishly, moving up the near side of the bed.

"You needed a smile. Bren, it's over."

"You... Do you really think you should've done that? You really hurt your mother."

Cassidy had seen the signs her mother was not fully in accord with her father. "But he planned to take everything away from me." She exhaled and gestured at the document as she looked back up. "Thank you."

Brenna shook her head and grasped Cassidy's hand. "I don't know what for. If it hadn't been for me, your parents wouldn't have gone off the deep end."

"My parents honestly don't understand, Bren. If he comes at me with a lawyer, I'll fight him." Cassidy took a moment to watch as Ryan pulled himself onto her bed. "My relationship with them has apparently been nothing more than a facade. They say all the right things, but they don't really believe I'm capable of making my own decisions."

"Mommy?"

"Yes?"

"Can we go home now?"

"Not yet, Ryan." Brenna said with a staying hand across Cassidy's waist as she tried to push herself up for a hug. "Mommy may be stronger than she thought, but she's still very delicate." To Cassidy she said earnestly, "You should sleep, you know. We'll do this paperwork later."

Brenna's hand settled for a moment on Cassidy's chest. Through the bandages, Cass felt a sense of security from the gentle reassurance of the touch.

"Why don't you want to do this?"

"Why do you really want me to?"

"Bren, I..." She looked at Ryan and paused, tickling him lightly across the ribs as he sat listening intently. "Ryan, could you...?" She was at a loss what to suggest, but she wanted to talk to Brenna seriously for a moment and she didn't need little ears taking it all in.

Brenna helped. "Ryan, why don't you go and get the pictures you drew?"

"I'll be right back!"

He slid from the bed quickly, causing the mattress to move. Cassidy inhaled and exhaled shallowly to combat the pain, trying to minimize the movement of her jaw.

"Thank you," she gasped.

After he was gone, Brenna settled carefully on the edge of the bed, searching Cassidy's face. The concern and the love shining there told Cassidy she had made the right decision.

"Now tell me—why do you want to do this?"

"In less than four months, you have become closer to me than anyone else in my life. You care for my son as if he was your own. You've charged in on my behalf in situation after situation. I love you. I want you to have the protection of knowing you have the right to be with me when you need to be."

"I don't understand. The Health Proxy is designed to protect you."

"What don't we have that other couples do without question?" Cassidy asked. She saw Brenna fidget at the word "couple", and understood her bashfulness about it. "You think I don't know what you did to get to stay with me here?"

"What?"

"About forty-five minutes ago, before I had the nurse get you. I'd been out of it so long, I asked for the news on the TV to ground myself a little." She paused. "We're the third story on HNN's Entertainment segment."

Brenna sighed. "After the questions I got downstairs, I figured something had come out."

"Yes," Cassidy said gently. "You and me."

With a sad chuckle, Brenna slipped her fingers around Cassidy's. "Are you mad at me?"

"I'm worried for you. And me, a little. You had to hide out in a bathroom. You only got to stay with me because you announced our relationship. It was hard enough on you telling Thomas and James. It won't help with Kevin and your divorce. It shines a very public light on our family." Cassidy laid her bandaged hand on Brenna's thigh. "I liked it when it was sort of our secret."

"I know. Me, too."

Cassidy smiled as Brenna bent forward, lightly brushing her mouth across Cassidy's lips.

There was a knock, interrupting their conversation. Brenna swiveled. "Yes?" She turned back, identifying their visitors to Cassidy. "It's Paul and, I guess, the head nurse." Cassidy nodded; Brenna stood and gestured the lawyer and nurse to the bed.

"Ready to proceed?" Paul asked. "This is Carrie Meeks, R.N., director of the hospital's nursing staff."

"Hello," Brenna greeted with a courteous nod.

From the bed, Cassidy echoed, "Hello. Thank you."

"A lot of people don't think of these things 'til times like this. You're looking like you'll recover, though," Nurse Meeks commented with a generous smile. "So. You're assigning her your Health Proxy?" She looked from Cassidy to Brenna.

"Yes, I am."

Carrie nodded, her tucked back brown hair bouncing lightly. "Sounds pretty definite."

Cassidy looked completely worn out by the time she had signed her last document copy. Brenna took the pen from her and studied her final signature line. "This is more complicated than getting divorced," she remarked idly. "Or married, for that matter."

"If you had been able to do that, you wouldn't need to do this," Paul reminded her, his hand resting gently on her shoulder. Cassidy smiled as Brenna's light eyes met his and accepted his support.

Ryan bounded back in with a sheaf of papers, followed by Cassidy's nurse.

"What trouble did you get into?" Brenna asked as he looked up with a broad, very pleased with himself smile.

"Not much," answered the nurse. "Just a drawer of adhesive bandages," she explained, lifting his shirt. "Seems he wanted to look just like Mom."

Across his stomach and chest, Ryan had haphazardly applied at least a dozen flesh-colored adhesive strips of various shapes and sizes. Brenna laughed, then covered her mouth to hide it. Paul, who was notarizing the documents as Carrie signed them, also chuckled.

"What is it?" Cassidy asked. Hearing his mother's voice and seeing Brenna's laughter, Ryan apparently decided it would be a good thing to show off. He climbed a chair so his mother had a clear view and showed off his bandaged stomach, lifting his shirt over his face.

"Ryan!" Cassidy looked at the nurse sheepishly. "I'm really sorry about this."

"No harm done."

"We won't let him out on the floor alone again," Brenna assured, steadying him with a hand on his arm. "Did you at least bring your mommy's pictures?"

He nodded and jumped down, jumping back up again with the papers in hand. "Here."

While Brenna helped Ryan show off his pictures, Cassidy submitted to the nurse taking her vital signs. "Best recovery I've seen in your kind of case," the woman said. "Fever's almost entirely gone and even your color is looking better." She smiled toward Brenna and Ryan. "Nothing like having family around, hmm?"

She patted Cassidy's good arm and breezed out.

Brenna's flustered expression made Cassidy smile faintly. Laughing would just hurt too much. "Nothing better," she agreed, catching her lover's gaze. "You are my family, Bren."

"I envisioned that," Brenna admitted after a moment. Settling into one of the chairs, she explained. "You and Ryan stood with Thomas and James at—"

"With us where?" a young male voice asked.

Shocked pleasure suffusing her face, Brenna turned. The curtain moved aside and her two sons stood at the side of the bed.

"Hi," Thomas and James greeted together.

Brenna rose quickly and swept her sons into a hard hug, one boy in each arm. She kissed both cheeks before pulling back. "What on earth are you doing here?"

"Well," Thomas started, "we haven't seen you in almost two days. I thought we should." He held up his bus pass. "So, after school we got on the Transit."

Brenna hugged and kissed him again.

"Besides," James added wryly, "there seem to be fifteen zillion reporters who figured out where we live." He looked around. "They can't come up here, right?"

"Oh no." Brenna brushed her fingers over James' cheek. "I'm sorry." She urged the boys closer to Cassidy's bedside. "What did they say to you?"

"What's it like to have a gay mom? Did she date anyone before this? And what do you think of Ms. Hyland?" James shrugged. "You know—the usual stuff."

The usual stuff? She was surprised by his nonchalance. "What did you say?"

James studied Cassidy for a long moment before he answered. "I haven't had one long enough to know. Yeah, guys. And, Ms. Hyland's better'n all of 'em."

"You are amazing." Brenna shook her head in disbelief.

"He shrugged again. No. Man, you are. Mom, I saw the news. That man is enormous, and you just attacked him?" The unspoken "I'm impressed" was clear in James' voice.

"You saw Mitch on the news?" Brenna asked.

"Yeah. He was arraigned this morning. Assault. He was given a fifty thousand dollar bond and a court date next month."

"He's out of jail?" Brenna's voice conveyed the same alarm Cassidy felt. "Only assault!"

Thomas nodded. "Actually, I ... We thought you should know. The police came by as a courtesy to report that he made some threats against you during his release."

"Then why isn't he still behind bars?" Bren asked.

"Apparently making a threat isn't sufficient grounds. You have to go down and press stalking charges before they'll take him in again."

Cassidy watched Brenna sit down hard, hand covering her mouth, her eyes pained. Supportively she squeezed her hand, frustrated the bandage prevented full contact. She cursed Mitch for the shivers she felt from Brenna.

So focused on Brenna, it took Cassidy another minute to feel Thomas' scrutiny. "Yes?"

"What exactly happened? Are you going to be all right?"

"Your mom probably knows more details, but I can tell you I hurt pretty much everywhere." Energized by the concern of people she knew cared, Cassidy tried to shift herself up so she could talk more normally.

Brenna's hands were abruptly on her shoulders. "You better

stop moving so much," she chided, easing her back down again. She reached up and pulled Ryan into her arms from the chair. "Come on. Why don't we all go and let Cassidy sleep?"

"Bren, wait." Cassidy turned to the boys. "You go on ahead. She'll be right there."

"What's up?" Brenna asked, leaning close as Cassidy looked up. She could see the shadow of the other woman's attempts to cover her anxiety.

"Please be careful," Cassidy urged. "Mitch is resourceful."

"I'm going to call the studio and request a security detail for you."

"Not me, you. Bren. The news reports... He knows where you live." She gestured toward the silent TV on the opposite wall. Brenna looked up. They both saw the tag line at the same time: KTLA News. Live. The neighborhood's welcome sign was clear in the background.

"Thank God, Thomas and James came here," Brenna breathed.

The captioning revealed the rest of Don Deering's story:

Fantasy took a turn into reality as colleagues became lovers. Ex-husbands, ex-boyfriends, even neighbors and friends are stunned as two stars emerge from the closet.

Deering had obviously done some digging. Cassidy recognized footage from interview sessions the Pinnacle PR Department wouldn't have approved for print, of her and Brenna answering questions, standing casually, even intimately close. Deering had also covered Ryan going missing at the Sports Warehouse. Video rolled of the women and their sons in the parking lot after the ordeal.

Was this the beginning? the caption read.

More recent video followed. For the first time, Cassidy saw the pandemonium surrounding Mitch's attack. The playback froze on a shot of Cassidy's untreated, battered face and Brenna holding her bruised hand just at the edge of the frame.

Will this be the end?

Deering concluded his sensationalist report with a few actual facts, notably their public roles and respective ages.

Brenna groaned. Cassidy brushed her fingertips through the woman's soft hair as Brenna lowered her head. Cassidy whispered, "It doesn't matter to me. I love you."

Despite the bandages and the pin in her jaw, Cassidy judged the tender kiss more than passable. She murmured her appreciation before Brenna pulled away.

Deeply affected, the other woman's voice trembled. "Think you can stay out of trouble until I come back?"

"When?"

"After I've gotten the boys in bed. I don't think I could fall asleep knowing you're here alone."

"Don't," Cassidy said. "Call Rachelle, or Terry. Go to a hotel. Don't go home, Bren, please. Not with Mitch out there."

"He can't scare us if we don't allow it."

"He's apparently not content with just scaring anymore."

Brenna's expression told her she had accepted the warning, as she nodded.

"All right. I'll talk with someone at the lot tonight." She kissed Cassidy's forehead lightly.

Cassidy let the tears from her physical pain fall quietly as she watched Brenna leave with the three boys. Closing her eyes, she adjusted the covers and tried to sleep, despite the worry plaguing her.

CHAPTER SEVENTEEN

DESPITE THE hot afternoon sun, the boulevard that led to Pinnacle's gated entrance was thronged on both sides by picketers. Brenna's Mountaineer crept carefully through the surging crowd and the microphone-waving reporters. Waved to a stop at the guardhouse, she rolled down her window, making the previously unintelligible din clearer and revealing both support and condemnation. Unable to completely ignore the menagerie, Brenna stole a glance to the left, where, from the positive tenor of their signs, the pro camp was gathered. Many shot her a thumbs up and pumped their fists in the air. Signs waved back and forth proclaiming "Grrl Power" and "Lanigan-Hyland: Pinnacle's New Power Duo." There were also "Get Well Soon, Cassidy" and "Best Wishes" placards.

An explosive noise went off behind the Mountaineer, making Brenna jump. Looking in the rear view mirror, she saw a protester running away toward the sea of signs decrying her, Cassidy, and the studio. Sentiments such as "God Decrees Time Trails Time is Up" and "No Gay Jakes" were waved at her. More damning and personal were "Play Gay—Play Dead", and Brenna fumed at the most hateful sign: "Mitch Hyland should finish the job."

"Are the writers planning to write this into the show?"

Brenna turned away from the signs and looked at her younger son.

"No. As a matter of fact, we just did an episode where Hanssen imagines a relationship with Raycreek."

"That's nuts," Thomas said. "Raycreek and Hanssen hardly talk."

"I thought you didn't watch the show," she teased.

He shrugged sheepishly. "I've caught it a few times. Enough to know that storyline definitely doesn't fit the characters."

"Cassidy agreed with you. She asked to rework some of the script and turned it into a delirium. She turned in a very good performance." Brenna held up a hand as the guard came to the window. "What was it?"

"Firecrackers and pop caps, but nothing up your tailpipe. Go on ahead."

"Thanks, Randy. Do you know where Victor Branch is right now?"

"He's been in the main offices with a lot of the production team all day. They're working out story line changes around Ms. Hyland's injury."

She reached out and patted the guard's shoulder. "Thanks. You have a good day."

"When you see Ms. Hyland next, tell we're pulling for her." Brenna smiled. "You be careful, too, ma'am."

Brenna checked her rear view one last time then drove through the opened gate. She guided the car into the authorized vehicles lot, pleased to see a blue-clad officer riding up and down the parking lanes in a golf cart. Security had obviously stepped up since the attack.

Should've been better before, she thought angrily.

"Time to find out how everyone else feels about recent developments," she said, mentally girding herself for the executives' questions. "Stick close, guys," she advised the boys.

Holding Ryan's hand, she led her sons through the foyer. Nodding at another security guard standing in the entry corral, she turned to the Television Division secretary who sat at a desk near a closed door. "Victor Branch around?" Brenna asked, and Cheryl Little wordlessly pointed toward the back offices. Not a good sign. Tensions must have everyone on edge.

In the back corridors, Brenna was self-conscious about the stares she received from open doorways. She drew to a stop at the end of the hallway and knocked firmly on the closed conference room door.

Answering the query from within, she said, "It's Brenna Lanigan."

Lonny Nickel answered the door. Looking harried and disheveled, he combed his fingers through his dark curly hair as he stepped back, gesturing her inside. He balked at the children's presence. "What're they doing here?"

"We're about to head home for some dinner. I thought you'd all–" She gave the room a visual sweep, finding Victor Branch at the far end, flanked by Michael Sassman, Susan Strom, and Cameron Palassis, "like an update on Cassidy's condition."

"Media's doing a fine job of that," Lonny snapped. "A domestic dispute has left one of our stars in Intensive Care, unconscious. Though," he conceded, "Terry did tell us she's awake."

"Off and on since about four-thirty this morning, yes." Brenna settled into a chair and gestured Thomas and James to take a seat on either side of her. Cringing from the sharp tone in Lonny's voice, Ryan pulled himself up in Brenna's lap. She automatically rubbed his back soothingly. "She is still in CCU here, rather than where her parents wanted her moved."

"What?"

"They wanted to move her to Missouri, but it's been worked out."

Cameron cleared his throat. "She's stable now?"

Brenna detected worry in his voice and provided more details. "Surgery went well. The EKG didn't show any lasting damage from her two heart attacks–"

"Two heart attacks!"

"Yes," she replied solemnly. "She had a lot of internal bleeding. Some of it put pressure on her heart. The surgeon spent most of his time plugging holes and draining fluids."

"God," Cameron exhaled, resting his face in his hands.

"I did a lot of praying," Brenna admitted unashamedly.

"But you're here, which must mean her prognosis is good?" Victor prompted.

"They'll probably move her to a general room on Monday. She'll be in the hospital for at least another full week."

"After that?" Lonny asked.

"She's got broken ribs and wears out very quickly. She'll need at least a month of at-home convalescence, and a brace when she comes back to work."

"So, no stunt work, then." Brenna shook her head. "Damn,"

Lonny fumed. "How are you for work?"

"I'll be taking care of Ryan for her, but I can report."

"Turn the kid over to his grandparents—"

"No!" Ryan exclaimed. "Not going with Grandma and Grandpa." He hugged Brenna hard.

She whispered in his ear, "I promise you'll be safe. I promise." That seemed to soothe him.

"What's wrong with him?" Lonny interjected.

"He witnessed some disturbing arguments between Cassidy and her parents," she explained vaguely. "And not only today."

"Oh." Lonny put his hands in his pockets. "We've moved childcare into an office next to Props. You can leave him there while you work."

"What have you got so far?"

"We're doing all the fill shots first. We gave one of your sequences with Brady—the first apprehension—to Chapman. Will can play it just as well."

"All right."

"Otherwise we're stuck. Could you come in Saturday to work with Brady on your other shots? His contract time was very narrow. We can't get him next week."

Brenna nodded. She had expected that. "Saturday bright and early, I'll be here."

"Are you going back to the hospital?" Cameron asked.

"Tonight." She remembered the most important thing she had to put in place. "I have a request."

"Something you want us to tell the press?"

"I don't want to issue any press releases until after I've talked with Cassidy again and we decide exactly what we want to say." She shook her head. "No, what I need now is someone for Cassidy's protection. Mitch got out of jail on bail this morning. If you don't hire a bodyguard for her, I will."

Victor tapped a folder in his hands against the tabletop. "You think he'll go after her again?"

"I'd bet on it."

Cameron added, "I agree. Before Cassidy's divorce became final, he was always calling, and he does fit the profile of a stalker."

Branch nodded. "All right." Brenna exhaled in relief. "There'll be someone at the hospital by third shift," he assured her. "Now, we need something from you."

The group fell silent as she looked from face to face. Seeing mostly consternation, she grabbed the subject by the proverbial horns. "I don't want to do a press conference."

"You need to give us something," Branch insisted. "The studio's being overrun."

"From what I've been able to piece together, Cassidy went to visit her family in Missouri over the holiday break. We'd begun seeing each other outside work. Her parents found out about it."

Lonny was flabbergasted. "So it's true? You're dating?"

"Wow," said Susan Strom, one of Time Trails set coordinators, who had been sitting quietly in the furthest corner. "This is going to be hot to handle. It crosses that fantasy/reality line fans have a hard time remembering exists anyway."

"I..." She looked at Cameron, who particularly seemed to be trying to ignore her. "We'd have liked it to come out under different circumstances." That was an understatement but these were not close friends, Brenna reminded herself. Details were not required, and in Cameron's case, unwelcome.

Lonny looked at his papers. "We'll help you draft a statement to the press, something to keep them occupied."

"I'll call my agent, and give you something for tomorrow."

Victor Branch shook his head. "Today. Your agent and also Cassidy's are cooling their heels in my office."

"I'm not going to get out of this, am I?" Brenna said with a sigh.

James spoke up. "Why is any of this anyone's business? They chased us out of our house, man."

Brenna put a hand on James' shoulder. "It's all right. He's right; I have to do this."

"All right, let's get the kids to Karen and sit you down with the agents. I'll tell PR they can assemble the press in media room 7."

"Understood." She pushed to her feet. "First I'm going to Cassidy's trailer to collect her appointment book. She needs to have her agent cancel her commitments for the foreseeable future."

"We'll send a runner over to take care of that. Get into my office," Branch snapped.

Brenna had been hoping for at least a short reprieve during which she could marshal her thoughts. She had no idea what she could say in answer to all the press questions. "All right. She's at Pasadena City General, CCU room 408." Brenna scribbled the room number on a scrap of paper and slid it across the table to Branch. "Can I at least talk to the rest of the cast first?"

Victor's expression told her he wasn't sure she wouldn't bolt.

Brenna was about to reassure him when Cameron spoke up from across the table.

"I'll walk with her," he volunteered. Turning to Brenna, he repeated, "I'll go with you."

Why on earth would he want to go anywhere with me? Brenna knew she was "the next man" after Cassidy ended her relationship with Cameron. If they were alone, he could say or do a lot of things Brenna was unsure she could deal with right now. Charitably, she did recall he went pale at the news of Cassidy's heart attacks. Maybe he only wanted private confirmation Cassidy was recovering. "All right."

The walk from the executive offices over to the sets for Time Trails had never seemed quite so long. Brenna wanted to both hurry to see the others, and hang back, because she was still trying to piece together where to begin in the press conference. She knew that no matter what prepared statement she gave, the media would harangue her with all the questions she didn't want to address, unless she gave them something else to satisfy them. *Pack of dogs*, she thought uncharitably. *Have to throw them a reasonably tasty bone so that I can jump in the other direction while they're gnawing that to bits.* Cameron shuffled along, his hands shoved in his pockets, his head down. Thomas kept looking from her to the writer, stumbling occasionally as he shortened his strides to avoid tripping over either of them.

Ryan circled, occasionally catching Brenna's hand and asking to see Mrs. Grinaldi. Finally Brenna stopped. "Thomas, do you remember the way to the Prop department?" She caught Ryan's hand and put it in Thomas'.

Thomas nodded. "You're sure?"

"We'll be there shortly, but I think maybe we'll be quicker if Ryan gets some playtime in, instead of crawling on the rigging." Bending over, she hugged Ryan. "You be good." She brushed her palm over his cheek. James held back for a moment, looking from Thomas to Ryan, who he clearly didn't want to spend a lot of time with, and his mother and Cameron. She raised her eyebrow at him in question.

"You need someone with you, though," he said.

Brenna shook her head. "I'll be fine. You don't want to face the press any more than I do."

Cameron stood in silence until James was also gone, having

followed after his brother.

"You're pretty good at that," he said. "No wonder Cassidy appreciates you."

"Cameron, don't do this. To me or yourself," she advised kindly.

He tried for nonchalance. "I'm just saying that I... I can see why she loves you." He shook his head. "I don't... I just can't get into kids."

"That isn't why she stopped seeing you," she said quietly.

"How could you know? Have I been the topic of some pillow talk?" he jabbed.

"It isn't like that."

"Damn you," he growled. "One stupid script and she's crawling into your bed." He stabbed a finger at her. Brenna ignored his anger, knowing it stemmed from his hurt. "I used to be the hero. Me. I collected her from that airplane when she was barely able to walk. I saw to it she got treated. She cried on my shoulder every night as I helped her in and out of the brace. Don't you wonder why no one ever saw her out of makeup or out of costume that first month?" He inhaled. "The costumer was the only other person who knew."

Brenna nodded. It all made sense. Ribs took so long to heal. Cassidy never moved much in those early months because she was hampered by the brace. What Brenna had thought a corset had instead been a rigid medical aid.

Cameron was not finished with his rant. "And you! You of all people. You froze her out! Now this—you and her? How does that work?"

Ashamed, Brenna's gaze slid away from his. Cassidy had never mentioned the early days or demanded an apology for Brenna's cold shoulder treatment. She was content to take their relationship forward, leaving the past behind. That seemed to be the way Cassidy lived her life—always in the moment and focused on one thing at a time. Completely. She could be on a set totally in character, to the point that there had been a guest actor who thought Cassidy was a cold fish when she was in "Hanssen mode."

Or she could be totally into you. Brenna recalled being captured by swirling pools of blue eyes on a moonlit mountain night. She inhaled sharply, recalling the last time she and Cassidy had made love. *Was it only two days ago? It feels more like a lifetime.* Her arms suddenly ached with the desire to hold Cassidy again as she cried out in pleasure, the sound making Brenna feel like the queen of the universe.

Hearing Cameron shuffle impatiently beside her, Brenna returned her attention to his question. "You're right. I don't deserve that she should love me, but she does."

"Do you think I could visit her?" Cameron asked. "I know what you said in the office, but..."

"Cameron, I don't know that I would if I were you. She's weak, tired. If she's still upset at you, it might not be the best thing for her to see you." She offered an olive branch. "I can ask her, though."

"She amazed me, taking up with you," he said reflectively, apparently taking her offer to heart. "I thought we were pretty compatible."

"When you treated her like a trophy instead of a person, Cameron, it was over." The look of bewilderment on his face told Brenna that he had no idea what she was talking about. "I don't expect you to understand; you've gotten too used to controlling things. Cassidy has an infectious sense of wonder, and despite her rapid rise in this business, she's not cynical. She's intelligent and insightful. She makes me feel this is all still worth it, that honest love still exists. I'd forgotten."

"Sounds like you had a mid-life crisis," he snorted.

"Maybe I did. But she's worth a crisis."

He still looked completely baffled. They reached the stage door and Cameron pulled open the door to the soundstage. "We'd better make this quick."

With a sigh, Brenna entered ahead of him, then hung back until she heard the director call, "Cut!"

Rachelle stumbled toward her chair. Right behind her, Brady bounced a little and smiled as he looked up. "Hey, Aunt Brenna!"

She held the two chairs as the actors flopped into them. "Hi, Brady."

Rachelle looked up. "Bren!" She glanced beyond Brenna to see Cameron lingering beside a camera. "Cameron?"

"Hi." Brenna smiled and grasped the hands that reached toward her. "Working hard?"

"They rearranged some scenes to free up you and Cassidy, so, here we are," Rachelle explained. "We got our calls at five a.m. I'd barely put my head on my pillow. Will's tickled, though. He got some of your scenes with Brady."

"I heard," she said. "I'll be in on Saturday to finish up my part."

She glanced up at Brady. "Are you all right with that?"

"Sure," the young man answered readily.

"Is your dad around?" Brenna asked, thinking about how abruptly Max had left the hospital.

"Came through a little while ago, but haven't seen him since."

"Okay. I'll call him later." Brenna patted Rachelle's shoulders. "I have to run."

"Tell Cassidy we're pulling for her."

"I will. She woke up about four-thirty, actually."

"That's good news. How did the morning go with her parents?"

Brenna frowned. "Her father thinks she deserved it," she revealed quietly.

"Son of a bitch," Rachelle exclaimed with heartfelt emotion.

"They almost got the doctor to agree to move her to Missouri. While Cass was unconscious, they had the medical control. I argued long enough for Cassidy to wake up and take control of things herself."

"What did she do?"

"She named me her health proxy." Brenna caught Rachelle's raised eyebrow. "She'd had another heart attack. I couldn't let her parents do something she clearly didn't want. It's kind of made things more ... permanent between us."

"Sounds like it. What did her parents do?"

"Gerry Hockman fumed, threatened to sue, and then stalked out of the hospital. I have no idea where they are now."

"Where's Ryan?"

"Ryan needed to run off a little steam. It got pretty stormy at the hospital. I think he's nervous and upset, but being around my sons seems to make him feel secure. All three boys are with Mrs. Grinaldi right now."

"So the home front is weathering the press storm?"

"James says there's crowds around our house, which is why they came to the hospital—to get away for a while."

"Shall I tell you what we've been doing to help?"

"Don't tell me. I've been painted as the matriarch of the troupe. My concern over Cassidy is no more or less than what I showed to you, or Rich, or anyone else, when you all had troubles of your own."

Rachelle chuckled. "Nobody's buying that."

"I know. Branch has ordered me to do a press conference. Within the next hour."

Rachelle stood up quickly. "I'll ask for a break. We'll be there to support you."

Brenna sighed. "Thank you." She looked at Brady. "If you see your dad..."

"I'll have someone find him. We'll be there too."

"Thank you." Brenna reached out to give Rachelle a hug, but Rachelle grabbed her and kissed her cheek firmly, startling her.

"Keep your chin up. I'll have as many of us there as I can manage."

"I... Thank you, Chelle."

"See you in an hour."

Brenna walked out of the soundstage area, followed by Cameron. "How much of that stuff about her parents are you telling the press?" he asked.

"As little as possible. Her parents don't deserve the fifteen minutes of fame, and I won't do anything to help Mitch's case by airing it in the press. I want us left alone."

Cameron didn't respond. Brenna inhaled the crisp January air and slipped Cassidy's trailer key out of her purse. She mounted the steps quickly, but the key did not easily fit. Bending down, she examined the lock and noticed scoring around the cylinder. A chill skittered down her spine and she took a step back.

The noise of a golf cart approaching startled her. Turning, she saw a young man in bright blue shorts and a white crew shirt—a Pinnacle runner—driving up to the trailer.

"Hey, Ms. Lanigan."

"Hi. What's up?"

"Mr. Branch sent me to get some of the flowers and stuff from Ms. Hyland's trailer to send over to the hospital."

"I'm here to collect some things she might like myself."

"Give me a hand then?" he asked.

Brenna nodded and stepped back as he moved up the steps. He had the same trouble with his key. The rasp of it in the lock, not settling the tumblers, made her nervous. "Maybe you ought not to..."

He bent away from her outstretched hand and peered into the keyhole. "Looks like something's been jammed in there." He tried the knob. "Dang, it's already unlocked." He pulled the door wide. The knob clicked suddenly in his hand and Brenna grabbed his shoulder, yanking him backward. "Hey!"

Brenna peered around the edge of the open doorway. When nothing jumped at her from the dark interior, she shrugged sheepishly. "Sorry. Guess I'm a little jumpy."

"Yeah, guess so." The runner stood, brushed himself off and reached inside for the switch, flooding the interior with light. "Just flowers and cards everywhere."

Everywhere was right. Several arrangements had been knocked to the floor. The pots lay cracked and flower petals were strewn around. "Well, I'll take these," she said, scooping up a stack of postcards and telegrams and dropping them in her purse. "You get the flowers that are still in decent shape; I'm going to grab her appointment book."

"That was one of the things I was told to find. I was delayed getting out here—couldn't find a cart. All the security folks seem to have 'em." The runner was already hefting several arrangements.

Brenna searched Cassidy's desk and found a combination appointment/address book. "I'll be right back." Stepping out into the sunshine again, she spotted someone else coming up the walkway.

"Can I help you?"

He held out an electronic signature pad. "Making a delivery to Cassidy Hyland." he explained. "I was told her trailer was unlocked and just to put it somewhere there's space. Apparently there've been a lot of deliveries?"

"Yeah."

She read the company name, Flowers Unlimited, and his name, Jim, on his lapel.

"I better get the delivery inside." He started to turn away.

"Wait. I'm a friend of Ms. Hyland's. I'm going to take some of the flowers and cards and things to her. Why don't you leave it with me?" As an afterthought, she asked, "Who is it from?"

"Well, Ms. Hyland's supposed to..."

"She's in the hospital. Who is it from?"

He read the delivery information. "Mrs. Gwen Talbot, 1402 Sycamore."

Brenna nodded, familiar with Cassidy's neighbor. "I'll take the flowers directly to Cassidy. She'll enjoy them."

"But the delivery..."

"You've made it." She grasped the electronic pad and signed her name. "Thanks, Jim." She nudged him back around the end of the trailer where he had set down his package.

There were flowers... but Brenna laughed as she identified the logo on the side of the two-foot tall bucket. "God, that'll send her into catatonia!"

"It's our Chocolate Lover's Bouquet." She hefted the arrangement and sniffed the flowers, distinctly overlaid with the blessed scent of rich chocolate. "It's supposed to be for the recipient," he added with a grin.

"Of course." Brenna dropped her chin and shifted the "bouquet" onto one hip, holding out her freed hand to shake his. "Thanks."

As she headed again for the trailer steps carrying the bouquet, Cameron shook his head. "What the hell?"

"Flower delivery." She nodded toward the delivery man who had started back toward the main buildings. She eased a small wrapped piece of chocolate from the side. "Fortification before I face the press." Surprisingly, Cameron laughed.

CHAPTER EIGHTEEN

BRENNA ENTERED Victor Branch's office and saw Ray Aruth sitting primly, his briefcase open on his lap. Next to him sat a woman Brenna didn't recognize. "Hi, Ray." She turned to the woman and held out her hand. "You must be Cassidy's agent. I'm Brenna Lanigan."

The woman shook her hand. "How is Cassidy?"

"Recovering slowly. It'll be several days yet."

Her own agent still hadn't spoken. "Ray?"

"I'm just here to deliver this," he said, tossing a packet of papers toward her.

She caught it with consternation.

"What's this?" She flipped the first page over and was surprised to see the contracts for the English project Celtic Queen staring up at her. "Voided?" She studied the language appended by the production team's legal representative. "But why?" She looked to Ray for an explanation.

"They want a particular type. You are no longer it," he stated bluntly. "I spent the holidays convincing them to wait for you, saying you were going to be perfect for the role. That you were not pigeon-holed in sci-fi, that you were going to give the project the maturity to bring it spectacular reviews." Ray was tense and aggravated, and didn't care if it showed.

"But I am all those things. I'd have given my complete attention to every tiny detail. Cass and I—"

"Cass and you are the problem," he snapped. "When they decided on you for this film, you were a mature married woman with two kids, the epitome of respectability." He snatched the contract and it crumpled in his tight grip. "Now you are a philandering woman with a lesbian following. That is not what this project wanted from you! Your divorce isn't even final and she's living with you!"

"Actually she's still in the hospital," Brenna said slowly. She swallowed her surprise and hurt at Ray's bluntness. "Thanks for asking."

"The agency doesn't care. You threw away a golden opportunity, for what? For sex? People sleep their way into roles, not out of them."

"This is ludicrous. I'm still the same actor," she chafed. Would people now expect her to only play a gay woman, or that she would only draw gay people to her projects? "Who I love doesn't affect what I can do," she said with asperity.

When she looked at Ray, she found not the ally who had helped her continue to find roles when she had hit the "deadly 4-0," but a man who was just as disappointed in her as the industry now appeared to be.

"There has to be some other reason," she insisted. "Did they find they preferred Sarandon or something?"

"No, they have decided to go with an unknown Scottish-born actress who has been circulating in their Royal Shakespeare Company for twenty years."

The information left her nothing with which to salve the wound. The producers really had decided against her, plain and simple. She clasped her hands around her knee to still their shaking. "What did you try to change their minds?"

"Nothing."

"I see." She stood, turned away from him, exhaled and brushed her fingers through her hair. There was really very little to say. Not looking at him, she asked as plainly as he had spoken to her, "Do you wish to terminate our contract, as well?"

Out of the corner of her eye, she saw Ray pull out another document and her heart sank.

"We foresee that any prospects you might have had will now dry up," he said. "The agency has decided to drop its representation of you."

Roll with it, she counseled herself. You've been in more difficult situations in your career. On the heels of that was the abysmal thought that maybe this actually was the worst. She looked at him, but he was looking at the paper he held out rather than at her. "Do you agree with them?" she asked, accepting the paper.

"I thought you were a good investment when we first acquired you," Ray said neutrally.

"Now you don't think so."

"Why didn't you come to us to handle the publicity on this?"

"This what? My personal relationships were changing; it had nothing to do with my career."

Ray was incredulous. "In six months you went from being married to having an affair with a co-star—a woman!—and you didn't think you'd need publicity management?"

Looking at her situation from the outside for a moment, Brenna realized she might feel the same as the agency did. However, she wasn't outside of it. She was inside, and she was happy. But it was true that her divorce was not finalized. Defensive, Brenna said "It wasn't my intention to have my relationship on the front page of every newspaper in the country."

Ray shook his head. "I thought you were more savvy than that." His words were a final indictment.

"Will the agency be... making a public statement?" she asked. How much more could she take?

Ray shook his head. "Embarrassment is not something we desire, either. Our other clients might get antsy."

"Do you represent any... gay clients?" she asked.

Again shaking his head, Ray said, "If we are, none are out, but the Bormanis Agency prefers a stable of mature clientele in any case."

A label for which she apparently no longer qualified. Brenna exhaled. "Right." At least she could be mature about watching her career self-destruct. "My portfolio?" she inquired, as she snatched up a pen from Victor's desk and signed her name to the agency's dismissal papers.

"I will have a courier deliver all your properties to your home address."

He wasn't even going to bring it himself. Ray was washing his hands of her quickly, cleanly, and quietly. Brenna kept her gaze down so he would not see her eyes shining with unshed tears. She pushed the paper back to him, holding out the pen. Taking it, he signed his name below hers.

"Thank you for the time you spent on my behalf."

"You're welcome," Ray said. He would not meet her eyes.

There was a long silence between them. Finally Ray turned, collected up the signed documents and his briefcase, and hurried through the door.

"Ms. Lanigan?"

Brenna turned with a start. She had forgotten the presence of Cassidy's agent. "I'm sorry for that, Ms. ..."

The agent stood and held out her hand. "Natalia Gardner. My friends call me Talia." Brenna took the hand in surprise. "Looks like you need my help."

"I am going to give a press conference in about half an hour. You were here to help with Cass' side of things."

"I think I can help both of you." Talia nudged Brenna into the chair vacated by Ray. "We can manage this exactly the way you and Cass want."

"What does the studio want me to do?"

"The studio told us..." Talia's gesture included the absent Ray. "Well, I'll finish what I was asked to do," she said, resting her hand on Brenna's knee. "To say whatever it is two formerly straight actresses can say to quiet the damn reporters so they'll leave the set alone except on media day."

As anxious as Brenna was, the statement sounded exactly like Victor Branch. Delivered by this woman, it made her laugh. "That sounds exactly like Victor. All right." She sobered. "Trouble is, Cass isn't out of the woods yet, and I'm pretty frayed around the edges. I am quickly realizing that I had never considered what it means to be gay—until one of our directors made me see that I could become Hollywood's newest poster child."

"So you've considered it for about five seconds." Talia nodded, seemingly completely unfazed. "All right, I can work with that."

Brenna shook her head. "How did Cass find you?"

"She looked in the Yellow Pages under damage control," Talia replied. "I helped her and Cameron Palassis keep her news all positive while she was divorcing Mitch."

"So you knew about her being abused?"

"Yes, and we will get through this new challenge together as well." Talia resumed her seat beside Brenna. "Now, I've got some ideas here about where to start."

"Let's hear them." Brenna scooted her chair closer to Talia's, looking over the woman's arm as she withdrew a yellow legal pad and a pen.

The large auditorium-style room frequently doubled as a full feature screening room for pre-release movie showings for all the big reviewers. Now Brenna stood in the wings, leaning hard on Talia's arm and wishing she had time to call Cassidy to watch their "coming out" on TV. She might have dared to bring their sons to stand with her, but Talia had advised that the boys be kept away. They didn't want to prompt questions about how the new family would go forward, just deal with the disruption to the sets, the beating Cassidy had received from Mitch and its presumed cause, the relationship she and Cassidy had begun.

Looking at the small note cards Talia had carefully printed as they settled on the order and nature of the questions they would answer, Brenna exhaled nervously. Talia had warned her not to perform. "They need to see the real you, Bren. That's the only way they'll believe every word you say and leave you alone."

The media is too damn interested in our lives, Brenna thought angrily. *Why don't they just get their own?* She took a deep, calming breath. She had to get through this, needed to get back to the hospital and see to Cassidy's care. What was important now was to find out what it would take to make Cassidy fully well again. And this press conference was standing in her way. Best get it over with. She straightened her back.

Talia patted Brenna's hand and smiled encouragement. "You handle this the way I know you can, and I'll represent you from here on out."

Brenna felt a small portion of her load lifted from her shoulders. "Thank you."

Standing room only, it seemed every member of the entertainment-interested press, television, radio, and internet were in attendance. There were hand-held recorders, video cameras, production cameras, pens and pads or palm-sized computers in nearly every visible hand. There were still cameras on tripods, a few hanging around the necks of still more reporters edging in around the outskirts of the bucket seating.

"Victor's going to speak first, then I'll go." Talia winked. "Then you can wipe the floor with them."

Brenna laughed and the tension in her back miraculously vanished.

There was suddenly a large hand on her right shoulder, making Brenna jump. Victor looked down as she looked up.

"Ready?" he asked.

"As I'll ever be," Brenna allowed.

"You have the skills to do this," Victor said. "So do it." He stepped forward.

Talia leaned closer. "What was that about?"

"Victor once told me that nothing I ever do is accidental."

"Really?"

"I dumped a bowl of punch on a man who was aggravating Cassidy and made it look like an accident."

"Is the man still alive?"

"Yes."

"Then I'd say 'brava'."

Victor's appearance at the podium raised the noise level momentarily and Brenna calmed herself as the flashes from cameras gradually stopped. Raising his hands, Victor said, "All right, everyone, take a seat. We all know why we're here, and I am finally able to say that we can give you some definitive, accurate information."

Brenna turned at a hand on her shoulder and

Rachelle Cheron smiled. "We're with you." Behind Rachelle stood Sean Durham, Will Chapman, and Terry Brown. A little further back, Brady stood with his father Max. Brenna bit her lip to keep from bursting into tears as her friends all gave her a thumbs up.

She turned back to face the crowd, the show of support putting a little more steel in her spine.

Victor continued,

"...not going to treat being gay as some pariah condition. Far too many people who work in this industry know it isn't. You're here because two presumably straight actresses have revealed they are having a relationship, and a very private grievance harbored by a former spouse landed one of those women in the hospital."

"So let's get on with it!" someone shouted from the gallery.

"Regardless of the imagined reasons for it, there is no excuse for spousal abuse," Victor said. "This studio should have done more to protect Ms. Cassidy Hyland from her ex-husband. That fault we accept, and studio security procedures have been updated as a result of this terrible incident."

"So you're sorry. We get it. Move on!"

Victor's glare could have immolated the man on the spot. He did not rise to the baiting. "Ms. Hyland remains in the hospital. Her condition has been upgraded from critical to serious, and she will likely be moved from CCU to a private room on Monday. We have her agent, Natalia Gardner, to address questions of Ms. Hyland's condition." He stepped away from the podium and Natalia moved up to take his place. "Thank you, Mr. Branch. As Ms. Hyland's representative, let me go on record stating that this studio has handled this terrible situation with as much attention to Ms. Hyland's medical needs as possible. Cassidy sends her thanks, and she promises to be back at work as soon as her doctors allow."

Brenna listened as Talia outlined the extent of Cassidy's injuries, as well as congratulating the studio for immediately bringing her parents in from St. Louis. Brenna could debate how good that action had been, but it played well to build the studio's image of being family-oriented and also a supportive employer for an injured employee.

"Ms. Hyland and Ms. Brenna Lanigan and their colleagues spent more than eighteen months working side by side, long days and often long into the night, to bring Time Trails' dramatic adventures to the American viewing public. The show is a ratings bonanza every time this cast comes on screen." Talia shuffled cards in front of her, signaling her plan to change points. "But their private lives have never played out on that same screen and been held up to public scrutiny."

Brenna was surprised to see Rachelle step forward as Talia turned to the wings. "Ms. Rachelle Cheron's pregnancy last year was hidden from the cameras—for the simple reason that her character was not pregnant."

Rachelle nodded at the crowd as she stepped back past Brenna. She stopped briefly to give Brenna's hand a supportive squeeze, unseen by the gathering. Brenna turned her attention back to Talia, impressed with the woman's quick thinking.

"In this same way, an actress' sexuality is her own private affair." There was a wave of snickering sounds. "Yes, this was an affair," Talia repeated. "And it came as much of a surprise to the two women involved as it has to you now over the last few days."

Sure she was about to be called forward, Brenna cleared her throat and waited.

"Cassidy Hyland is a young beautiful woman, a tempting sexual icon to men everywhere. That was the primary purpose of her being cast in Time Trails almost two years ago—a key male demographic got juiced every time she appeared." Talia danced quickly to her other point. "Her vivid acting skills made scenes crackle with energy and intelligence."

Talia turned to Brenna. "And women began to fall in love with her too." Brenna stepped forward at the nod from Cassidy's agent. "Competition is the heartbeat of so many in Hollywood, so much so," Talia pointed out, "that Brenna Lanigan and Cassidy Hyland fell in love, and didn't even know it."

Talia grasped her hand and pulled her to the podium. Brenna felt the notecards crumpling in her clenched fists and stood waiting for her eyes to adjust to the white lights that were blinding her. For the first time she was unable to be outside of herself, to see herself do all the right things and walk herself through this event.

Brenna blinked, and then said the first thing that came to mind. "I didn't know it was possible to feel this way." She paused. "About anyone.

"Some women... Me," she corrected. "I grew up like most Midwestern girls, expecting to finish high school, marry a nice man, maybe have a career, definitely have children, and raise them to send them off into the world on their own someday."

Brenna looked at the first card which read, "Expectations." She lifted her gaze back to the reporters. "I wanted the career so badly, I left home at 18, determined to make or break it in New York. The children and the husband could come later. But I understood that they would come."

She looked over her shoulder, wishing to see her sons there, but finding a smile from Talia, and beside her, Rachelle. She lifted her eyes briefly to the ceiling and thought of Cassidy. "It never occurred to me that I would want, or need, anything else."

She looked back at her cards. The second read "Things I want and need." Brenna smiled. "But I did want and need other things. I needed understanding. I wanted the outdoors. I needed to act. I wanted my children's health and happiness. And I wanted to find someone who wanted these things too." She inhaled and exhaled to settle the nerves making her palms damp. "I tried twice but failed at my marriages to two men. Not all of it was their fault; a great deal of it was mine. I hadn't learned how to express what I wanted and needed in ways they could comprehend, and deliver on. I had begun to believe the 'Men are from Mars, and Women are from Venus' claptrap about the differences between the sexes. I had women friends, and I had men as lovers. I was resigned to the fact that I wasn't going to find one person fully capable of being both." She let the smile be born from the warm glowing core of herself, growing and growing until she could only laugh a little to release the full feeling. "But I was dead wrong. There was someone out there for me capable of being both a friend and a lover. I just never expected it to be in a female package."

Looking down at her notes, she saw the next card read "Cassidy." The name said everything to Brenna. "Cassidy," she began, "is beautiful." She shook her head. "I couldn't even look at her for long before my heart was in my throat and I wanted to stammer, feeling completely inadequate next to her. So I never managed to talk to her for any length of time."

"You sound like a teenager!"

Brenna laughed at the characterization from the reporter.

"Yes, I did. Acted like it, too." She shook her head. "Cassidy had her own reasons for trying to reach through that impasse between us." She looked up. "I will be forever grateful that her son turned five.

"I've known many actresses over the years, and this is not a slight to a single one of them," she went on carefully. "When Cassidy looks at Ryan she loves her son. Her home is a child's home. She organizes her life around caring for him. She made the choices she's made because she refused to see anything harm him."

"You fell in love because of children?" came a shouted interruption.

"No. We became friends because of that."

"So how did you fall in love?" someone called.

"It wasn't quite like falling over a log," Brenna chuckled, "but it was just as amazingly unforeseeable and that simple. Think back to when you met your own partner, husband, wife, a boyfriend, a girlfriend. How did you know it was love?" She formed a picture of Cassidy in her mind and spoke to it instead of the crowd before her. "When you have that feeling, there's no mistaking it. Even if you'd never expect it, when she takes you in her arms, there's doesn't even have to be a kiss. Something inside you meets something inside her, and for the first time, everything you touch, everything you say, everything you are... is whole and solid. You're real."

Cassidy's image faded from her mind and Brenna stepped back.

There was a short ring behind her and she turned to see Talia opening her cell phone.

"I think this is for you," Talia said, holding out the phone to Brenna with a smile.

Brenna frowned at the unplanned interruption but took the phone. "Hello?"

"You made me real too."

"Cass?" She turned away from the podium microphone to keep her conversation private.

Cassidy's voice was breathy, strained. "I was watching the news...Saw Victor... Talia... You... You're beautiful, Bren."

Brenna felt her balance steady. "Cass, you sound tired."

"Yeah, I..." Cassidy's voice trailed away and Brenna held the phone tightly, just listening to her lover breathe over the open line. "You...shouldn't be alone."

"I'm not. You're here with me. I'll be back later. You go to sleep."

"'Kay."

"I love you."

Brenna heard nothing over the line for the longest time until finally she heard a click. Either Cassidy had ended the call or given it to a nurse to do so. But the buoyant feeling of knowing Cassidy was coherent stayed with Brenna as she closed the cell phone and handed it back to Talia. "Thank you."

"Any time."

Turning back to the podium, Brenna smiled. "Any questions?"

Hands immediately shot into the air.

Chapter Nineteen

Thomas shifted a black checker, jumping one of Ryan's red ones. Across from him, Ryan Hyland squirmed in his chair at the folding table. Unable to concentrate on his next move, he realized he couldn't wait any longer.

"Miss Karen," Ryan said, "could I go to the bathroom?" He carefully turned around in his chair to find Mrs. Grinaldi.

The woman with curling black hair and a friendly smile looked up from her magazine and met his gaze. "Do you remember the way?"

He nodded but Thomas offered, "I could take him, Mrs. Grinaldi."

Ryan frowned. As much as he liked Thomas, he knew how to go to the bathroom. "I'm big enough to go by myself," he said.

"He'll be fine, Thomas," Mrs. Grinaldi said. "We're safe here."

Ryan walked out of the room and looked up and down the hallway. To the right was the door out into the sunshine he could see peeking through the window. To the left would be where the bathroom was, around a corner. He walked quickly, finding the door labeled MEN.

He pushed it inward and stepped into the first empty stall, closing the door. A few minutes later he was tucking in his shirt when he heard noises as another door opened.

"Ryan?"

He frowned. That did not sound like Thomas.

"Ryan, are you here, son?"

Leaving the stall, Ryan looked up into the familiar face. "Daddy!"

"Shhh, son." He pulled off the baseball cap that hid much of his face and crouched. Ryan noticed that his shirt label said "Jim." "How are you, buddy?"

"Fine, Daddy." His daddy's face looked scratched up, but he wasn't crying, so Ryan decided the scratches must be makeup. Since Mommy wore costumes and makeup to pretend to be somebody else, maybe his daddy was doing that too. "Are you playing dress up?"

"Something like that," was the answer. "Come on. Let's go." His father looked quickly over his shoulder then down to the end of the stalls. "We don't have a lot of time."

"Are we going home? You didn't come by the hospital and see Mommy."

"No. I had some things to do first," Daddy said.

"I'm gonna tell Miss Karen that you and me are going to see Mommy. I can tell Thomas I got to see my daddy!"

There was a knock at the door. "Ryan?" His daddy stood quickly and backed away from the door. "Ryan," said the voice. "Are you all right?" Ryan reached for the door handle just as it opened inward. "You're taking too long. Mrs. Grinaldi sent me..." Thomas smiled at Ryan. "There you are."

"This is my daddy!" Ryan introduced proudly, stepping back and gesturing. His daddy stepped forward.

Thomas looked startled. "What the...? Holy shit! James!" Thomas stumbled backward through the open door, and Ryan watched his daddy chase after him. "Ow!" Ryan howled when his shoe was caught in the closing door.

"James! Mrs. G!" Thomas bolted, yelling, "He's here! He's here!"

Ryan pushed his foot free and watched his father run for the door leading to the outside. "Daddy! Wait, Daddy!"

Thomas skidded to a halt as he heard the outer door open. He pushed open the door to Miss Karen's room and yelled, "James, he's here!" Then he turned around and spotted Ryan still by the bathroom. "Ryan, are you okay?"

"Why'd you scare off my daddy?" Ryan pouted. "We were going to see Mommy together."

"Ryan, we are going to see your mom again tomorrow. Tonight

it's too late."

"That was my DADDY!"

Miss Karen came out into the hall and called him back into the classroom. "We'll wait right here for your mother," she said to Thomas. "I'll call Security." She ushered Ryan and Thomas back into the small room, shut and locked the door. "Come on."

Ryan sat down in a chair in the corner and tried to figure out what was happening. "Will Daddy come back for me?"

There was a sharp banging on the door. Karen looked through the window and quickly unlocked it, letting in James, who said, "He got out through a side door. I couldn't catch him."

"Daddy!" Ryan pulled at the door.

James pulled him away from it. "Ryan, stop!"

"I want my daddy!"

"Ryan, man, your dad is bad news. C'mon." He tugged on Ryan's arm.

Ryan pulled away from him and ran to a table, where he sat down and cried.

Ryan was still sobbing when Brenna arrived with two men from Security, and he would not come to her when she called. "What on earth happened?" she asked.

Thomas frowned. "He saw his father."

"I thought I asked that the news be kept off." She rose to her full height. "I ask you to do one thing—"

"We did what you asked!" James intervened. "Shit, Mom, listen. Mitch Hyland came here. He was going to take Ryan away. What the hell was Thomas or I supposed to do? We weren't going to let him take Ryan."

"Mitch was here?" Bren swallowed hard and her face blanched. "He was here?"

Thomas stepped forward again. "Yeah, caught up with Ryan while he was in the bathroom."

"You confronted him?"

"I didn't plan to," Thomas protested. "Ryan was taking too long and when I went to check on him, I found him with his father."

Brenna studied Thomas for a long moment and noticed a bruise just beginning to discolor his cheek. "He hit you?" she growled, brushing it with her fingertips.

"No. I stumbled backward and hit the wall." Thomas squeezed

her hand. "It's all right. He's gone."

She crossed her arms over her chest and muttered, "Now he knows I have Ryan." She shook her head.

"Mom, call the police."

"I know, James," she assured her younger son. "I am going to talk to them, but you all need to be safe first."

Thomas sighed. "Where?"

"With us?"

Brenna turned to see that Will Chapman and Terry Brown had followed her over from the press room when a security guard had alerted her to an "incident" with the children.

"You ran off in a hurry. Is everyone all right?"

"There's been a little excitement," Brenna downplayed. "Hang on."

As Will and Terry talked quietly with Thomas and James, Brenna tried to reach Ryan. He had stopped crying, but he continued to sniffle as he rubbed at his runny nose and eyes.

"Ryan, it's time to go home," she coaxed. She took a box of tissues from Karen. "Come on, let's clean up." He sniffled hard once and rubbed his nose on his arm, looking at her, his eyes narrowed. It was the same furrow his mother had when she concentrated. "Are you tired?" It was well after six o'clock. He shook his head. "Hungry?"

"Yes."

"Well, I've got some food at home. Do you like soup and sandwiches?" He turned up his nose at her. "How about just peanut butter and jelly?" He nodded, but still would not move toward her. "Are you scared?" He nodded. "Because of your dad?" He nodded again. "I'm sorry," she said. "He won't be coming back again."

"Why not? What did I do wrong?" he asked, tears brimming in his eyes.

"You? Ryan, no, you did nothing wrong," she said emphatically.

There was a long silent stretch of time as Ryan thought. Brenna wanted desperately to hug him, but she held back, waiting.

"Did Daddy really hurt Mommy?"

Ryan's voice was filled with an uncertainty and hesitation a five year old should never have. Brenna couldn't help the tears that formed in her eyes.

She swallowed past the lump in her throat. "Yes, he did. I'm sorry."

"Why did he?"

"I don't know why. I just know I don't want the same thing to happen to you. Your mom wouldn't want that either." She could see the upset and confusion in his expression. She had to give him the time to come to grips with his emotions on his own, if he could.

When at last he spoke, his voice was small, but it held a tendril of hope. "Miss Lanigan?"

He stood up and walked to her. Resisting the urge to wrap her arms around him, she responded cautiously, "Yes?"

"Do you love me?"

She kept very still. His father no doubt said he loved him. Will Ryan believe me or not? "Yes, I do love you, Ryan. So very, very much."

"Can I see Mommy?"

"Of course you will see her," Brenna soothed.

"Now?"

He obviously wanted to ask his mother who he should be trusting, and Brenna was sorry she had to make him wait. "Not now." He looked up past her and she realized the others in the room had come up behind her. "Do you think you can trust me just a little longer?"

Ryan didn't answer but she held his gaze for a long moment. When she finally broke the connection and looked back over her shoulder, Brenna met Will's eyes. "I'm going to send you to a friend's house for tonight, okay?" Chapman assented with a nod. "Thomas and James too?" she asked the big man. He nodded again. "Ryan," she smiled at him, "do you have a favorite movie?" The boy nodded. "Do you think my sons would like it?"

"Star Wars: Episode One," he said. "Do they like pod racers?"

Brenna looked up imploringly at Thomas, and he supplied the clincher. "We love the pod race." Ryan beamed. James groaned, and Thomas took Ryan's hand, leaving her watching the three boys head for the door with Terry following close behind.

Will put his hands on his hips. "Are you sure?"

"Mitch is obviously following me. I've got to separate myself from the kids until we get him back under wraps."

"He's certainly bold," Will commented. "I can't believe he came back here."

"He looked pretty bad when I last saw him. You'd think he'd attract attention."

"We're a studio. Hell, maybe he came in with an extras call. Or passed his scratches off as the results of a bar fight."

"Doesn't exactly speak well for our security," Brenna said.

"You can't worry about that now. Security will look for him. What's next for you?"

"Well, we're done with the press for now. I hope it holds them. I want to get back to the hospital."

"You need company."

"No, I don't."

"That wasn't a question." Will lowered his voice. "We have to split up. Get a plainclothes officer, take the studio limo, but don't go into town alone, Bren."

"He's not after me; he's after Ryan."

"As long as he thinks you have Ryan, you're a target."

"Maybe we can use that to our advantage," Brenna mused. "What if I lead him to someplace the police can grab him?"

"How will he find out where you are?"

Despite the seriousness of what she was suggesting Brenna couldn't suppress a chuckle. "That's the easy part. I'll let the press follow my every move."

CHAPTER TWENTY

THE SUBURBAN community where Brenna made her home sloped down from foothills. The single lane streets wended away from a tiny, exclusive business district, ending in loops and cul-de-sacs where driveways departed through tight clutches of trees toward some famous and not-so-famous homes. Built before the age of cookie-cutter construction companies and when land tracts were more generous, each home spoke, if not necessarily of the current resident's character, at least of their tastes in post-modern Spanish art deco or classic European villa, or of some other bygone Hollywood era.

Despite the high concentration of celebrity homes, and the lack of gates at the entrance roads, the paparazzi tended to remain clear of the area. Until this week. Their numbers had swelled from two or three photographers, to dozens of news stations following the single press statement by Pinnacle Pictures two days earlier:

"Cassidy Hyland, accompanied by Brenna Lanigan, both cast members of our Time Trails series, was transported to Pasadena City General for treatment of injuries sustained in an encounter with Hyland's ex-husband. Shooting on the series Time Trails has been temporarily suspended."

Everyone knew the history of the two actresses. If not, it was widely documented in interview archives. Before the public had completely recovered from the revelation that Mitch Hyland's attack had been provoked by a jealous rage, news crews following the women to the hospital caught a juicy sound bite: Lanigan declaring to a desk nurse, "I'm her lover." Now most of the studios were carrying Brenna Lanigan's press conference. Don Deering wanted a full interview and was determined to get it.

As the KTLA van stopped before the private home, it became just one more amongst the dozens of news vans lining the small street and milling reporters with still cameras. The hospital had been crowded. Don had asked one question, then, getting no answer, he decided to wait until things died down a little, hoping Lanigan would come home. Straightening his tie, he hopped down from the passenger side. His cameraman and driver, Lou Phillips, set the hydraulic on the transmitter and pulled his camera from the back, hooking it into the feed with a quick cable connection.

"Shit, Don." Lou looked around. "I thought you said we'd be first on this."

Don shushed him. "What's going on?" he asked another reporter.

"Studio unit reported Lanigan is on her way here."

"To make a statement?"

"Had a full press conference at the studio. So... not sure," the reporter admitted.

Damn. Don knew he had sensed something when dealing with the two women almost five months ago. He had been covering their mishap in the Sports Warehouse. Now they had admitted they were lovers, and he possessed some of the earliest footage of them intimately close, likely just as their relationship was starting. He wanted to get one or both of them alone for an exclusive perspective piece.

"I'm going to get the lay of the land," Don said to Lou.

"Gotcha."

Lou settled against the side of the van and shot a few minutes of establishing footage, as Don got a feel for the character of the neighborhood and the house he was approaching. It was a cozy, ranch-style home done in hand-hewn stone and wood fascia with a big front picture window. The shutters were stained rosewood, picking up the dark reds in the drapes. Lanigan had a very homey personality, he suspected, imagining there was a fireplace at the end of the stone chimney where she probably curled up. "Nice place," he commented aloud.

He crossed the lawn, peering briefly through slats in the privacy fence, unable to determine the lay of her backyard. He heard an engine and quickly hurried back to the public easement.

A delivery van from Flowers Unlimited pulled up alongside the mailbox, and a delivery man slid out. "What's going on here?" he asked as Deering joined him.

"Waiting for the lady of the house to come home," Don supplied. He was surprised to see scratches and a bandage on the man's nose. "I didn't know the world of flower delivery was so rough."

"What? Oh. Yeah, well a guy didn't like that some other guy wanted flowers delivered to his girl."

Deering shrugged. "I gotcha. Take it out on the messenger. Hope you got in a few good licks."

"Yeah. Well, I've got to deliver this. Can't leave it out here."

The muscular shoulders shrugged. Don couldn't help thinking the man's blue jacket looked just a little tight. Must work out and the company hasn't gotten him a new uniform yet.

Noting the man's name tag, Don offered advice, "Jim, she's not home. But there's word she's on her way." The man shrugged away from him and opened the back of his van, pulling out a bouquet and starting up the front walk. "Where're you going?" Don followed the delivery man up the drive and along the walk to the front door. "We aren't supposed to be up here."

"To deliver this." Another car drove into the cul-de-sac. Don glanced over to see a green Mountaineer garnering all the camera attention. Behind him, he could hear the delivery man trying the knob.

"I told you..." The man's shoulders blocked him and the front door opened. "How in the hell...?" Darkened blue eyes met his and a strong hand wrapped around his throat, dragging him inside the house.

Brenna anxiously studied the news assembly. It seemed every outlet she had left behind at the studio had dispatched a unit to her home. She sat in the back of a studio limo; the driver, however, was from the plainclothes division of the LAPD.

"I'll walk you to the door." He keyed the in-car radio. "This is Unit 1-9. Move in to the Lanigan address," he said into the microphone. "Let's hope our boy took the bait."

He moved the car forward steadily despite the crowding cameras. Once they were inside the Lanigan property line, the press fell back. He stepped out first and opened the door. When she got out of the car, like a sea crashing, everyone surged forward, thrusting microphones and portable recorders and cameras in her face.

"Ms. Lanigan! How did the fight with her husband start?"

She sighed and put her hand up defensively. "It's late. Don't you all watch your own news?"

Not being indulgent sorts, the reporters stayed. "What's next for you?"

"A little sleep. Please."

With the officer watching her back, Brenna turned around and pushed her door open. Distracted by the crowd, it didn't register that she had entered without benefit of the key. Letting the officer in behind her, she shut the door between herself and the press, resting her forehead against it as she set the lock.

"I'm going to check through the house," the officer informed her.

She nodded wearily. "Fine." There had been no sign of Mitch. If he hadn't heard the news reports meant to bait him to her house, he could be anywhere. She wondered if he had headed for Cassidy's home instead. Their children should be safe with Chapman, but maybe she'd better call.

She tingled at the sudden realization that she had included all three boys in her thought. *Our children. Mine and Cassidy's.* Wearing a wide smile, she started toward her bedroom.

There were the sounds of a scuffle ahead and two figures emerged into the hallway from her bedroom. At the sight of her, Mitch struggled against the cuffs behind his back. "Where's Ryan? You were supposed to bring the kids home."

"They're all safe, away from you."

She put her hand on the officer's arm. "Be sure you find out how he got on the studio lot looking like a reject from a fight film."

"Will do, ma'am."

She started past him to her bedroom, but he stopped her. "You shouldn't go in there, ma'am. I'm going to call for the paramedics."

Brenna blinked, then went to her bedroom doorway and looked inside, stifling a gasp at the sight. The reporter, Don Deering, his face black and blue, lay unconscious across her bed.

CHAPTER TWENTY-ONE

BRENNA LANIGAN'S exhausting morning had begun before dawn and now, with the sun high overhead, she had begged off of meeting her coworkers at the commissary in order to spend lunch with someone very precious. She pushed the door closed behind her with a satisfying thud. Walking past the bathrooms which opened onto the corridor, Brenna slipped her arms free of the heavy military-style vest which she wore over a light gray cotton undershirt. Her mood lightened at the sensation of air circulating on her skin.

"How's things today, Ms. Lanigan?"

The guard was seated at the desk in the corridor. Bestowing a warm smile on him, Brenna's eyes brightened from gray to a deep blue as she stopped next to him. To her right was a pair of swinging double doors, a large sign beside them stating "Props". "Great now, Harry," she answered, Behind him was a single door, inset in the wall and painted the same light gray of the walls. She stepped past him and grasped its knob.

"Enjoy your lunch," he said. "I'll keep it quiet out here for you." He wrote her name on a check-in pad and checked his watch before writing her arrival time next to it.

"Thanks." She turned away, pushed inward on the door, and entered the brightly painted room. The sound of her entry did not go unnoticed. As she rounded the edge of the door, a small blur hurtled toward her. Her reflexes, admirable for a woman over forty, allowed her to catch the blond five-year old under his outstretched arms.

"Hi!" followed by a rapid series of questions, and news about his day, assailed Brenna's ears. She pulled Ryan's slender body into her own, instantly even less tired because of his enthusiastic greeting. Small arms wrapped around her shoulders and warm lips pressed a wet kiss on her cheek.

Her eyes grew moist and she pulled back to looking into his glowing eyes. "It's good to see you too," she said, brushing her fingers through his thick hair. He's almost due for a haircut, she thought. "What's for lunch today?" she asked him.

"Mrs. G and I are making peanut butter and jelly sandwiches," he announced with pride. He tugged on her hand as she stood up. "Come on."

"Of course." Walking across the room behind him and carefully moving around the little tables, Brenna saw Karen Grinaldi standing beside a kitchenette counter, complete with undercabinets and a sink. Behind the caregiver was an oven inset in the wall.

"Good afternoon, Bren," Karen said warmly. "Do you have a long break?" She reached out a steadying hand to Ryan's back as the boy stepped up onto a footstool in front of the counter and reached for a jar of grape jelly.

"Long enough for sandwiches and milk."

"And cookies." Karen smiled. "Ryan wanted to bake some this morning."

"They're peanut butter too," Ryan added, glancing away from his task of upending the jelly jar over the bread.

Both women moved to stop the mess before it happened. Karen grasped the bottom of the jar, beginning to turn it upright, while Brenna caught an errant glob of jelly in her cupped hands.

Ryan looked sheepish. Brenna smiled and said quietly, "Oops."

"Sorry," he answered, his smile faltering.

Brenna cleaned her hands at the sink. "No harm done, but remember, when you're working, you can't let yourself be distracted."

"I'll do better," he assured her gravely.

She kissed his cheek. "I know you will."

With renewed determination and the smile returning to his face, Ryan went back to his task. One at a time he put the three sandwiches on the cutting board and Karen cut each in half. Brenna collected three plastic cups in different primary colors and filled each with milk from the refrigerator.

Carrying two plates, with Karen carrying the third, Ryan led the trio over to a child-height table and carefully set one plate in front of each chair.

Brenna set the milk cups down and turned to take a seat, only to find Ryan pulling out the one next to her leg. "For me?" she asked. He nodded. Seating herself, she adjusted to the tiny proportions and watched Karen do the same.

Ryan settled quickly onto his own seat between them.

He looked at Brenna expectantly, waiting for her to taste it first.

She examined her sandwich, the bread lumpy in several places over extra thick globs of jelly. "It looks wonderful," she declared with a smile.

Ryan beamed as she bit into a corner and chewed thoughtfully. "Good?" he asked.

She swallowed and cleared her mouth with a sip of milk. "Delicious."

Ryan giggled and took a bite of his own sandwich. Karen had already consumed half of her own lunch while Brenna played out her ritual with Ryan.

I need this time together as much as he does. Brenna felt her fatigue fading as she ate her sandwich and watched Ryan rush through his. As soon as they finished lunch, they could move on to the next phase of their time together—a phone call to his mother who was still in the hospital, a stay now concluding its second week.

Brenna had taken over caring for Ryan, bringing him with her to and from the set each day for Karen's child care services. But the lack of contact with his mother wore on Ryan, and on Cassidy, as well. So they had arranged to make the midday call to keep mother and son connected.

Ryan was already carrying his plate and cup to the sink as Brenna finished the last bite of her sandwich and the dregs of her milk. "Ready?" she called.

He ran over to the cubbies and pulled out his bright orange backpack, searching through it until he came up with a small cellular phone. The phone was Cassidy's, another connection between mother and son, and the number for the hospital room where Cassidy recuperated was programmed in the quick dial.

"You know how to call," Brenna said.

Ryan quickly pressed the button and put the device to his ear, his face lighting up by degrees as the phone rang. "Hi, Mom!" he said brightly when the call was connected. His face contorted into a frown. "Are you feeling okay, Mommy?" There was a pause, and Brenna wished she could hear the reply. "Oh. Okay. So you've been sleeping?" He nodded, obviously echoing his mother's affirmative reply. "I made Ms. Lanigan lunch again." He smiled. "Yes, she always likes it."

Brenna rolled her eyes as she held out her hand. "Ryan, may I talk to your mother?"

Ryan looked from Brenna's face to her outstretched hand, then informed his mother, "I'm giving you to Ms. Lanigan now."

Brenna smiled at his grown up tone. "Thank you," she said graciously. Ryan cocked his head, as if to listen. She shook her head and he dashed off. She waited until he had grabbed a bucket of toys off of a shelf. "Cass?" As she spoke into the phone, her voice softened with concern. "Rough day?"

"Therapy is a bitch," the woman on the other end admitted, her voice sounding sharp and breathy. While Cassidy Hyland might tell her son everything was fine, she and Brenna had been through too much, learned too much about one another, to ever be able to cover up personal pain for long. "But they are letting me check out today."

"Do you want me to cut out of here now?" Brenna asked. It was atypical of her work ethic to leave the set early for anything other than a catastrophe, but Brenna's priorities had been significantly reordered since the near fatal attack on Cassidy. She would definitely leave early if Cass needed her. There was a moment of silence and Brenna recognized it as Cassidy weighing the pros and cons. "I can settle you at home and come back later," she added as an inducement.

"You can't afford the time away from the set. I've upset the schedule enough." Cassidy exhaled. "What time do you think you'll be done?"

Brenna shook her head. "I can be done now."

"I'm not in any shape now... just took the Percocet."

In the background, Brenna heard the sounds of Cassidy adjusting her position in the bed. Brenna felt a sharp desire to be there to adjust her pillows, anything she needed. Then the television began to buzz in the background.

"Don't depress yourself with the news," Brenna said.

"Look at that," Cassidy remarked at the television. "At least we're no longer the top story every day."

"Maybe midnight is a better check out time. Less press," Brenna pointed out.

"I still can barely walk," Cass grumbled.

"I know. We'll work together on that," Brenna said gently.

"Brenna, I shouldn't go home with you."

"Why not?"

"You've taken so much on with Ryan. I should just get a Home Nurse."

"It's no bother, Cass."

"But you're doing so much. It's not fair."

"I want to do this."

"But—"

"Cass, please. It's all right. You're not going to impose. I'll enjoy having you at home."

"What about the press?"

"Damn the press. Your health comes first."

"All right."

Despite her agreement, Cassidy sounded frustrated.

Brenna could also hear the washed out quality that signaled Cassidy falling under the influence of the strong pain medication. She called Ryan to the phone. "Ryan, time to say bye."

He yelped a cheerful, "See you tonight, Mommy," into the phone and handed it back.

Brenna's smile filtered into her voice as she offered her own sign-off. "Having you home will be wonderful. You'll see. You'll get well much more quickly with me taking care of you than you would with some impersonal home health person. I'll see you tonight. I love you."

"I love you, too." Cassidy's murmur faded and then there was only the click of the connection closing and Brenna pressed the end button on the cellular.

"Is Mommy ever going to get better?"

"Yes, she is," Brenna replied firmly. "We just have to help her a lot."

"Should I stay at home and take care of her?" he asked. "I could. I don't have to come here."

"Darling, you do. As much as your mommy needs help, you can't take care of her."

"I want to help," he declared stubbornly.

Brenna smiled at his endearing expression, so much like his

mother's.

"You do. Just by loving her as much as you do." I can speed things along just a little. I can make sure the afternoon filming session goes damn efficiently. "Will you be ready to go when I come at dinner time?" He nodded emphatically. "All right. I'll see you then."

She looked at the wall clock and realized the call would come down soon to report back to the set. "I have to go."

"Wait!" he said suddenly, running to the counter and picking up a small, semi-round lump off of a paper towel. "You forgot your cookie."

She took it and kissed his cheek. "Pack up the rest and we'll give them to your mommy for dessert tonight. I bet they will be the perfect medicine."

Ryan beamed, and Brenna steeled herself for the afternoon's work ahead. As she left the child's haven, she tried to set aside her personal life for her professional one.

Brenna sat waiting for the stagehands to reset the stage after the explosives experts had done their job. There were still two more takes, just for camera angles. It was well after six. It would very quickly be after eight if they didn't get everything on the first try. While she could not always count on others to not miss a cue, or to take it in their heads to initiate a harmless prank, she usually could count on herself to get it right. Two of the first four retakes had been necessary because she missed her blocking, stepping toward the wrong follow-up speaker or turning to look upstage when she should have looked downstage.

It was just too damn hard to concentrate. She heard Cassidy's tired voice over and over in her mind, and her heart and body screamed to be with her lover, soothing away the pain, rather than on set. Besides, she felt Cassidy was still uneasy about staying in Brenna's home for the rest of her recovery.

"Brenna? Bren?"

A voice penetrated the fog.

Uncurling her fist from under her chin and looking up dourly, she met the inquisitive gaze of Terry Brown. She saw her reflection in his dark-as-night eyes and picked up her chin. "Are they ready?"

"Are you?"

She started to push to her feet, but he restrained her with a light push against her shoulder. "What?" she asked.

"Do you want to rehearse the scene again?"

"I know it cold," she said wearily.

"But—"

"Terry, I want to get this done."

"Maybe you shouldn't have come back yet. It has only been two weeks since—"

Brenna whirled on him and growled, "Don't."

Terry's expression grew somber, silently expressing his thoughts.

She spun toward the set. "Let's get this over with."

A reporter stepped up to them. "Do you have a minute?" he asked.

Brenna took in his appearance with a quick top-to-bottom sweep of her eyes. Pen behind his ear, Dockers pants, and a brown polo shirt were fairly typical of the rag reporters, who tried to look like nothing so much as an underpaid stagehand. She tried hard to push a smile onto her lips. "We're due on the set," she said.

"I just wanted to ask Mr. Brown a question. Have you been pleased that the production schedule has spread the work out more evenly amongst the whole ensemble since Cassidy Hyland's injury?"

"More work?"

"Yeah, there were complaints when she first got here that a lot of the screen time was taken away from folks like you and," he nodded toward where Will Chapman and Sean Durham stood, arms crossed, also waiting for the set to be reset, "and those guys."

"We are all a team," Brenna said uneasily, though she suspected where he was going with his question.

"You didn't think so a year ago."

He was looking for a quote, and sniffing hard. "Things change," she said without elaboration.

"Yeah, a starlet getting beaten by her ex doesn't happen every day."

Terry stepped forward abruptly, grasping Brenna's arm which she had almost swung at the reporter. Unobtrusively, she released her fist slowly. "No, it doesn't." *God, this man is an idiot.*

"Work will be waiting for Miss Hyland when she is able to return. Now," Terry said, "we have to get back to filming." Gently laying a hand on Brenna's arm, he steered her toward Sean and Will, who had stiffened when the reporter broached Brenna and Terry.

The reporter called after them, "Would you take a swing at

Mitch Hyland in open court, Ms. Lanigan?"

Yes, I would take a pickaxe to Mitch Hyland if I could. Terry's reassuring squeeze on her elbow encouraged her to clamp her jaw tightly shut.

"What's up?" Sean asked Terry when the two joined them.

"They want me to say something about Cassidy," Brenna said. "All week, if it isn't about the show, it's about whether or not, as her lover, I knew her ex-husband was after her. I wish they'd cut us a break. She's only getting out of the hospital tonight."

"That's good news."

"Yeah, maybe. She's not real happy about it. Her therapy's still going well, but mostly I get the feeling she doesn't want to come home to my place."

"Why not?"

"She has her own."

"Obviously that's still bothering you," Sean ventured. "You need to work it out. Go to the hospital early. Talk. Leave the work behind and tend to your heart's needs for a change."

Brenna shook her head. "I have to finish this first." Squaring her shoulders, she turned and preceded the group to the set.

The scene being taped had as its focus the ensemble's absent member played by Cassidy Hyland, Lieutenant Christine Hanssen. At first, the schedule had been juggled, rotating episodes focusing on other cast members so that they were shot earlier in the schedule. Eventually, the studio had to acknowledge the absence of the Alliance's regular crew member. They were also beginning the arc of episodes leading to the end of the series.

As she tried to be the stalwart Commander Susan Jakes, it was not helping Brenna's concentration to think about why Cassidy was absent, and would remain absent for at least another three to four weeks. Her blood still boiled at the least reference to the incident where Cass had been beaten nearly to death by her ex-husband Mitch Hyland. She was losing her customary control.

She was walking a simple corridor scene with Will Chapman playing Lieutenant Raycreek, her second in command. This was the third take. The first two times her mind had drifted and she had missed cues. On the surface, their exchange was just a discussion of a terrorist conflict which had caused Lieutenant Chris Hanssen to be ordered back to her original fighter squadron. But Brenna could not help but play it deeper, as deeply as her emotions ran, for herself and for Susan Jakes who had been smoothing over her relationship with Christine Hanssen, the rebellious young officer now missing in the disputed territory.

"What does Command say?" Jakes asked.

"Nothing good." Raycreek shook his head. "Neither side is allowing any teams into the area to verify anything."

"What is the latest estimate of casualties?"

"The terrorists detonated a multi-ton device. The tectonic shockwave registered as far as the Gobi. Deaths already number in the hundreds of thousands."

Without looking at Raycreek, she asked, "Were you able to reach Hanssen's wing command about her last known coordinates?" As she waited for potentially bad news, Jakes swallowed hard and stared at her fingers spread against the wall, holding her up.

Raycreek's hand started for her shoulder but her expression narrowed as she looked over at him, and he abandoned the gesture meant to reassure. "Yes," he admitted.

She spun away from him, as much to distance herself from the fatalistic word as to bark her next command. She hit the communication panel on the nearby wall. "Creighton, this is Commander Jakes. Inform HQ that we're planning a mission in aid."

"Yes, Commander," came the voiceover reply from Terry Brown, off-stage as the tactical officer, Lieutenant Creighton.

"Sue," Raycreek started.

Jakes cut him off with a silent glare then turned to the communication console again. "I want every document concerning every ship and troop movement for the last two weeks. We're going to plan this down to the last microsecond." Her chin came up, daring Raycreek to challenge her decision. He didn't.

"I'll alert you when we have the data," he said. As she strode away, he turned to watch her go.

Off camera, Terry Brown and Sean Durham did the same. Brenna went off-camera at the other end of the set with her back to the camera. As she shed her portrayal going around a corner, they could see the instant the sturdy lines of Commander Jakes shattered into the softer lines of Brenna Lanigan.

"Cut and print that!" Mike Landau, the episode's director, yelled from behind Camera 2, which had been tracking down the corridor after Jakes.

"Oh, thank God!"

Brenna's exclamation made everyone chuckle.

"Collect Ryan before you go," Will teased.

She turned and waved her thanks, restraining herself from running away from the set. She would be with Cassidy in less than thirty minutes. And they would be going home together.

Chapter Twenty-Two

CASSIDY WATCHED with detachment as the nurse checked her vital signs. For the moment she felt relatively pain free. The brace she now wore offered support to her while she sat up in the bed. Her left arm, held in the nurse's hand as she timed her pulse, was only a little chilled. Early in her recovery her fever had fluctuated so often that she wasn't sure she would ever be consistently at normal temperature again. She felt weaker than she wanted, dependent on too many people to do things for her.

She wanted to go home, but at the same time knew that going home required her to be able to handle so much more than simply her own healing: being Ryan's mother, being Brenna's lover, trying to deal with Thomas and James for longer than a few hours. She wondered where she would find the energy for it all.

The door opened and the nurse said automatically, "Visiting hours are over."

Cassidy grinned as Brenna appeared around the edge of the door. "We're here to take her home."

"In the middle of the night?" the nurse objected.

"Yes, actually. I have her release papers right here." Brenna held them out blindly toward the nurse; she only had eyes for Cassidy. "Hi. We're a little early, but I couldn't wait any longer to see you."

"I'm still here," Cassidy said grumpily.

"You're sitting up and everything, though," Brenna praised. She realized the nurse was still standing by the door, and said, "That's all we need, thanks."

Waiting until the nurse was gone, Cassidy admitted, "A combination of the Percocet's residual effects and the brace."

"Mommy?"

Cassidy smiled at him hugging Brenna's leg. "Hi, sweetheart."

Ryan started to leap on the bed, but Brenna caught him before he could move the mattress with his intense forty-five pound body. "We're taking Mommy home. You can do that later," Brenna assured him.

Cassidy nodded her thanks.

"I haven't packed anything yet."

Brenna shook her head. "Don't worry about that. I've got it." She started by fetching the overnight bag from the closet. "What do you want to wear?"

"No belts, ties, heels..." Cassidy shook her head, "but I desperately want out of this backless number." She plucked at the hospital gown.

Brenna chuckled. "All right. How about these?" She held up a pair of Cassidy's sweatpants, trim fit but with a drawstring waist. When Cassidy nodded, Brenna added,

"Doesn't really match, but I brought a button up shirt. Thought maybe we could get it on you without aggravating your chest too badly."

The thoughtfulness made Cassidy regret her earlier carping. "I just don't want to impose on you."

"I do understand your wanting to be on your own, but this isn't... It can be temporary. Though I'd really love it if you... stayed."

"Promise me you'll let me pull my own weight?" Cassidy inched her legs over the side of the bed; her knee still ached but at least her legs mostly worked. She stretched against the strain in her lower back and tried to adjust her position. Her weakened arms and a whirling dizziness made her close her eyes, stemming a seemingly unstoppable tide of tears.

Brenna moved forward, resting her hands on Cassidy's quivering thighs. "When you can lift something more than your own feet without help, we'll talk. All right?"

She slid an arm around Cassidy, who slowly lifted her uninjured right arm and managed to return the embrace. Cassidy's immobilized left arm, with the custom brace around her wrist and hand, was secured with Velco straps to the front of the body brace.

The heavy material was lined with hardened plastic ribbing, thwarting her aching need for closeness and comfort.

Awkwardly she rested her cheek against Brenna's shoulder and let the tears fall. Brenna stroked her hair and placed soft kisses against her brow and temple. "I'm sorry for being grumpy. You've done so much for me."

Brenna placed her palm under Cassidy's chin and gently tilted her head upward. "I love you. Nothing, but nothing will ever change that."

As Brenna pushed Cassidy along the corridor in the wheelchair, Ryan walked alongside, holding his mother's hand and talking non-stop. Cassidy tried to shush him a few times, then gave up trying. She frequently reached up over her shoulder to caress Brenna's hand on the handlebar. They said little to one another since they were surrounded by hospital security, two of whom checked outside the door while two waited with them.

"All clear," they reported.

"All right. Let's go home."

"I'm ready," Cassidy murmured. Out on the landing, she waited while Brenna pulled open the doors and buckled Ryan into the car seat in the middle of the center bench seat. When she started to push herself up onto her feet. Brenna was quickly at her side. Cassidy's intention was to push Brenna's hand away, but, muscles shaking, she grasped the strong forearms instead. "Thanks."

"You're welcome."

Brenna supported Cassidy as they slowly walked the few steps to the car. Grasping the frame of the door and bracing her hand on the front passenger seat, with Brenna's assistance Cassidy boosted herself inside. Seated, she reached for the shoulder harness, stopping in only a few inches when she discovered the limits of her mobility. Brenna handed her the buckle from the harness and Cassidy gratefully pulled it across her chest and waist, closing her eyes as she pushed in and heard the buckle snap into place. The effort just to get this far had been exhausting.

Brenna walked around the car and got into the driver's seat. "Thanks, fellas," she called with a wave.

"Thank God there was no press to see that," Cassidy said.

"They're probably all waiting at home." Cassidy groaned. After the car engine started, Brenna's hand slipped over Cassidy's and gave it a reassuring squeeze. "Hang in there. Won't be long now."

Thankfully there were no members of the media lurking around Brenna's home. She pulled Ryan out of the car first, cradling him in her arms as she unlocked the front door. Crossing quickly through the house, she put him down in the spare room, stripping him without waking him, and tucking the sheets around him before she went back out to the car. Cassidy was leaning against the side of the SUV.

"What are you doing?"

"Being stupid," Cassidy muttered. "I got up, hoping I could walk a few steps on my own."

Brenna hugged her, holding her up at the same time. She felt the moment Cassidy gave in to her exhaustion and leaned on Brenna's strength. "All right, let's get you inside."

She helped Cassidy from the car to the wheelchair, shouldered the overnight bag, and moved toward the house. Leaning down to Cassidy, she asked, "Are you still bothered about staying here?"

"I'm not used to being able to depend on anyone but myself, Bren," Cassidy groused. "I guess that's why it's a difficult thing for me to do."

"So, it's just general grumpies. You're no longer upset with me?" Brenna turned the wheelchair around and backed Cassidy into her home.

"I know you're right. I can't take care of myself at home."

"There was always the option of a home nurse."

Cassidy frowned. "You were right about that too. It'd be a stranger."

Brenna smiled. "Besides, I think you'll enjoy the baths I give you."

Cassidy laughed, then clutched her side. "Damn that hurts. But thank you."

"You're welcome." Brenna wheeled Cassidy down the corridor to her bedroom. After pulling the sheet down, she helped Cassidy onto the bed, arranging her feet, and pillows to support her. "How's that?"

"I'm fine."

"Well, let's get your clothes off."

"I'm looking forward to you saying that when I'm well again."

"Trust me, I will." Brenna kissed her, brushing her fingers under Cassidy's chin, lifting her head gently.

Slip on shoes slipped off. The sweatpants had to be worked off over the bandages and brace, but Cassidy was stalwart throughout the process though Brenna cursed herself several times for not being careful enough with this or that movement.

Brenna undid the line of buttons and pushed it back off Cassidy's shoulders. Cassidy then pulled off the Velcro strip securing her left arm to her brace. "What do you want to wear to bed?"

"I usually wear an oversized t-shirt, but I don't think I can get my arm into one."

"Do you want a button up shirt then? A robe?"

"Maybe a robe."

Brenna retrieved a terrycloth robe from the inside of her closet door. "How's this?"

Cassidy nodded, and Brenna eased her up and helped her push her arms through the roomy sleeves. As she tied the belt, Cassidy used her good hand to cover Brenna's on her waist.

"Thank you."

"You're welcome." After stripping off her own clothes, Brenna pulled on a nightgown under Cassidy's appreciative watchful gaze.

As Brenna settled onto the bed far to the other side, Cassidy fingered the strap securing the brace to her left hand and wrist. She was leery of losing the support, but the doctor had assured her it could come off at night. And, God, how she wanted to hold Brenna.

Finally she pulled at the strap and loosened the contraption.

"Are you sure?" Brenna asked.

"I don't want to inadvertently hit you with it in the middle of the night." Cassidy tentatively flexed her fingers, just one at a time. She lifted her arm and placed her hand on Brenna's shoulder, letting her fingers roam the skin, her fingertips warming as she traced Brenna's collarbone and then caressed up her throat to her cheek. "Can we cuddle?" she asked.

"Are you sure we should? I don't want to hurt you."

"You won't. I just need to hold you against me. Please."

"All right." Brenna gingerly arranged herself, and Cassidy, so that their bodies were touching. Her lower leg arranged over Cassidy's thigh, her palm resting on the thick vest fabric encasing Cassidy's chest, just above her heart. Her head settled against

Cassidy's shoulder. No weight, just contact. She pressed her lips to Cassidy's clavicle. "How's that?"

Cassidy's right arm lifted carefully behind Brenna's back and she held the bare shoulder, stroking the silky skin around the narrow strip of cloth. "Much better." Cassidy pressed her lips to Brenna's hair. Their eyes met; Cassidy studied her lover's features, seeing that dark circles had formed. "Go to sleep."

"You too."

"I will eventually. Just want to hold you. Let you sleep." Brenna's kiss on her shoulder made Cassidy smile. "Do you want something to help you sleep?"

"You're the only drug I need right now."

Brenna's blush was endearing. "I've never been called a drug before."

"Both a stimulant and a muscle relaxant." Cassidy chuckled. She felt herself losing the struggle to stay awake.

"Love you, Cass."

Chapter Twenty-Three

Brenna exhaled as the directed called, "Cut!" For what seemed like the first time in weeks, she was actually pleased with her performance. She lowered herself into a canvas sling chair, hands folded contemplatively over her stomach.

When Terry Brown reached past her for a small towel that rested on the arm of her chair, Brenna impishly snatched it up, grinning broadly as she ducked under his reach and darted behind the chair.

His eyes were smiling as he gave chase. Dodging one another, they bounced around the small area until she cut left and he intercepted her. Wrapped up in his arms, she patted his face with the towel, grinning all the while.

"Thank you," he said.

She kissed his cheek. "Thanks to you and Will for insisting I leave early the other day to take Cassidy home."

"We didn't want to ask about that. Amazingly, we saw nothing about it on the news. So you had a trouble-free trip home?"

"Yes, the press was mercifully absent. She's settled in at my place. She was as out of sorts as I was about our disagreement. I discovered that I was only listening to what she said, rather than what she meant." She added, "She does want to do more for herself, but that doesn't mean she doesn't want my help at all."

"How's her actual health?"

"She's weak, but her mood's brighter already now that she's out of the hospital. The physical therapist will start coming by on Monday. And today, she asked me to leave Ryan with her when I went home for lunch break."

"Then she's definitely feeling better."

The episode director, Mike Landau joined them. "I'm sure you know we nailed it all today."

Brenna nodded. "Thanks again. Is there something else?"

"No, I was just finishing my notes for editing, and looked up to see the crew had vacated, except for you two. It's after ten. You should go home."

Brenna looked at Terry. "Why don't you come by and see Cassidy this weekend? It'll make her smile."

"You keep her to yourself for a while. I really have to take my mug home to see the wife for the weekend."

"All right."

"But I will visit eventually, I promise." Terry hugged her and left the set.

Turning back to Mike, Brenna said, "I, um, haven't talked to the writers recently. Any word on what's coming?"

"You mean whether they are writing Cass in or out?"

"I know she wants to come back."

"What are her chances of being sufficiently recovered to return before we wrap here?" the director asked. "What does her doctor say?"

"I'll ask Cassidy if I can go with her to her next appointment to get a better idea of his prognosis for the time frame of her recovery," Brenna decided.

"Then let us all know." Mike put a hand on Brenna's shoulder and, though younger than her, looked at her with a fatherly concern that Brenna found somewhat unsettling. "Frankly," Mike said, "I do hope Cass comes back. The two of you are among the best couples I've directed."

Brenna's brow furrowed. "That comes through in the film—that we... Cass and me... we're a couple?"

"I've seen a few in front of the camera who were able to hide that they hated each other's guts. But they were automatons. You and Cass, though, you two had sparks crackling between you right from the start, eighteen months ago. Recently, the sparks became flames and I thought..." When Brenna's gaze slid away from his, he asked, "Did I say something wrong?"

"Just... I'm embarrassed, I guess."

"Don't be. There are a lot of people who envy the passion you display." He tucked his hands into his jean pockets. "Some of us wish we could find something like that for ourselves."

Brenna heard the wistfulness. "Mike?"

"Closest I ever came, I think, was Esteban, a Spaniard I met in '91. Hot bod, great smile..."

Mike's gay? Brenna's eyebrow hitched in surprise.

"Forget it. Anyway, it's great to see someone really making it work. Anytime you and Cass want a place to hang out, I've got a place in Redondo."

After Mike left, Brenna remained alone on the set for several minutes. Hands on her hips, she tried to figure out why she felt surprised by his revelation.

As far as she knew, no one else on their set knew that Mike Landau was gay. There were members of the crew who were openly gay, like Justin, a stylist in Makeup, or Melody Capstan from Props, who wore their orientation like a badge of honor.

It suddenly hit her that Mike was seeing her as "one of us", a safe person to share his thoughts with. If the stage crew saw her that way, would it be very long before fans had that same perception? Being a gay role model was one role she knew nothing about.

The sound of the front door opening stirred Cassidy awake. Sitting up slowly, she looked around the living room from her reclining position on the couch. Blinking sleep from her eyes, she checked the clock and saw it was just after eleven-thirty.

At first she thought it might be Brenna arriving home, but when James walked in, she realized that having a chance to talk to him alone was probably a good thing.

Around ten o'clock, decidedly late for Ryan, Cassidy had stopped their cathartic snuggling on the couch and had taken her son into Brenna's extra room to put him to sleep on the futon there. What had formerly been the Lanigan boys TV and game room had become Ryan's space almost completely. It was strewn with toys more appropriate to the preschool child than the two high school boys, and so she had leaned against the door jamb watching over him as he tidied up his scattered belongings. Despite being exhausted when he finished, Cassidy had looked on the clean room with pride and praised his effort, then settled him down to sleep.

What was bothering Cassidy was that Ryan had also found a

ticket stub for an art show in the downtown district, and she decided that this might be a good opportunity to ask James about it. He was past curfew. She wondered how many nights he had been out so late while his mother was tied up on the set or sitting with her at the hospital.

"Miss Hyland?"

Cassidy looked over the back of the couch to see James depositing his backpack on the floor. "Hi, James. Did you have a good evening?"

Brenna's younger son pushed his hand through his light brown hair. "Yeah. I... was out with some friends."

"Fridays are definitely prime for that," she said easily. "Your mother will be glad to know you're home safe."

"Is she home already?" The thought apparently worried him, if his anxious look toward the bedrooms was any indication.

"No, she's not home yet," Cassidy replied, and he visibly relaxed. "So, did you see another art show?" When he stiffened, she held out the ticket stub. "I came across this when I was putting Ryan to bed."

James took the stub from her and gave it a cursory glance. "Has Mom seen this?"

"No. Is this where you were tonight, too?"

James debated with himself, but apparently her non-confrontational tack was working. A little warily, he answered, "Yeah. I... I, um, have a few pieces showing there."

Cassidy smiled; that was great news. "I saw the portrait you did of your mother." She had even coaxed Brenna into mounting the painting and hanging it on the bedroom wall. She considered it a wonderful view to focus on while lying in bed,.

Warmed by her reaction, James settled on the couch next to her. "These aren't like that."

"Different medium?"

He nodded. "And different subject."

"Are you trying to sell them?"

"Hannah says I could. I guess that's why I go, to see... well, to see who's looking at them and what they're saying."

"Hannah?"

"Hannah Shropshire." He fished in his pockets and Cassidy became aware of his clothes. He was dressed quite sharply, in a pair of black Dockers pants and a slightly large matching black cotton, button-down shirt with a single breast pocket. His typical attire for school would have been a white polo shirt and faded blue jeans. Finally he passed her a small business card. "She's the gallery owner, a friend of my art teacher."

"Your art teacher recommended you for a showing?"

"Along with other kids," he said. "It's an Arts for Education campaign."

"But it's not sponsored by the schools, is it?"

James shook his head. "That's why I've been glad Mom doesn't get home early. She'd have a cow if she knew it was unchaperoned."

"What's the subject matter?"

James dropped his head as he considered his answer. "Teen life," he said finally.

Cassidy looked at the card in her hand, which mentioned not only the gallery but the show title: Sex, Drugs, and the American Teen Experience. She closed her mouth tightly. Oh, boy.

"Am I grounded?"

"I don't have the authority to do that. You should tell your mother, though."

"I'd be grounded faster than an electrical line. I wouldn't get a chance to explain."

"Maybe if you talked to me, you would."

Cassidy looked up, as James turned around abruptly, their gazes settling on Brenna who was just entering the house and taking off her light jacket.

"Hi," James said warily.

"Did things go smoothly on the set?" Cassidy asked quietly.

"The set is fine," Brenna answered briskly, striding forward. "So, where have you been?" she asked her son.

James ducked his head and Cassidy recognized the gesture as one that Brenna often had when she was unsure what would be best to say. "Go on," she encouraged James with a cautious pat to the back of his shoulder.

Standing up, James turned to his mother and said, "I was at the Isis Gallery." His mother's expression didn't change. "It's an art gallery off Simon. I... They're showing a few of my pieces."

Brenna's fingers tapped on the back of the couch, and she looked down at the fabric for a long moment, breathing deeply several times before speaking. "All right. Have you been going there every night?"

"Nobody's been here. I didn't think it would hurt anything," he muttered.

"Not hurt anything! James, what if something happened to you out there? Would anyone know to call us?"

"Bren." Cassidy's initial call went unheard, so she called louder, "Bren!"

"What?"

"I've already talked to him about this. I've handled it."

Brenna turned away but Cassidy clearly saw her anger. She knew that most of it was a result of James' actions, but wasn't sure that some of it wasn't reserved for her intervention.

"Thank you. Tomorrow I want to go see this gallery," Brenna said after a minute. James swallowed, but nodded. "Good night, James."

"Good night, Mom."

Brenna waited until James was out of sight before speaking again. "Cass? Why did you do that?"

"Because I was here. You said "us" when talking to James just now. You want us to be a couple, Bren? I can handle a broken curfew."

"But you're..." Brenna gestured widely.

"Not his mother?"

"I wasn't going to say that. You're still mostly flat on your back."

"All I did was talk to him." She winced a little as she pushed herself into a better sitting position.

"You're supposed to be recuperating." Brenna plunked herself down next to Cassidy on the couch, and Cassidy stretched out an arm, encouraging Brenna to snuggle up against her but Brenna balked. "I don't want to hurt you."

"I'll live. I need a hug as much as you do." Cassidy closed her eyes in contentment as Brenna's body moved against hers. The weight was light, but the solidity of her lover beside her filled her eyes with tears. "I've missed you. Being at the hospital, I frequently had visitors, the nursing staff at least, but I still missed you. Being home and having Ryan to talk to for much of the day was nice, but..." Cassidy lifted Brenna's chin. "I missed you. I haven't hugged you since our first night home."

"We really have to remedy that," Brenna acknowledged. "I miss you constantly. Knowing you're here, though... I have been better able to keep my mind on task."

"So shooting went well?"

"Yeah. Mike Landau's looking forward to us being back on set together."

"Really?"

"Says that when he's watching us together, it gives him hope he'll find his own lover."

"Mike's gay?"

"Seems so."

Cassidy laughed. "We're role models."

"Scares me to death."

"Come on, what's difficult? You just keep loving me and I'll keep loving you. We'll figure out how to parent the kids together and be absolutely model citizens. Maybe we can single-handedly turn the public tide for gay marriage."

"That's not likely."

"We're bound to be asked sooner or later," Cassidy persisted.

"Would you marry me, really? I have a terrible track record."

"Bren, your track record has been for running the wrong race." Feeling Brenna's heartbeat under her palms and the warm flesh through the thin shirt, her mind turned to more immediate interests. With an intent look, she leaned close and brushed her lips against Brenna's. "I'm ready for bed, aren't you?"

Brenna helped Cass up with a hand under her elbow. They walked together down the hall and entered the master bedroom, closing the door behind them with a click.

CHAPTER TWENTY-FOUR

CASSIDY AWOKE feeling more rested than she had in weeks. She lowered her gaze to the woman lying across her shoulder. Brenna was awake, a peaceful smile on her lips as she traced her fingertip lightly along Cassidy's clavicle. Unable to see the clock, Cassidy wondered how late they had slept.

"What..." she began, stopping as she realized her mouth was dry. She cleared her throat and summoned some moisture. "What time is it?"

Brenna lifted her head from Cassidy's arm and her blue eyes sought out the clock on the nightstand behind her. "Just about seven-thirty. You can go back to sleep." Brenna lowered herself down to snuggle against Cassidy's shoulder. "Most strenuous thing we have today is to spend the day together."

Cassidy turned onto her side and wrapped her arms more snugly around the smaller woman, then nuzzled Brenna's hair.

With Brenna moving faintly against her, their breasts making contact as each breathed, their feet entangled, Cassidy felt her body gradually awakening, a pleasant experience until her bladder became uncomfortable. She reluctantly kissed Brenna on the forehead and pulled her arm free from underneath the other woman. "I'll be right back."

Propping herself up on one elbow, Brenna watched as Cassidy rolled over, located her slippers with her toes, and pushed off the bed. She stopped at Brenna's vanity to take the robe hanging over the back of the chair, removed her brace and put on her robe. Brenna enjoyed the vision of lean, smooth curves, a generous rear, and softly defined shoulder and back muscles. Brenna's fingers itched to explore. "Need a hand?"

"No, I'm fine," Cassidy answered distractedly as she made her way to the bathroom and settled on the toilet, leaving the door ajar so she could hear Brenna.

"Since you've got the brace off, why don't we bathe this morning?" Brenna asked. "You haven't had anything more than a sponge bath in three weeks."

"Sounds divine."

"So what do you want to do today?"

"Didn't you want to go see that art gallery owner?" Cassidy reminded.

"I do, but I can do it later when you're napping."

"A little sunshine would do me good."

"You want to come?"

"I want to know what James is involved in too."

"Wouldn't it be too exhausting?"

"Not if we take the wheelchair."

"You hate that thing."

"I'd hate being out of the loop more."

Brenna stepped into the bathroom and kissed the top of the blonde's head as she passed Cassidy. "All right."

"Thanks for understanding."

"Thanks for sharing."

Closing the bathroom door, Brenna went to the tub and started the water. From underneath the bathroom sink, she retrieved a small jar of crystals and checked the label.

"Are you allergic to any scents?"

Cassidy leaned over her shoulder. "No. Why?"

Rotating, Brenna kissed her. "Aromatherapy," she said, taking a handful of the crystals and bringing them close for Cassidy to sniff. "Lavender," she identified. "It's very relaxing."

After filtering the crystals through her fingers under the running water, Brenna returned to looking under the sink. From a small wire basket, she took a natural sea sponge as large as her fist and a bar of clarifying soap. She placed both in a niche in the wall of the tub and stood. Turning, she offered her hand. "Ready?"

Dropping her robe, Cassidy stepped carefully into the tub and

Brenna steadied her as she gingerly lowered herself to a sitting position. "The water temperature is perfect," Cassidy said, swishing her hands and forearms through the silkiness.

Brenna's hands slid along her legs, from thigh to calf and back again, lightly massaging the muscles before lifting each leg out of the water and scrubbing it with the natural sponge.

Cassidy moaned softly in appreciation as her body flowed with energy. The washing was thorough, between toes, over knees and ankles. An excited quiver started low in her abdomen as gentle fingers moved along the inside of her thighs and closer to her sex.

However, Brenna clearly was not working to arouse, only to energize and relax. When her legs were settled back under the water, Cassidy felt like she was floating. When Cassidy opened her eyes, Brenna was pulling her nightgown off over her head. A moment later she stepped into the tub behind Cassidy, bending her knees around Cassidy's hips and cuddling against Cassidy's back as she stretched forward to retrieve the soap and sponge again.

"Now for the top," she said.

Soon Cassidy's stomach, arms, sides, and breasts were tingling from Brenna's detailed attention. She leaned forward, wincing just a little as her stomach muscles tightened.

Standing up, Brenna pulled down the showerhead and Cassidy's shampoo. The scalp massage that accompanied the shampoo and rinse left Cassidy nearly asleep.

"You are so good to me," she murmured, tucking her arms around her knees as she rested her head on top and felt Brenna's hands, slick with soap, begin to knead her back.

She was feeling lighter than air when all motion stopped. Brenna's hands rested on the flare of her hips and Cassidy could feel the other woman's hair and cheek against her back.

"Ready to dry off and have some breakfast?" Brenna's breath caressed the back of Cassidy's neck sending shivers of pleasure chasing up and down Cassidy's spine.

No," Cassidy replied bluntly. "I wish I could do this for you."

"I'm glad you enjoyed it."

Her lips lingered on the base of Cassidy's neck. Brenna rose and helped Cassidy from the tub. Seated atop the toilet lid, Cassidy accepted the thick green fluffy towel and said, "I can do this. You finish your own bath."

Cassidy admired the wet beauty as Brenna scrubbed herself clean. Wiry legs, dainty feet, taut abdomen and smoothly muscled shoulders received the attentions of the sponge. Brenna refused Cassidy's offer to do her back, and soon she had finished shampooing and rinsing her hair, and was rising from the water.

As the damp woman stepped from the tub, Cassidy pulled Brenna toward her and wrapped her arms around Brenna's back, pressing her face into the valley between twin handfuls of breast and licking at the warm beads of water. "I can't wait to make love to you again," Cassidy whispered.

Mindful of Cassidy's limitations, the two shared a kiss of promise and then set about getting dressed. Brenna quickly donned a pair of jeans and a three-quarter-length sleeve, pale violet cotton cling top. Cassidy's supply of clothes was limited, and while the day promised to be sunny, it was still February. Brenna helped her back into a button up shirt, secured the orthotic brace to her left hand, And then helped her step into loose jeans. Lastly she pulled the body brace around Cassidy's stomach and chest.

"I should probably strap this up tight for the support today," Brenna said, suiting action to words. "Do you want a sweater over that?" Cassidy nodded and Brenna found a long, overly large cardigan she wore when she curled up in front of the fireplace.

The two women emerged from the bedroom and Cassidy followed Brenna into the kitchen, where they found Ryan and James finishing a breakfast of cereal. Each accepted a good morning hug from Ryan and a cautious, "Morning," from James.

"Muffin, bagel? Some fruit?" Brenna asked Cassidy, looking through her cupboards and refrigerator.

"Juice and a muffin would be fine." Cassidy reached into a tin and pulled out a blueberry mixed grain muffin. "You?"

"Same." Brenna poured two glasses of apple juice while Cassidy collected two small plates and a second muffin. Together they walked back out to the table and took seats side by side opposite James and Ryan.

James was quietly spooning down his last bite. Ryan, however, noticed there was something different and bubbled over enthusiastically, "You got dressed nice today, Mommy! So we're going home?"

"We're all going downtown," Brenna said. "To see James' work at the art gallery."

"What about Ms. Hyland?" the young artist objected to his mother.

"I can use the wheelchair," Cassidy said. "We need to get out and about, and your mother's right—we should check out the art gallery where you've been spending your time."

"Everyone?" James squeaked.

"Why can't we go home?" Ryan asked. "You're all better."

Brenna said sternly, "Yes, all of us."

"I am feeling better today," Cassidy acknowledged Ryan, "but we can't go home just yet. Why do you want to go home?"

"I want my toys."

"You have toys here," Cassidy pointed out.

"I miss Ranger. Can we bring Ranger here?"

Brenna shook her head. "The Talbots are taking good care of Ranger."

"Why can't he come here?"

"This house isn't set up for a dog," Cassidy explained.

"Can I go stay with Ranger?"

Cassidy wondered where Ryan's distress was coming from. Was it just the dog? He had first asked about his toys, only asking about Ranger when that excuse was challenged. Asking directly, however, probably was not the best approach. Next to her, Brenna was quiet. A dimple had formed in her cheek where the other woman was clearly biting to stay quiet. Under the table, Cassidy reached out and gently squeezed Brenna's thigh.

"We're going to see some artwork that James made," Cassidy said, wondering whether her son could be distracted for the time being.

"Why?"

"Because that's what we've chosen to do," his mother said patiently.

"When can I choose?" he asked.

Cassidy looked over to Brenna. "Tomorrow?" she queried.

"Thomas will be home tomorrow morning," Brenna said. "He's supposed to be at a FIRE session until then."

Nodding, Cassidy offered to Ryan, "How about a trip tomorrow afternoon to see Chance? I can call his mom tonight."

Ryan frowned. "I have to wait 'til tomorrow?"

"Yes," Cassidy said firmly.

Brenna didn't say anything but Cassidy knew her mood had shifted; she seemed upset. The auburn-haired woman tucked her hair behind her ear as she looked down at her wristwatch and pushed away from the table. "I guess it's time to go."

CHAPTER TWENTY-FIVE

FOLLOWING THE directions James gave from the back seat, Brenna drove into an area of Los Angeles that Cassidy was sure she had never seen before. For an "underbelly" of the city, it was pristinely clean, and historic looking.

There were café style eateries mixed in among the storefronts. Each business had its name on a wide canopy, shading the doorways in a variety of colors.

Brenna stepped out of the SUV looking around in curiosity before she assisted Cassidy into the wheelchair. Cassidy noted one place in particular and looked up at Brenna to suggest, "Want to try Mata Hari's Mediterranean for lunch?"

"We may want to placate them with pizza or burgers afterward." Brenna nodded toward the children.

Cassidy noticed Ryan's frown, matched by James' frown beside him, though neither was looking at the other.

James started south down the wide sidewalk and Brenna followed, pushing Cassidy as Ryan skipped between them.

By the time they reached the gallery, Cassidy was grateful that Brenna had paid so much attention to massaging her lower back. While she felt her muscles had tensed during the ride over the uneven sidewalk, the pain was nowhere near the usual levels. I might just manage this, she thought as James stepped back and Brenna wheeled her inside the open door.

The wide open door had a glass inset that was covered with every manner of printed flyers, signs, and business cards, almost obscuring the gallery name etched in the glass—Isis Gallery.

Inside, Brenna lowered her sunglasses from her nose and turned slowly to take in the layout. Cassidy received a warm smile as their gazes intersected, but Brenna's smile immediately vanished into the seriousness she usually reserved for her performance in front of the camera as her gaze continued around the room.

The lighting was track style, selectively placed to illuminate the art pieces—those hanging from the various dividers and walls, as well as the sculptures posed on boxlike stands in the open spaces. The walk areas were mostly in shadow and Cassidy saw a few figures moving among the displays near the back. A person would have to practically be on top of another to make any sort of identification.

Only in the front area was the lighting better, due to the sunlight streaming through the front glass windows.

At a small counter to one side, next to a battered metal cash box stood a young man, probably no more than sixteen, who was dressed like someone out of the Dillinger era of gangsters and Prohibition. His pressed suit pants were midnight black, his vest the same single color, v-points on each side of the vest lining up exactly with the creases on the slacks. He wore shined patent leather shoes.

"How many tickets?" he asked, as Cassidy continued to study him. His voice was young, not quite fully changed. Nodding down at Ryan, he added, "We have an art room for the younger kids. Only thirteen and up can go through the displays with a parent."

Brenna stepped forward and the young man stopped his ticket spiel when her business tone declared, "We would like to see Hannah, please."

He looked confused for a moment then looked up at James shifting from foot to foot behind the woman's shoulder. "Got another piece, Jamie?"

Jamie? Cassidy was surprised. Even his mother did not call him that. Brenna had noticed it too, if the narrowing of her eyes was any indication.

James took a step to the side then forward. "I, uh, don't have another one yet, Micah. I, uh, this is my mother." He gestured awkwardly and somewhat dismissively to Brenna beside him.

Micah looked down from Brenna to Ryan again. "Thought your brother was older," he mused.

James turned red and his expression darkened in anger. Before he could speak, Cassidy interjected, "James' brother is older. This is Ryan, my son." She gestured out to the gallery area. "We're friends of the family and came to look at James' work."

Micah did a double take when he looked at her more closely. Finally, though, he simply nodded. "His work is among the best my mother has ever seen."

"How did his work come to your mother's attention?" Brenna asked, looking relieved to finally have an opening.

"Jamie's art teacher is my partner."

A mellifluous voice reached them all just as the generous figure of a woman blocked the light through an open doorway behind Micah. The woman stood still a moment, holding her hands open against the door jambs as if to give everyone a moment to adjust to her presence. At last she stepped up beside Micah and rested her thick forearms on the counter. "So you're Jamie's mother." Her hazel eyes held a twinkle.

Brenna bristled. "James," she emphasized, "says you want to sell his work. I like to know the people my son deals with."

Brunette ringlets bounced in a dark halo around the woman's head as she nodded and reached out a hand as big and meaty as any man's. "I'm Hannah Shropshire. I own Isis Gallery, and I have collected and sold art for almost twenty-five years."

Brenna did not take the woman's hand. "In L.A.? I've never heard of this place."

"We've only been here since September. Connie, Micah, and I moved to L.A. in August."

Brenna continued to keep her hand to herself, despite Hannah's ready openness, and Cassidy recognized that her lover was determined not to give an inch. "And your 'theme' for this showing?"

"Happenstance," Hannah answered. "Connie's students have been my main resource, though I have shown a couple of featured private artists."

"What happens if something does sell?"

"James would receive the money from the sale. The gallery would take part as a commission. Visitors are constantly asking about several of Jamie's works. Two in particular," she added as she stepped back from the counter.

"He's only 15," Brenna objected. "He paints in his spare time. I've never seen—"

"Your son's work belies his age. The style is a merging of

Durban's and Rye's vivid realism with an atmosphere of the fantastic, reminiscent of Vorhees or Pinot."

Hannah Shropshire was tall, Cassidy realized; the woman loomed over Brenna and herself in the wheelchair.

"Are you all right, ma'am?" Hannah asked her.

"Yes, thank you." Despite what sounded like a distinctly English name, Cassidy got the impression from Hannah's dark thick hair, and Mediterranean coloring that she was actually Italian. She had the vaguest accent in her speech.

Hannah was talking again, and gesturing them to follow her.

"Why don't you come with me?"

His voice anxious, James interjected, "Hannah?"

Hannah stopped and studied his face a moment with deep affection and compassion. Finally she said, "Don't worry."

Micah took Ryan into the children's art room while Brenna pushed Cassidy after Hannah and James, catching up to them as they rounded a separator wall which made an alcove of about fifteen square feet of space against the building's back wall.

Each of the three walls held framed oil paintings, eight in all. The middle three caught Cassidy's attention. There were noticeable differences in their style and yet, somehow, the content and complementary nature clearly made them a group.

Brenna stepped around a free-standing statuary and read the identifying placard to the right of the sequence of works: "Jamie Logan, Los Angeles."

He's not even showing his artwork under his given name.

Cassidy studied the first of the three, from right to left, and found a nightmare leaping out at her from the dark heavy layers of paint. The subject of The Animal Man was figuratively human, male genitalia bulging but hidden beneath tight, spandex-looking shorts. The wild feral feeling came from the fact that the eyes, a deep sea green, had the elongated pupils of a cat, and the facial muscles stood out in strained relief from the snarl of lips pulled back from dog-like canines. Bare-chested, the body had the physique of an attacking bear on its haunches, even the arms and hands drawn wide had fingers tensed and extended claw-like.

Cassidy could not look at the entirety very long, moving her gaze over it in pieces, marveling at the sensation of being grabbed and mauled which it evoked.

"It took my breath away when I first saw it as well," Hannah said from behind her. Cassidy's gaze jerked away with relief to look at the gallery owner, catching Brenna doing the same, obviously equally entranced. "I thought the artist who created it must be tormented."

"It certainly seems to be saying that," Brenna said dryly. "James, where did this come from?"

He opened his mouth to say something but Hannah drew their attention to the second painting.

Where the first painting had seemed dark, heavy in the oils, the second was light and airy, the colors spread thin like gossamer. Where the first bespoke hideous nightmare, the second seemed an attempt to put the beauty of heaven itself on display. A hulking shadow lay prone, rays of light defining themselves arrow-like and piercing the body. The figure seemed to block the light to the lower left corner of the canvas, where the shadows deepened around a thin figure with the suggestion of a quiver of arrows on its back.

If the first canvas had made Cassidy hold her breath, this second made her sigh and stare, and search the shadows for the identity of the beast-killer.

She was startled again as Hannah introduced the third painting.

"This one came to us last week," she said.

The angelic and profane styles of the first two seemed to have merged on this canvas. Less stark than The Animal Man and more solid than Pierced, Woman Rise depicted the figure of a woman with sunlight bright hair stepping through shadow, half in light and half in darkness, her back to a figure behind her. Much of her upper body remained in shadow. Her legs stepped out, as though over some threshold, breaking through to a light that captured every detail of the muscles in her legs, the tendons in her feet, the sharp relief of a skirt wind-blown around her hips.

Covering her mouth, Cassidy was surprised to realize the image had moved her to tears, as two tracked down her cheeks and were caught at the corners of her mouth.

Beside her, Brenna had lost her edginess. "James," she glanced to the second and first paintings, then back to the third. "I never expected... this." She gestured helplessly. "You created these." She brushed her hair from her cheeks, discreetly brushing at her eyes.

Cassidy reached for Brenna's hand to say something but lost her thought when Brenna's hand found hers first.

In a steady voice, Brenna asked Hannah, "What offers have you had for them?"

"Mom, you can't buy them," James pleaded.

Brenna regarded him for a long moment of silence. "You want to sell them."

"Not to you."

Hannah shook her head. "I haven't set a price on them. One of the interested parties is an associate docent at COMMA."

Cassidy prevented herself from giving a low, impressed whistle. The California Museum of Modern Art. Brenna's fingers squeezed harder and Cassidy brushed her thumb over the back of Brenna's knuckles. Their eyes met; Brenna nodded, so slightly that it was imperceptible to anyone other than Cassidy

She turned to her son. "James," she said, "do you need me to sign anything?"

His face lost its deep anxiety, shattered by the onslaught of a giddy smile. "Does this mean I can keep coming here?"

Brenna looked to Hannah. "If I can count on you being supervised."

"Anytime he wants to use my workroom, I'd be honored," Hannah replied.

"I will expect you home by ten on school nights," Brenna said, sealing the agreement by sharing a handshake with Hannah. "And you have to keep up with school."

"Since James is under eighteen, I do need your permission to use his name on the sales orders," Hannah said to Brenna. The two started back to the front of the gallery. James reached for Cassidy's wheelchair handles.

"How are you doing?" she asked him.

"I didn't expect this. She really likes them."

"They're amazing, James." She paused then asked, "Will you continue to use the pseudonym?"

"Do you think that bothered Mom?" he asked.

"Maybe a little. But you don't have to hide anymore."

"I like that my paintings are not being hung simply because I'm Brenna Lanigan's son."

"Well then, maybe you should keep the name you're using."

They stopped at the counter, where Micah was waiting for them.

"So, man, what's the word?"

Jamie shrugged, still a little dazed at the unexpected turn of events. "Looks like she's going to let me sell them."

Micah's face split into a wide grin. He offered a high five, which James returned.

Cassidy looked up to see Hannah and Brenna emerging with Ryan. Her son was liberally spotted with a rainbow of colored chalk dust on his face, arms, and hands. Micah had thoughtfully put a small smock on him, though.

"Thank you," Cassidy said as Micah leaned back against the door jamb.

"No problem. Maybe we'll see you around here more often."

CHAPTER TWENTY-SIX

THEY WERE having lunch at a round table inside the Mediterranean café Cassidy had suggested earlier, and James sat next to Brenna, quiet now. He had been so animated with Micah, who was clearly a friend for all the right reasons and not just because his mother was a celebrity. It was clear that Micah and Hannah both considered James someone special because of his talent and for who he was as an artist. Brenna tried not to stare at James with the awe she felt. She had imagined such a different scenario for explaining his late nights. She felt as if she was rushing to catch up with understanding her younger son, and felt guilty about missing the changes he was going through.

He looked up from his menu. "Mom?"

She tried not to smile too widely. "Yes?"

"I'm really going to sell those paintings?"

"Signed, sealed, and soon delivered," she quipped with a smile. "Jamie Logan is off to a grand start."

"Does that bother you?" he asked. "That I used a different name?"

She knew that James had always been the least comfortable with her celebrity. It was no wonder that he presented his work under a pseudonym, though she had been bothered by that revelation at first. "I guess I was surprised as much as hurt, but I know why you did it."

He looked down at his plate then back up at her. "I was worried that would hurt you."

"Before or after you worried the subject matter would shock me?" She resisted the urge to reach over the table and grasp his hand, grasping Cassidy's instead as the blonde put a hand on her thigh.

"Before. Was it really shocking?"

"That first one was definitely out of a nightmare. Vivid."

James considered that. "Thank you."

"You're welcome." Brenna smiled and squeezed Cassidy's fingers. "So, how do you see this working?" she asked James as the waiter delivered their drinks and a cutting board holding a crusty loaf of bread.

"I've been sticking around after school in Ms. Vetter's room; now I can hitch a ride to the gallery with her."

"Don't impose. It might be out of her way."

"It isn't. Hannah said that James' art teacher is her partner," Cassidy reminded.

Brenna felt embarrassed at the surprise she felt. "Oh. Right."

"Are you ready to order?"

Brenna turned her attention to the waiter attending their table. Wearing pantaloons and an open vest over his bare chest, he looked first at Cassidy and then at Brenna with dark eyes almost black in his olive-toned face. However, his accent was distinctly Southern Californian. She smiled.

"I want a burger and fries," Ryan declared.

"This isn't Mister Burger, Ryan," Brenna corrected gently. "But I think you'll like the braised chicken."

She glanced at Cassidy.

Other than her reminder to Brenna, Cassidy had been quiet since they had left the gallery. Brenna remembered their hands clasping in front of James' third painting, and the sheen of tears she had seen in Cassidy's eyes. She squeezed the captive hand. "Is that all right, Cass?"

The blue eyes that drifted up from the menu obviously had not been focused on the food list. They held the faraway look that Brenna had come to recognize as Cassidy wrestling with something painful.

Cassidy closed her eyes and shook her head. "Excuse me," she said as she struggled to her feet and left the table.

"Hold on, I've got it." Brenna quickly told James, "Two salads.

We'll be right back."

In the bathroom, Cassidy was in front of the handicapped accessible sink, instead of in a stall. "Cass?"

Silent, Cassidy cupped her hands under the water flowing from the faucet. Bringing her palms to her face, she dampened it and then her neck. When her gaze intersected with Brenna's in the mirror, she exhaled.

"Cass, why didn't you say you don't feel well?"

Turning away to pull off a paper towel for her hands and face, Cassidy answered, "Because I didn't want to argue with you about going home."

Brenna lifted her hand to Cassidy's shoulder and cupped the muscles gently, feeling the tension holding the blonde tight as a bowstring. "It's your first day out. What's the crime in admitting you're tired?"

Cassidy breathed out against her shoulder. "Now that I'm out of the hospital, it's harder to remember I'm not well," she admitted wryly.

"We'll go home right after lunch."

"We should get back out there." Cassidy lifted her head from Brenna's shoulder and leaned into a comforting caress of fingers brushing over her cheeks. "I'm sure James is tired of making Ryan keep his hands to himself."

"He'll manage."

"He's not Ryan's brother, Bren. Didn't you see his expression when Micah mistook Ryan for Thomas?"

"I think Micah was pulling his leg. They seem pretty close."

Cassidy sat down on the small chair next to the sink. "He looked like he was angry."

"He apparently has an outlet for that now," Brenna mused. "James really surprised me today," she added. "I was sure I'd find something else."

"He has amazing talent," Cassidy agreed. "I remember telling you I thought that portrait he did of you for Christmas was very professional."

"Guess you were right. He's about to get paid for it. That's pretty professional." Brenna crossed her arms over her chest, shaking her head in amazement. "I never noticed it really." She looked at Cassidy. "I almost missed my son growing up."

Cassidy lightly stroked her fingertips over Brenna's cheek just before tilting her head up and capturing Brenna's lips in a tender kiss. The contact was a slice of heaven. Cassidy lifted her chin and deepened the kiss with the tip of her tongue entreating entrance. Brenna gasped and opened her mouth.

"Well, I never!"

Surprised by the interruption, Brenna released Cassidy's lips and turned see the back of a woman leaving the bathroom. "Apparently she was not expecting a show," Brenna said lightly.

Cassidy chuckled, and kissed Brenna's temple before wrapping an arm around Brenna's waist. "Let's get back to our sons."

Returning to the table, Brenna found Ryan making a crumbly paste of his bread and several pats of butter. She sipped her water with studied calm as she caught the disdain on the face of a woman staring at her from another table. When the woman turned to whisper something to her male companion, Brenna put down the glass with a heavy thud.

Cassidy grasped her wrist. "Don't."

"Something wrong?" James asked.

With precise care, Brenna loosened her wrist from Cassidy's grasp, lifted her napkin and patted her lips with it. "Nothing," she told James. Looking over his shoulder, she caught sight of their waiter with a tray balanced on his palm. "Here comes our lunch.

Still, Brenna could not completely dispel her upset at the cutting behavior of the woman in the bathroom.

After lunch, the group stepped outside to the sidewalk. Cassidy slipped her sunglasses from her purse and saw Brenna doing the same. "You want to see what else is around here?" she asked, shifting in the wheelchair,

"No, you need to go home. Thomas is probably due home any minute now, anyway."

CHAPTER TWENTY-SEVEN

HEARING A car's motor, Brenna looked up from her script reading. As she processed that the vehicle was not just passing by on the street, she also realized that it had pulled into her driveway. She looked over to her right to where Cassidy was reclining amid a pile of cushions at the opposite end of the couch.

The blonde's bare feet were tucked up beside Brenna's hip. Brenna had given them, and Cassidy's lower legs, a massage earlier. Ryan lay partially on Cassidy's chest with his head butting up against his mother's chin. Both were sound asleep.

Putting down her pages, Brenna went to the door. Looking through the peephole revealed a blue SUV parked on the driveway and a large African American in a tan uniform walking around the back of it. He was facing away from Brenna, so she could not see his face.

A moment later, the man reappeared, talking to someone who was following behind him. Brenna instantly recognized Thomas, though he was looking down at the ground, concentrating on moving his feet with the precarious aid of crutches. She was out the front door in a flash.

As the door opened and his mother burst through the doorway, Thomas stopped and looked up sheepishly. "Hi, Mom."

Searching down his body, which was dressed in a sleeveless shirt and hiker's shorts, Brenna focused on how he held his left leg slightly bent, keeping the weight off of the foot that bore thick wrappings, though it did not look to be in a cast. "What happened?"

"I took a spill during the hike. My ankle's twisted."

"That's all it is, ma'am. We just came from the hospital."

Brenna looked at Thomas' escort and recalled her manners. "I'm sorry. I'm Brenna Lanigan, Thomas' mother. You are...?" She held out her hand.

"Sergeant Leroy Abernathy," he answered, shaking her hand. "I'm one of Thomas' instructors at FIRE. Nice to meet you."

"The Forestry program?" Brenna clarified.

"Yes, ma'am. We were out on Nativity Ridge studying the game tracks when Thomas fell."

"Leroy helped me wrap up the ankle and we trekked back to town for the x-ray. I decided I wasn't going to be much good to the group with a bum ankle, so I asked him to drive me home."

"Thank you, Sergeant Abernathy," Brenna said.

"No problem. Damn fine man you've got, ma'am. Hurt like a bi—" Leroy cleared his throat and corrected himself before continuing. "Hurt real bad, but he handled it real well."

The man blushed, which surprised Brenna.

She almost told him she had said worse herself, but decided against creating that level of familiarity between them. "Thanks again for bringing him home."

"Yes, ma'am." Abernathy clapped Thomas on the shoulder. Thomas patted the hand in return and the two shared a smile. "Take care, man. See you next weekend."

"I'll be there," Thomas promised.

Brenna remained quiet beside her son as they watched Abernathy back out and drive away.

"Well, I'd better get inside," Thomas said.

Brenna held the door for him. "Cass is asleep on the couch with Ryan. Do you need anything for pain?"

"Whatever they injected in my ankle seems to be taking care of the pain for now."

"Where are the hospital instructions?" she asked.

"In my backpack."

He nodded to his right shoulder and she lifted the bag off, waiting patiently as he shifted his weight so that he could get his arm free of the strap without dropping the crutch.

"Any prescriptions?"

"Said not to use aspirin, but over the counter stuff should be fine if I need anything."

"All right, let's get you settled and then I guess we've got everyone home for dinner for a change."

Inside, Cassidy had awakened. Seeing Thomas' predicament, she moved out from under Ryan and sat up.

"Hey, you're up," Thomas greeted brightly.

"Hey, you're down." Cassidy's nose crinkled as she quirked a smile at him. "What happened?"

"Twisted my ankle." While his mother took away the crutches, Thomas' powerful arms braced against the side and back cushions and he lowered himself to the couch. He looked over at Ryan sleeping. "What'd you do to tucker him out?"

"You first," Brenna requested, leaning over the back of the couch. "The whole story, please."

Thomas shook his head but smiled. "I'm a klutz."

"Really?" Cassidy sat down next on another chair. She was a little surprised. Accidents could happen, but Thomas was one of the more agile and athletic individuals she had met. "So how did it happen?"

Thomas leaned back into the cushions, getting comfortable before he started his tale. His hands illustrated points in the air as he excitedly recounted it all.

"We went up to Nativity Ridge to talk about the animal tracks, habits, and behaviors. There's a loose trail up there. Lindsey Carmichael jumped when one of the guys startled her with a wiggling snakeskin, and she leaped into me. I slipped in the loose rocks, and as I was trying to regain my balance, I landed with my foot half in one of the rat snake holes that dot the trail."

"Snakes?" Brenna repeated with alarm. Cassidy reached over and took her hand.

"Not there at the time, I swear." With a smile, Thomas lifted his hand in a Boy Scout salute. "I just turned the ankle." He thrust his thumb over his shoulder. "Abernathy was right there, practically caught me before I hit the dirt. We wrapped it up, and he and I hiked back down to get it x-rayed."

"You got away without breaking your ankle. You're lucky," Cassidy complimented.

Thomas grinned. "Yep." He shook his head. "I would have liked to impress Lindsey, though."

"I'm sure you did," Brenna said.

"Mom, I fell on my ass in front of everybody."

"But you prevented her from falling too."

Thomas cocked his head in thought. "You're right." His dust-covered face split into a wide grin.

Brenna patted his shoulder and straightened up. "Well, you rest that ankle. I'll start dinner."

"Need some help?" Cassidy asked.

"No. I just thought I'd put together a casserole."

Cassidy pushed to her feet with her uninjured right arm. "Doctor says I have to move around some."

"But you spent all day out."

"You did?" Thomas asked.

"A little sunshine goes a long way," Cassidy said with a smile. To Brenna she added, "I promise I'll sit down if I get tired."

"I'll put a stool from the breakfast bar in the kitchen."

Cassidy sighed. "All right."

After collecting the ingredients, Brenna took down the cutting board. "I'll chop."

Working the can opener for the soup stock, Cassidy sat on the breakfast stool next to Brenna. From their position, they could see Thomas settling back, lifting his foot onto the tabletop. His gaze turned to Ryan, and he was soon lightly rubbing the back of the five year old's calf.

Apparently smelling the aromas of the cooking vegetables when Brenna seared them in a wok, James appeared, smiling at his brother until he noted Thomas' injury with some alarm. "What happened to you?"

"Snake hole," Thomas said. "How's your weekend been?"

Flopping down on the couch, James blurted, "A damn sight better than yours. Mom's agreed to let me sell my paintings."

"That's great!"

Obviously, Thomas was not surprised by the revelation about the gallery showing. Brenna frowned. *What else am I going to be the last to know?*

Cassidy nudged her. When Brenna met her gaze, Cassidy asked quietly, "Are you mad that Thomas already knew?"

"I just thought I knew my sons a little better than I apparently do," she whispered back.

"Well, maybe my convalescence can give you some down time too."

Ryan woke and Cassidy watched Thomas begin wrestling with the boy on the couch. Leapfrogging over Thomas's waist, Ryan slammed into James, and Cassidy held her breath.

"Squirt, I am not a trampoline," James said, easily picking Ryan up. But he only gently tossed him in the air toward his brother. "Here, catch."

Thomas caught Ryan, who laughed. "Wanna go hit some balls outside 'til dinner's ready?"

"I'm not very good," Ryan said.

"We'll teach you."

"Chance says Daddies do that."

"Well," Thomas said, "dads and... almost big brothers."

"Brothers?" Ryan asked.

"Yeah. C'mon, Slugger." James urged Ryan out ahead of them, and Thomas followed after them relying heavily on his crutches.

James picked up the bat and glove from just outside the door, while Ryan grabbed the ball.

Brenna stopped Thomas. "Almost big brothers?"

"Yeah."

Nothing else needed to be said. Brenna stepped back as he shifted his weight, then her gaze followed him outside.

Turning back to the kitchen, Brenna's saw Cassidy leaning on the kitchen wall, her mouth open in surprise. Brenna reached out and caressed Cassidy's chin, then slipped her arm behind Cassidy's head and gently pulled her down for a kiss. Drawing back, she said with a smile, "Hi, Mom."

Cassidy responded happily, "Hi, Mom."

EPILOGUE

IT WAS a beautiful Saturday, and Cassidy was sitting on the swing by the pool deck in Brenna's back yard. Two weeks had passed, two weeks of Brenna taking Ryan with her to the set while Cassidy continued to recuperate. Today Brenna was out running some errands, and Ryan was working on his batting. Since Thomas and James had taught him how to swing at the baseball while it was resting on a batting tee, Ryan had been practicing diligently ever since.

Gently swaying to and fro, Cassidy sighed deeply. She hadn't heard anything from her parents, not to follow up on her recovery or pursue the legal trouble her father had threatened. Obviously her words had had an impact on him. She suspected it would be some time before she could expect her father's civility, or want to give it to him in return.

As she watched Ryan with pride, occasionally calling out her approval, she felt a surge of relief that Mitch's custody of Ryan would never again be an issue. Her ex-husband had been arraigned on attempted murder charges, for his attack on her and also that of the flower deliveryman he had assaulted and robbed of his clothing and ID in order to camouflage his presence on the set. The battered man had been found unconscious in a bathroom stall near the prop room.

Cassidy shivered at the realization of how close she had come to losing Ryan. She watched him protectively as he ran after another batted ball. He looked stronger to her now. And he was less dependent on her. She realized that in the fall, he would be starting kindergarten, and, she suspected he would be physically and emotionally ready.

Looking into the clear sky, Cassidy realized it was quickly turning into evening. Brenna had said she would be gone only a short while, but had been gone for more than three hours, missing Cassidy's physical therapy session. That was worrying. She usually made it a point to be available during PT in case the therapist had instructions for follow up.

As if on cue, Cassidy heard the sound of an engine cutting off out front. She could hear the sliding door of the SUV opening, and suddenly there was barking.

The side gate to the back yard clattered and opened. Ryan ran to it as Ranger, Cassidy's Dalmatian, bounded inside, pulling Brenna behind him. He stopped as soon as he spotted Ryan, eagerly licking the boy as Brenna released the clip of the leash and secured the back yard gate.

Brenna coiled the leash around her fist and walked across the garden path toward Cassidy. "I'm back," she called.

"I can see that. Are you sure you want to have Ranger here?"

"If my begonias survive, I'll live. But I thought it would be good for Ryan." Brenna sat down on the swing as Cassidy shifted to make room.

"You didn't have to do this."

"I did." Brenna wrapped her arm around Cassidy's shoulders and they melded together. "Ryan was miserable here with all his things at your house."

"After you get off work, you've been stopping there with him and letting him pick something to bring over here every day for a week."

"But it wasn't anything that he really wanted."

Cassidy nodded her recognition of Brenna's perception, and then Brenna kissed her. "And, I have something for you."

"Something for me? You brought over half my closet last week."

Brenna handed over a pamphlet. "It's a birthday present for you."

"My birthday?" Cassidy rubbed her forehead as she considered the revelation for a moment. "I'd forgotten."

"You've been sort of... distracted. Then again, that's what a lover's supposed to remember, right? Birthdays, anniversaries, special occasions."

Cassidy looked at the pamphlet. "So, what's this?"

"A weekend vacation package for your birthday. I haven't booked it yet, I wanted to talk to you first, but... I was remembering back... in January, when we were talking about our plans after Time Trails. I was thinking about a ski weekend."

"Kind of out of the question," Cassidy said, indicating her wrapped ribs.

Brenna kissed her then, indulging them both in the taste and feel of their passion rising. "I don't ski either," she admitted, "but I thought... snowed in in a luxurious lodge... Irish coffees... curled up by a fireplace..." She punctuated her description with breathy kisses down Cassidy's throat.

Cassidy cleared her throat. "Sounds... warm."

"I thought so."

"The doctor did clear me to return to work in another week."

"So, no snuggling by a fireplace until after we're done shooting?"

Cassidy shook her head then kissed Brenna's nose before moving on to taste her lips. "How about when Time Trails is over, we plan another family camping trip?" she suggested.

"Every day will be a vacation with you here," Brenna said, "but going away together would be really nice."

The noise of feet thrashing through flowers caught both women's attention, and they looked over in time to see Ryan go sprawling in a flower bed along the far side of the pool while Ranger bounced enthusiastically around him.

"I'm sorry about the flowers," Cassidy said. She called out to Ryan, "Ryan, bring Ranger out—" Brenna's hand on her arm stopped her.

Brenna teared up. "It's... not important. Please?"

"It is important, Bren. I told you—"

Brenna swallowed and shook her head. "He's just a boy."

"With a big dog!" Cassidy winced as her sharp tone caused Brenna to recoil. "My place is Ranger-proofed. Yours isn't."

"Maybe we can find a doggie daycare—"

"Brenna!"

Brenna burst to her feet and turned around. "I need this to work out!"

Clasping Brenna's hands between her own, Cassidy pulled

Brenna back down into the swing. "It will. Be patient. A lot has changed in such a short while; we all need time to adjust. Thomas starts college. Ryan starts kindergarten. We can find a way. Together. But you can't just make the choices, or assume all the responsibility, or suffer quietly when something you love is being trampled." She gestured toward the flowers. "We'll take Ranger back to Gwen and Lou tomorrow." She cupped Brenna's cheek as her lover wiped her eyes.

"Everything's moving so quickly," Brenna said wistfully. "I can't believe Ryan starts school in the fall. Have you decided where you'll enroll him?"

"The school where Gwen teaches serves my neighborhood."

"But that's all the way across town."

Cassidy saw Brenna's hesitation. "It's where we live," Cassidy said quietly, knowing where the conversation was going. "I should go home soon."

"Just because you are able to go doesn't mean you have to move out. I thought we were doing well. We love waking up together. We get Ryan ready together..." With a wince, Brenna resigned herself.

Cassidy rubbed Brenna's shoulder. "It'll be spring soon. I have things I need to do."

Brenna sighed. "It's more practical for you to stay—"

Kissing Brenna's forehead, Cassidy feathered her fingertips through the delicate auburn hairs at Brenna's temple. "Not very romantic, I know." She eased back, drawing Brenna's gaze to her with the earnestness in her tone. "I want to stay with you. Part of me loves how it's been these last weeks too. We are already a family, Bren." Cassidy shook her head. "But I feel...we missed out. This wasn't what either of us planned. I missed out on courting you. I want to have all the romance, all the dating, all the time together that has nothing to do with being practical."

She lifted Brenna's chin. "We'll make all the plans—camping, what our next jobs will be, where Ranger will live—we'll decide those things together. Then..." She kissed Brenna, tasting her mouth with leisurely sweetness. Brenna's soft moan of arousal made her smile against the bow-like lips and Cassidy eased away. "When the time is right, we'll move in together, and I'll make you mine officially."

She softly growled the last words, feeling the shiver of pleasure course through her lover and the pulse pounding in Brenna's throat. Her smile deepened as Brenna's cheeks turned pink and she closed her deep blue eyes, struggling against her emotions. Cassidy wrapped her arms around Brenna's back and tucked her closely against her body.

"I'm already yours," Brenna murmured, her voice husky and her breath brushing Cassidy's collarbone. "Everything about you makes me fall in love a little more deeply each day." Brenna traced the small dimple in Cassidy's chin.

"Talking with Kevin about your divorce today got me thinking about marriage, Bren." Cassidy looked up at the sky. The sunset was beginning to paint the cloud-dotted sky in deepening blues, pinks, and purples. She cupped her hand over Brenna's in her lap. "I intend to have your whole family around you when we marry, and I haven't even met most of them yet."

Brenna's expression, uncertain and briefly panicked, suggested she wasn't as keen as Cassidy on the idea of having a formal ceremony. Cassidy knew she'd guessed right: Brenna had been letting her take the messages from Kevin in order to avoid facing her family.

True to form, Brenna shifted the focus away from herself. "What about your family?"

Cassidy's eyes stung with tears. She closed her eyes and felt Brenna's fingertips brushing the tears away from her cheeks. "That's not fair," she murmured. "You and your sons are the only family that matters to me," Cassidy said earnestly when she opened her eyes.

Brenna moved out of Cassidy's embrace and clasped her hands between her own smaller ones. Planting gentle kisses on the knuckles and into the palms as she gently opened the fists, she said, "And you and Ryan are the only other family that matters to me." The words were spoken like a vow. "So..." Brenna's inhalation pushed her chest against Cassidy's briefly. She exhaled. "If you want to meet my extended family, we'll plan it..."

"...together." Cassidy smiled. "We can accomplish anything together."

"Together sounds just perfect to me," Brenna sighed. "If I have to wait a little while before we're together all the time, I can do that. I love you, Cass."

"I love you, too, Bren."

Cassidy returned Brenna's kiss and then coaxed her head onto her shoulder as Brenna started the swing moving with a gentle push against the ground. Facing westward, they swung and snuggled, watching the sun slowly setting.

It is now 2013 as I write this. We in the LGBTQ community have come a long way with our struggle for civil rights and legal recognition of our relationships and families. In 2001, when I was first penning the drafts of Turning Point and Turn for Home, much of what my characters struggle through was very real. Today it is no longer an issue in many parts of the world. Whole generations no longer hold onto a bigotry regarding sexual orientation. However, there are still places today where it remains a struggle to come out and to become who you were meant to be, where a person is denied the right to love and create a family with whomever she chooses. This is Brenna and Cassidy's story – fiction to be sure – but shares their struggle so no one will ever forget what once was reality for so many.